Bury the Lies

Copyright © 2022 Jane I

Published by The Peapod Press

All rights reserved. No part of this book may be reproduced in any form, or by any electronic or mechanical means – except for the inclusion of brief quotations in articles or reviews – without written permission from the author.

ISBN: 9798366391771
Cover photo © 2022 Jane Phillips
Cover design © 2022 Amy Phillips
First edition 2022

This is a work of fiction. Names, characters, places and events are products of the author's imagination. Any resemblance to actual persons, living or dead, is purely coincidental.

Books in The Burials Series

Bury the Truth

Bury the Lies

# Mary

would have been thrilled that her namesake is developing into a formidable woman.

But kind, always kind.

**Acknowledgements**

This is Book Two of a series, so I can thank the same people! My City University friends, Vicki Bradley, Paul Durston, Vicki Jones and Fraser Massey have been with me for the long haul – reading and re-reading as the book developed. The long-prose group at Cambridge Writers and Sian Salkeld have helped by reading drafts. Special thanks must go to Jane Woodnutt and Paul Durston for line-editing and finding all the spelling errors, grammatical howlers and typos that my several readings had missed. Amy Phillips stars again as my High Priestess of On-line Anything. And Glyn is still making me tea.

**About the author**

Jane Phillips is a psychologist. This gives her an unhealthy interest in the criminal mind. To counterbalance, she has a husband, two children and four grandchildren. They do their best to keep her on the straight and narrow.

# Chapter 1

Monday 12th November 2012

Ben whistled as he unlocked his front door. He smiled at his poor rendition of Danny Boy. It represented the last vestiges of his long, dark connection with Northern Ireland. The decision now made, he was ready to purge himself of his guilt.

In the hall, the answerphone was flashing. A job, he hoped. He needed something mainstream, something boring and beautiful in its simplicity. Idly, he pressed the button. That whining pseudo-voice droned its anodyne message just at the edge of his consciousness, 'You have one new message. Message received yesterday evening at nine forty-five.' The machine clicked and he was immediately alert. He flinched, as he listened to a voice he'd never expected to hear again. Its usual stentorious tones were absent. It whimpered, 'Benedict. Help me – please. They're going to kill me. You're the only one I can trust.' There followed a clattering and thumping, a cry, and silence, before the buzz as the line went dead.

That evil bastard. That lying toe-rag. That oily, pathetic apology for a human being. That wretched man was trying to worm his way back. He owed that man nothing. But, even as his brain was saying 'No', Ben knew that he would have to go.

At their last meeting, Dobson had said he feared for his life and Ben had walked. This time he couldn't. Not a second time; not with those noises off. He'd have to investigate and tell that squalid specimen of humanity that there would not be a third time. He looked at his watch and did a quick calculation. Just past six. If he biked to the College, he could be there before six-thirty. He quickly scribbled a note for Katy, picked up the emergency torch and set out for the city centre.

At that early hour, Cambridge was silent and beautiful; still dark, still asleep for the most part. A gentle, misty rain was swirling but it didn't slow his cycling. By exceeding the speed limit, he arrived at the front portal of St Etheldreda's College at twenty past six. He glanced up at the windows and counted across to Dobson's rooms. Bright light shone out and Ben's heart missed a beat. Dobson had never been an early riser, a fact known to everyone. Ben shivered, as the cold seeped into his bones.

Without alerting the porter, he wheeled his bike into Front Court and dumped it out of sight. Hell to pay if it was found before he retrieved it. He mounted the stairs three at a time and gently pushed the door to Dobson's outer office. It swung open with the smallest of creaks. It was unlocked – an ominous sign. He waited. No sound. By the light from the stairwell he could see Mrs Jones's ultra-tidy desk. He played his torch over the room. It looked exactly as it had on his last visit. He smiled briefly at the thought of Mrs Jones thanking him for standing up to Dobson. He inched towards the door of Dobson's inner sanctum. No sound emerged. The 'No Entry' red light glimmered through the gloom. A bar of bright light shone under the door. Ben put away his torch, took out a pair of latex gloves and slipped them on. Dobson's door was closed. He listened again, then slowly turned the handle. Not locked. This door was silent as he eased it open.

Light flooded his eyes and, for a moment, all he could see was the mass of papers strewn at his feet. Then he saw that every light in the room had been turned on and the room had been turned over. A break-in, but no sign of Dobson. Typical, thought Ben. He's probably buggered off back to his place in Trumpington and I'm on a fool's errand. And again, Ben wondered why he'd come. He owed that man nothing.

He stood at the door and surveyed the mess. The fusty bookcase was empty and all those ancient tomes had been discarded on the floor. The files of paperwork, usually stacked neatly on a shelf, had been hurled into an untidy pile. The drawers of Dobson's desk were upturned on the sofa and their contents scattered. Ben's one thought now was of the paper that he had seen Dobson put into that top desk drawer last summer; the paper that Ben had helped Stanley Murdock's solicitor deliver to Dobson following Murdock's death. The scene of destruction enveloping this room indicated to Ben that finding that paper had become paramount.

He advanced into the room, stepping carefully to minimise disturbance. He went straight to the desk and looked inside. He could see nothing untoward. He put in his hand and felt around the empty shell. His gloves were thin but they still impeded his search. Then he felt a small ripple on the underside of the desktop. He played his torch over it and smiled. Even in the intense beam of the torch, it was almost impossible to discern the alteration to the wooden desk. Dobson had colour-matched his safe place using wood veneer but had not taken it quite to the edge. Ben looked for something to prise it away. Dobson's paperknife would be ideal. He dug at the edge of the veneer, being careful not to damage the desk or whatever was hidden. It came away easily, revealing just the paper that Ben had expected. A swift glance showed that it was similar to his – the one he'd acquired from Stanley Murdock's possessions and which how resided in the fire-proof box in his bedroom. He folded this second list and put it in his inside pocket, then replaced the paperknife and discarded the piece of veneer on to the pile of books.

So, where was Dobson? At the first sign of trouble, had he retreated to his house in Trumpington, as Ben had surmised? Ben looked around – nowhere to hide. He'd never been into the further room. He imagined it to be Dobson's bedroom when he slept in College. He tiptoed over and tried the door. It swung open without a sound.

Beyond was carnage. Dripped arcs of deep red were sprayed across white walls. A dark red pool had congealed on the wooden floor. In the middle of that pool, Dobson sat, propped against the far wall, a deep gash across his throat and a knife handle protruding from his chest. His dead eyes stared straight at Ben.

# Chapter 2

Ben retreated to the stairwell and took several deep breaths. He'd seen thousands of dead bodies, hundreds of victims of violence – people who had died a horrible death. He'd recently buried one of them. But it had been a long time since he'd seen a victim in situ. He knew what he must do, but first he had to think through what needed to be said and, more importantly, to whom. After a minute's thought, he searched his phone contacts and tapped the number. It was answered by a sleepy voice. He had to wake her, and fast. 'Vin, it's Ben. Stop! Don't say anything. I've found a body. He's been murdered.'

As he waited for the police to arrive, he already had that skittering of excitement in his stomach. Since solving Stanley Murdock's murder, life had reverted to the humdrum, a day-to-day treadmill of everyday existence. Six months ago, he'd apprehended a killer and had, himself, braved death. Then nothing.

His thoughts turned to the meeting last summer, when he'd told Dobson precisely what he thought of him. And then he'd walked away never expecting to see that deceitful bastard again. Now he had a dilemma; what to tell the police and what to tell 'Chris'. They were the professionals, so the easy path would be to hand everything to them and get back to the day job. But, he couldn't. He'd hated Dobson but he'd had that call for help, he'd found the body, and he suspected that he knew more about the victim than anyone. There was a bond – a distasteful one, but a bond, nonetheless. And then he'd removed evidence. Now he needed to be involved – more than involved. That paper from Dobson's desk told him that he had to be the first to find the culprit.

He scanned its contents. It had more information on each person than his copy. Dr Clare and Professor Hallfield were there and others whose names he did not know. Some dates and times, some names and insinuations in the form of riddles. There was no doubt in Ben's mind that this was a blackmail list – sent on by Stanley Murdock, after his death, so Professor Dobson could continue to bleed those victims. But there was no evidence attached. Surely a blackmailer needed evidence?

The sound of heavy footsteps on the stairs caused him to stuff the paper back in his pocket. He knew that he'd have to talk to Chris before he could divulge anything beyond the most obvious. Murdock and Dobson had been Chris's people, after all, so Chris needed to know, and fast. Ben too had briefly become 'one of Chris's people'. He'd found the subterfuge of espionage so distasteful that he'd withdrawn from that role at the earliest opportunity – once he'd discovered Stanley Murdock's killer and made sure she was safe. Ben now had the feeling that he was going to be drawn back into that world. Bloody Dobson – why did he have to get himself killed.

The Head Porter was leading two large, plain-clothes officers as they puffed up the stairs. They were followed by Vin. Ben smiled. She was not at all out of breath and looked fabulous, even this early. He gave a slight bow to the company as they assembled in a crowd on the stairwell. He first greeted the Head Porter. 'Good morning, Mr Fisher.' He turned to the two overweight officers. 'Good morning Officers. I'm Ben Burton. I found the body.' He turned to Vin as the person in charge. 'Good morning, Chief Inspector. Sorry to have woken you so early.' He nodded his head towards Dobson's door. 'Professor Dobson has been murdered. I must apologise, I've compromised the scene.' He felt anything but sorry but thought an apology might be helpful. 'I got a call from Professor Dobson last night. He left a message on my answerphone saying he thought his life was in danger.' He looked towards Vin. 'I was out so I only picked it up this morning.' Looking at her, he tried unsuccessfully to erase from his mind the thought of her naked body wrapped around his. Last night, he'd been out and he'd been in, a complication in the circumstances. And he realised he'd been happy last night. Could be he was moving on. Could be.

'I got here somewhere between six-thirty and seven. I went into his study. It's been turned over. Then I opened his bedroom door and found his body. He's been stabbed and his throat cut. As soon as I found him I came out here and phoned you. No-one else has gone in since I arrived.'

The very large policemen who was taking notes asked, 'Before we go in, sir, how compromised?'

'As soon as I saw the upheaval in his study, I put on latex gloves but there will be footprints.'

The officer looked sceptical. 'Latex gloves. Who carries latex gloves? Can I ask why you had latex gloves?'

'Yes, of course, Officer. I'm an undertaker. I always carry gloves in case I'm called out when I'm not at home.'

'Ah. I see,' said the policeman. Though it was plain to Ben that he did not see at all. The officer tried again. 'And...'

'Enough,' said Vin. 'Thank you Sergeant. I can vouch for this man's profession. He is indeed an undertaker.' She turned towards Ben. 'Mr Burton, can you just confirm your actions inside those rooms?'

He'd already lied about the time and he was going to have to lie some more. He didn't know how much Vin or her officers understood of Dobson's Service connections. He shrugged in a way that he hoped would look apologetic. 'I was as careful as I could be. At first, I couldn't see any sign of Dobson so I thought – hoped – he'd been burgled and had gone home leaving it till this morning to tidy up. He'd asked for my help, so I thought I'd better check all his rooms. I stepped carefully into his study to try not to disturb things. I went round to the back of his desk to make sure he hadn't collapsed there. Then I opened the door to his bedroom but I didn't go in. I could see immediately that there was nothing I could do for him. I should think he's been dead about nine hours.'

The note-taking policeman looked sceptical and sounded dismissive. 'And how would you know that, Sir?'

Ben didn't like the emphasis on the 'sir'. He could feel his hackles rising. 'Officer, I deal with dead bodies all day, every day. You learn these things.' He didn't feel at all inclined to expand on this. After all, he had a perfectly logical reason for knowing the possible time of death. Then he relented. 'He left his phone message to me at nine forty-five last night. I could hear sounds of the break-in before the line went dead. I've put two and two together and I'm sure your people will confirm that I've come up with four.'

Before the sergeant could respond, Vin intervened. 'Thank you, Mr Burton. I'm afraid we're going to take up a lot of your time this morning. As you've contaminated the scene, you are required to go immediately to the police station to make a statement and we'll need to take all your outer clothing for analysis. We'll get a car to take you. Can you arrange for someone to bring a set of outer clothes, including shoes, to Parkside?'

Ben was immediately worried. He'd carefully removed evidence and he did not want it to fall into the hands of the police until he'd scrutinised it. Stripping at the police station might bring it to light. He quickly formulated a plan. 'Yes, that's fine.' He moved sideways, knocking into one of the burly policemen. 'Sorry. It's a bit crowded here and I can see that we're getting in your way. How about Mr Fisher and I go to the Porters' Lodge to await my escort?'

The DCI replied, 'Good idea. Put on these overshoes and keep them on until you're told otherwise. We'll also need to hear that phone message. Could you bring it to the station later this morning?' She turned, so only Ben could see her face, and she gave him a rapid and almost imperceptible wink.

She turned back and addressed the Head Porter. 'Mr Fisher, we'll need to talk to you before we go. And I'll need a key so we can secure the scene. We'll leave a uniformed officer outside this door. Can you provide a chair? Now, I'm sure there are people that you will need to inform.' With that, she proceeded to unpack her protective clothing and her officers followed suit.

Before Ben could make his escape with Fisher, there were swift steps on the stairs. A tall, slim woman appeared and looked quickly round the uncomfortable huddle on the landing. She acknowledged them all. 'Good morning. I gather that you are the police. I'm the Master here. What can I do to help you?'

Vin stepped forward and shook hands. Before she could speak, Fisher broke in. 'Master, I have some terrible news for you. Professor Dobson is dead.' He motioned towards Ben. 'Mr Burton found him just half an hour ago. I'm afraid he's been murdered.'

Ben watched the Master carefully. He always looked to see people's reactions on being told of a death. It told him a lot about them. The Master took a deep in-breath before she spoke. Ben was impressed to hear that her voice was steady. 'Mr Burton, a pity we're meeting in these extreme circumstances.' She took a pad and pen from her pocket and began to write a list. 'I must circulate a message to staff and students – one that will give the necessary details but will not alarm unduly.' She looked squarely at the company. 'A difficult balancing act.' She turned to Vin. 'What else should we do?'

'There is a procedure. We'll have an initial look, then I'll send in some scenes of crime officers to do a thorough search for clues to the identity of the killer. I'm afraid they will be here some time and will seal off the area – and that might include the whole staircase.'

'That would be difficult. Still, needs must.' The Master turned to Mr Fisher. 'Has Mrs Jones been informed?'

'Not yet. Mr Burton and I were just going to the Porters' Lodge to get started.'

'Good. Include my condolences, please.' The Master turned to Vin. 'Do you need me?'

'Can you just wait a moment. I've got a couple of questions before you go then you can get on with your damage limitation.'

As they descended the stairs, Fisher began tutting about poor Mrs Jones. From Ben's memory of 'poor Mrs Jones', he felt she'd not be too unhappy, as long as she still had a job to come to. But you never knew how a death would affect a person. He'd seen such a range of reactions that he was no longer surprised by anything. Fisher was still speaking. 'This is going to rock the College. And she's only been here a couple of months. What a welcome. She's not one to wobble, but even so.'

Ben assumed he was referring to the new Master. He supposed that the first woman Master of this College would not be one 'to wobble'. But he agreed that to have one of the Fellows murdered on site was indeed not the best welcome to her new job.

As soon as they arrived at the Porters' Lodge, Ben extracted Dobson's list from his inside pocket. He was taking a risk letting it out of his hands, but this was by far the lesser of two evils. He'd known Fisher for nearly thirty years and knew he could trust him, but he had to prepare the ground. 'This is a list of names. I was going to talk to Professor Dobson about it this morning but...' Ben grimaced at the thought of what he had seen of Dobson that morning. 'I'd rather leave it in your care than have the police going through it. You know, keep it within College. Can you keep it safe for me until I've been to the station and given my statement?'

'Of course I will, Mr Burton. Not keen on the police, myself, and I've known you, God knows how long, since we were both wet behind the ears. Give it here and I'll put it safe in my desk.'

Ben watched while Mr Fisher locked the offending list in his desk drawer. He listened while Fisher took down a set of keys from the board behind him and summoned one of the porters to take the keys and a chair to Professor Dobson's rooms, and not to say a word to anyone under pain of dismissal. Then Fisher phoned Mrs Jones and explained that Professor Dobson was dead and it was a police matter. They would contact her and she was not to come into work until further notice, or to talk to anyone, again under pain of dismissal. And yes, of course she would be paid, and did she need anyone to be with her? It seemed that she did not.

Fisher gave a nervous laugh. 'Well, she ain't grieving. Thinks it's suicide. I didn't put her right. Should I have, d'you think?'

'No. She'll find out soon enough.'

Ben's police escort appeared. He looked at the clock over the Wren chapel. Only seven-thirty. 'I'll call back later to see the Master. See if there's anything I can do to help.'

'Okey doke, Mr Burton. See you later. And I'll keep your paper safe from prying eyes.'

\* \* \*

At the station, Ben had given precisely the same statement as he had to Vin and her cohort. He'd removed all his outer clothes and was now wearing the odd assortment that Katy had brought in for him. At the station he'd managed to get the message to Katy that he might be some time and that she, Mo and Michael were to carry on without him.

When he arrived home, Katy was just finishing her breakfast. He looked at his watch. A quarter to nine. She waved a greeting. 'Hi Dad, saw your note. Heh! I saw that young cop at the station, the one who fancies me. Chatted him up and he was so indiscreet. Said it was a murder and you'd found the body. Then he clammed up, knew he'd said too much. Then he asked me out.

Might go. He's OK. Couldn't ask at the station. So, how did he die?'

'Stabbed and throat cut.'

'Yuk.' She pointed to the remains of her muesli. 'Good job I decided not to have an oozing ketchup sandwich this morning. You upset?'

He grimaced at the thought. It was just one more thing he didn't understand about 'youth'; how they could ingest and enjoy such unadulterated garbage. 'No, not upset. Unsettled though. You listened to the answerphone message?'

'Yeah, sounded heavy. You'll have to take it to the police. I expect Sarah'll be involved. Heh, Dad, be good if we could solve it first, like last time. One up on the cops, and one up on Sarah. When you seeing them again?'

'Got to go in with the phone this morning. Bit complicated. It's Vin who's leading the investigation.'

Katy spluttered into her muesli. 'Oh, Dad. You sure pick 'em. First you date a murderer, then one who's investigating a murder you discovered.' She wagged her finger at her father. 'You'll be getting a reputation.'

'Maybe. Anyway, I've got a bit of work to do before I go in. Can you tell Mo and Michael about Dobson. I'll fill in the details when I get there.'

'OK – but Dad, shall I tell them to be careful?'

Ben looked sideways at her.

'Like you're dangerous to be around? Joke, yeah?'

Ben pointed to the kitchen clock. 'Time you were going? I'll be in as soon as I can. OK?'

'See ya. And, Dad, didn't mean it about you being dangerous. It's just you do seem to attract danger these days.' She reached up and kissed his cheek. 'You be careful, eh?'

\* \* \*

When he arrived back at College, it was buzzing with students, dons, police and scenes of crime officers. Outside, a gaggle of journalists and photographers meant he had to fight his way through to retrieve Dobson's list from the Porters' Lodge.

Fisher handed it over. 'Been in my locked drawer. You can be sure that no-one's looked at it. Not our business. If it's to do with the dons, we stay clear. Let them sort it out themselves. Then we keep our noses clean, if you get my drift.'

Ben wasn't at all sure that he believed this. His memories from his undergrad days suggested that the porters knew everything and controlled most of the activity in the College. The academics had always been kept in ignorance of this reversal but the students had known who held the keys to the college, both literally and metaphorically. So he asked, 'I gather then that you looked?'

Fisher had the grace to look sheepish as he nodded assent. 'Sorry, Mr Burton, but you didn't say it was secret. And I won't pass anything on.'

'So what can you tell me?'

Fisher pointed to the list. 'These five are Ethel people – some high-ups. These three, I've never heard of.'

But there was no time to hear more of Fisher's views as the call came from the Master's Lodge that she could see them now. That excellent channel of communication had been cut off temporarily. He would need to revisit it.

\* \* \*

Ben hadn't been back to the Master's Lodge since that evening in the summer when his arm had been twisted to meet Chris. That had been Dobson's doing, getting him involved with the Services again. But it was only with the help of Chris, that he'd been able to solve the murder of Stanley Murdock and ensure that Josephine Finlay had not faced trial. Now, the old Master had been shuffled into a nice little sinecure in College and, it seemed, a dynamic woman had taken his place. He would have to contact Chris. It was not something he relished, and he had three bodies waiting to be buried.

'Mr Burton, Mr Fisher. Do come in.'

They stepped inside and were ushered into a well-equipped study. The Master's first question surprised Ben. 'How is Mrs Jones taking it?' He decided that this new broom might be just what this college needed.

Fisher replied, 'She's worried about her job Ma'am. Thinks it's suicide. I didn't put her right.'

'We'll have to reassure her. She's a long-standing member of the College staff. Of course her job's safe. Can you phone her for me? Put her mind at rest. I've sent an email to all members of staff and asked them to pass on the news to their students. I just said that Professor Dobson has died suddenly and the police are looking into the circumstances of his death. The rumours will flow. That can't be helped. Tell me, Mr Burton. How did he die?'

Ben had expected this question to come earlier. Either, this was one practical woman who had higher priorities, or she already knew. He replied, 'Stabbed, throat cut, and his rooms turned over.'

She immediately replied, 'Ah, as I thought, a burglary. Better not say any more than the basics until I've talked to the police again. Mr Burton, the police have informed me that you are an undertaker. They suggest I ask you to remove the body when they've finished here and deliver it to the pathologist. Can you do that for us?'

'Yes, of course. I came to offer my help, if needed. I'll liaise with the DCI.'

She nodded. 'I think I'll need to keep in touch with you.' Ben handed her his card. 'Thank you, Mr Burton, Mr Fisher. I believe I'll have a busy day.' She smiled a grim smile and ushered them out.

As the front door closed behind them, Fisher made a wry gesture. 'Cool customer, ain't she. The old Master would've been flapping about like a bat on heat.'

'Yes, looks like you've got a young and efficient female Master. Seems that equality's moving forward here, and about time. My daughter's always complaining about those "entitled white men". How have the Fellows taken it?'

As Ben asked this, he realised that he, too, was one of those entitled white men: white, middle-aged, Cambridge graduate. Time for a change in him too.

He tuned back into Fisher's spiel. 'Some ain't happy about being dragged into the twenty-first century. Rattled some of them. A bit of rear guard action's going on but she'll win in the end. But this murder's a nasty business. We've always been one of the more open colleges, letting in visitors. That'll have to change.'

Ben looked Fisher in the eye. 'You're assuming it was an outside job. Think about it. We both know Professor Dobson was disliked by everyone and hated by many. Could have been someone from inside College.'

Fisher shook his head vehemently. 'Mr Burton, I can't believe that. No, it's not possible. We're like a family here. That would be dreadful.'

# Chapter 3

Ben went back home before venturing to work. He had to compare the list from Dobson with the one he'd had hidden in his bedroom since Stanley Murdock's death. At the time of Murdock's murder, Chris had told him to bury all Murdock's incriminating effects with him. But Ben had ignored that order. He'd kept Murdock's blackmail list, a threatening note from Murdock to an unknown conspirator and a small key. Now, he placed Murdock's and Dobson's lists side by side on the kitchen table. In ten minutes, he'd made a detailed comparison. He was convinced that both were blackmail lists. The one he'd removed from Dobson's desk had fewer names, probably only people that Dobson knew. Seven entries appeared on both lists and Dr Clare had been added to Dobson's. The descriptions on Dobson's paper were more detailed than the one that had come from Stanley Murdock's safe. Dobson's list had more pointed insinuations so that Ben could begin to make a guess at some of the transgressions that had led to blackmail. He assumed that Dobson would have made the same leaps. Professor Hallfield was on both lists, as were the five Fellows of Ethel's, people who must have been known to Dobson. He counted eight names on Dobson's list and eighteen on Murdock's. And, of course, one of the names on Murdock's list, but missing from Dobson's, was Dobson himself. Ben wondered what hold Stanley Murdock had had over Dobson, and how he had extracted payment.

Ben suspected that one of those eight on Dobson's list had murdered him. He had no evidence on which to base this but it just felt right. The intuition that had led him to keep some of Murdock's possessions had served him well. Now, he would follow his intuition again. His first problem was that he had to gain access to each of Dobson's blackmail victims.

He put thoughts of Prof Hallfield and Dr Clare to one side. He knew, even though he had not been explicitly told, that they were having an affair; an affair complicated by the poor health of Peter Hallfield's wife.

He read through the other six entries.

18

*Professor Olaf Pedersen, July 2009, Not his native huldufolk at the end of this rainbow. Tie and dye – that's his hobby.
Dr G. Fursley, June 2005, Playing the good man in Scotland set the cat alight.
Professor H. Walpole, October 1961, Better to be under the bed than in it, especially when dealing with him who's not the sharpest.
Dr J. Hendrick, May 1991, Charles Rennie opened his doors for a second time – saved by the Three.
Dr J. P. O'Connor, April 1997, Should have been first in line. Your call Graham. And a good one.
Dr A. N. Taylor, 2011, They played the violin together for years but he's lost his bog-light, so now he's a target.*

The first five were known to Fisher – Ethel people. The last was a mystery. Ben could make out some of the allusions, and wondered what Dobson had made of them. He thought about his relationship with the dead man. Ben had felt a visceral dislike for Dobson from his first days as an undergraduate at Ethel's. This thirty-year feeling of antipathy had been brought to a head the previous summer in what Ben still thought of as the OK corral, when he'd told Dobson exactly what he thought of him. He'd felt better, partly because he hadn't stooped to hitting the man. Since then, he'd not given him a thought. But now Dobson was dead and he'd turned to Ben to save him. The least he could do was try to find the killer, and he had to protect Dr Clare. He liked her and, more to the point, he needed her.

He took out his phone and began to type the remembered email address; remembered even though he'd thought he would never have to use it. His message was terse. Another of Chris's informants was dead. He knew he wouldn't have to wait long for a response.

\* \* \*

Ben gathered Mo, Katy and Michael into the tiny kitchen at their undertaker's office. He noticed that Katy made sure that she was wedged in next to Michael in that small space. Another problem, and one he didn't know how to solve. After he'd told them what he'd discovered, Mo was the first to respond. 'You never liked him. And yer never told us why. Your business, I guess. But why come to you for help?'

'I guess he had no-one else to turn to. Nobody *liked* him. He didn't have any friends. He used people. Didn't give a shit about their feelings, trampled on them for his own ends. The academic world is full of rivalries. He made alliances, he made enemies. That's how he operated, and he was a liar and a thief. When I was his student, he stole my work and passed it off as his own. And I'm sure I wasn't the only one.'

Michael looked perplexed. 'Jeez – your man sounds a right gobshite. But if being a gobshite was enough to get you killed...' He paused for a moment. 'Did for my uncle though, didn't it?'

Only Ben and Chris knew of the alliances made between Dobson and Michael Murdock's Uncle Stanley. Stanley Murdock had indeed been a gobshite of the first order. But, as Ben knew, he had also been in the pay of Her Majesty's Government. He'd been an undercover agent in Northern Ireland and, as the saying goes, he knew where the bodies were buried. Where was bloody Chris when he needed him? He'd expected an immediate response but it had been an hour and still not a peep.

The front door pinged. Ben smiled. Back to normality. 'Looks like we have a customer. And we have work to do. All know what you need to do? Good.'

\* \* \*

Ben walked through to the reception area and saw the back of a blond head above the backrest of one of the swivel chairs. 'Morning, Chris. Took your time.'

Chris swung the chair round. 'Said you were turning into a pushy git last time I saw you. Saw the address and thought you might have changed your mind.' Ben shook his head and Chris shrugged. 'Anyway, offer still open. So you found the body, eh? And he'd asked for your help. Why would he do that?'

Ben's email to Chris had been to the point. He hadn't told him any extraneous detail, just that he'd found the body. So Chris must have got that from the police or from Fisher. Fisher was unlikely because Chris was an outsider, not from Ethel's. Ben knew that Chris had people he talked to in the Force – and elsewhere. Dobson and Murdock had been just two. And, Ben realised, he'd joined that list. One of Chris's informants. He liked that not one bit.

Chris continued, 'Doesn't feel like a contract killing. Wouldn't expect that anyway. Too low-level. And it would've been much cleaner. They were obviously looking for something. Any idea what it was?'

Ben didn't answer but posed a question of his own. 'You say "they". How do you know it wasn't a single assailant?'

'The Boys in Blue found two distinct sets of footprints – apart from your clod-hopping size elevens. Both go into the back room. One killed him while the other stood and watched. Seems they tried to get some gen from him first. Little nicks on his neck. See, my job is to make sure this has nothing to do with Murdock. And if it has, that nothing sticks.'

Ben opened the door that led to the back office. 'Give me a couple of minutes. I need to sort something for a funeral.' He closed the door behind him and quickly sifted through his memories.

Should he tell Chris that he'd not done what Chris had told him to do? When he'd buried Stanley Murdock, Chris had said, 'Bury everything. Put all the evidence underground. Bury the truth and forget the bastard.' But Ben hadn't. The gun had gone into the earth; he had no use for a gun. The worthless Swiss banknotes had gone but not the threatening note. The evidence that Stanley Murdock had intimidated and controlled his three offspring, that had gone too. As had the offspring, two to Brighton, one to God-knows-where. He'd disappeared from Cambridge along with his inheritance.

Contrary to Chris's orders, Ben had kept three items. He'd kept the note from Stanley Murdock threatening retaliation. He'd kept Stanley's list of names with its insinuations of wrong-doing and he'd kept the mysterious key. The list was the link between Murdock and Dobson. Yes, he'd have to tell Chris about the list. The key and the note, those he'd save.

He folded the two lists so the names of Dr Clare and Professor Hallfield were covered. He photocopied the two truncated versions then re-entered the front office and handed Dobson's copy to Chris. He pointed to it. 'I found this one hidden in Dobson's room. He'd done the usual trick of a veneer panel inside his desk. I'm pretty sure this is the paper I helped Josephine Finlay deliver to Dobson after Murdock's death.'

'Makes it doubly sure it was amateurs. Pros would have found this.'

Ben handed over the second list. 'This one was with Murdock's things.' In order to try to deflect questions, he added, 'Before you ask, Josephine's put me down as her next of kin. She still refuses to see me but Katy and my Uncle Mo visit her regularly. Dr Clare tells me she's making good progress. If it continues, they're thinking that she may be allowed visits out.'

The deflection seemed to have worked. Chris nodded, 'She did us all a favour when she killed that bastard. Murdock had become a complete nightmare. Got a cast iron alibi for Dobson though. Being in a nut-house is as good as it gets.'

Ben winced at the terminology. He'd forgotten just how uncouth this young man could be. Chris was looking through Dobson's list. 'Know any of these?'

Ben pointed to some names. 'These five are Fellows at Ethel's. My first task is to chat with the Head Porter. Known him for years. But I don't know any of these personally.' He pointed to the other name. 'This one, I don't know, but presumably Dobson did.' He then moved on to the longer list. 'The only other name I know on this list is Dobson himself. Seems Murdock was blackmailing him too.'

Chris seemed to be ignoring Ben's confession of insurrection. He tapped the paper in his hand. 'Hoped there'd be a Russian connection. Cambridge has history with the Ruskies and they're getting every-bloody-where these days. Interesting that the perps didn't find this. Definitely amateurs.' He turned back to Murdock's list. 'Some high-ups here though. Wonder what evidence there is – could be useful to us if we can find it. Helps to keep them under control.' He pointed to the faint line where Ben had folded the paper. 'Looks like Stanley had more victims in the past. Could be some have died.' He folded both papers and put them in his pocket. He looked at Ben. 'Now here's a proposition for you. How's about I make sure you're hired to bury Dobson. Then you can ferret around in that godforsaken hole of a college.

Lay odds they'll clam up for the cops. Their sort do. But they'll talk to you. You're one of them.'

Ben couldn't believe that, in one speech, he'd been offered a role in the investigation – which he wanted – and denigrated as an alumnus of a 'godforsaken hole of a college'. He decided to ignore the insult and go for the prize. 'I'll bury Dobson for you.'

'Good. Being an undertaker is such great cover. Don't know why we didn't think of it before. Any questions?'

'Yes. How much does DCI Wainwright know of your involvement?'

'Canny woman that. She'll have come across my name when she was in the Met. Worked a lot with her boss. They rated her. She'll go far. And I hear you've got your leg over. Lucky you. I've got my source at Parkside. Not her, wish it was. Mine's a bit flaky. Booze. Tell you what, put in a word for me, eh?' He scribbled a phone number on a bit of paper and handed Ben a burner phone. 'Contact number just for this job.' Without waiting for a response, he stood up. 'Got some sorting to do. I'll get back to you tomorrow.' As Chris reached the door, he waved the paper in his hand, 'This all you kept?'

Ben was immediately on his guard. That line had been thrown away far too nonchalantly. He lied, he hoped convincingly. 'Yes,' and to try to deflect further questioning, 'Now, is there anything else I need to know?'

'Nah. Just checking.' Then Chris added, 'You ain't much on discipline, are you? You know, following orders? Told you to bury every-fucking-thing. Bloody good job you didn't.'

# Chapter 4

*Scrub the soles of your shoes with bleach, then give them to a charity shop – Ely not Cambridge. Wash all your clothes – likewise get rid – Ely. Get rid of gloves in the river in Ely. NOW. Burn this note.*

# Chapter 5

Ben arrived at Parkside in plenty of time for his meeting with DCI Lavinia Wainwright. As he sat waiting in a soulless corridor, a friendly voice greeted him. 'Hi, Mr Burton – ooops, sorry, Ben. Forgot, I mustn't make you feel old.' Without noticing that her slip had indeed made Ben feel ancient, Pam continued. 'Haven't seen you for ages. Sarah tells me you're missing all the excitement of murders and stuff. I sure am.'

'Hi Pam.' Ben made room for Sarah's best friend to take a seat beside him. 'How's it going now you're a sergeant? Making you work hard?'

'Nah – not really. It's been dead boring since we were stood down from the Murdock killing. Still don't understand. I know we were coming up against brick walls and all that but still, we were shocked when the word came from on high to shelve it. It was definitely too early – must have been more leads we could've followed. Now it's one long round of paperwork. Sarah's on foot patrol, puppy walking. Got this new probationer who's dripping. Don't know how she stands it.'

Ben laughed. 'Me neither. She's never been the most patient of people. Maybe she'll learn.'

Pam's eyes gleamed. 'But heh, little birds were flying round the canteen just now saying there's been a murder at one of the colleges. Need some excitement.' She grinned. 'We're off out tomorrow, Sarah and me. Meeting up with your lovely Michael. He's a dish. I wonder if Katy wants to tag along?'

Ben was sure Katy would like to 'tag along' although he was equally sure she would not like to be seen as an afterthought. Yet again, he was worried about Katy. She was only eighteen and Michael was so much older. He liked Michael, and he knew him to be innocent of the crime he'd served time for. He was sure Michael was keeping his part of the bargain and was not encouraging Katy, but he didn't want her to become entangled with anyone from the Murdock family, or to be hurt. Sarah was able to take care of herself. She always had been. But Katy? Katy was so like her mother; he wished his girls had known her. As he was ruminating, DCI Vin Wainwright poked her head round the door. Pam jumped up, looking flustered.

Vin laughed. 'It's OK, Pam.' Vin looked at her watch. 'There'll be a briefing at noon. Can you be the messenger? Should be long enough to muster CID and any Uniforms you can find. See if there are any lurking outside. Dig 'em out from all those nooks and crannies where the smokers go. Back of the fire station is a good place to start. Off you go now.' As Pam scuttled off, Vin turned to Ben and smiled. 'Mr Burton – or should I call you Ben so you don't feel old? Do come in.'

As soon as she'd closed the door, he asked 'Have you got x-ray ears or is the corridor bugged?'

Vin spoke quietly. 'Neither. The walls here are paper thin – and Pam's got a voice that carries. Useful if you're on crowd control, and useful for me sitting quietly in here. Did you notice how close the water cooler and notice board are to my door? I had them moved, plus the bench and those few chairs. They often gather there in twos and threes and I find out what's going on. It's how I know where the smokers go, plus those who want to be off the premises when it suits them. Want a coffee?'

As she poured two cups, Ben looked round the spartan room. He'd never been in her office before. They always met well away from Parkside and nosey coppers. There was nothing here to give a hint of its occupant's needs or personality. The Vin he knew was absent from this room.

She lowered her voice further so he had to lean forward to hear. 'Pam's right. This place is a rumour-mill. After your statement this morning, they're sure you're seeing a married woman. They've checked phone records and the call from Dobson has been verified. And CCTV shows your car picking up petrol near me at the time of death. So you're in the clear. Relieved?'

'I would be if I'd ever thought I'd been a suspect. But finding the body? Suppose I must be.'

'We've been careful but I'll be surprised if they don't twig about us before long. Hyper-vigilant from now on.'

Ben grimaced. Part of his problem was hyper-vigilance so, hyper-vigilant was just what he was trying hard not to be. 'I think someone may have twigged already.'

'Had to happen, I suppose. There's one or two old hands who'd use anything they had on me. You met them this morning at the College. They want to keep me in the dark, send me down blind alleys so I fail. Don't know if it's because I'm a woman or they blame me for replacing Turnbull.'

'But Turnbull was a plonker.'

'Probably why they felt comfortable with him. They could get away with stuff they know I won't put up with. Please don't tell Pam or Sarah. Listening in is one of my ways of keeping up to speed. Now, bring me up to speed on this murder. Tell me what you know?'

'Before I do – any news on the knife?'

'Disappointing. Clean and new. Probably bought specially. And – as they say in the ads – available at all good hardware stores. So it's a dead end, pun intended.'

'And a bad one! Anyway, two things I need to talk to you about – the murder, yes – and MI5.' Vin raised her eyebrows but said nothing. 'I've brought in my answerphone. It doesn't have a removable tape like in the olden days.' He handed over a bag to Vin. 'Can you get it copied and back to me. Need it for work.'

She nodded and picked up her phone. After a short conversation, in which she said immediately twice, she asked Ben, 'Thirty minutes do? Tell me about the murder first, then about MI5.'

Ben relayed his tale from finding the answerphone message to finding the body, including the hidden compartment in Dobson's desk and its contents. He showed her the two blackmail lists. They were, to all intents and purposes, Stanley Murdock's and Professor Dobson's lists, but truncated as had been the ones for Chris. He saw her eyes widen. She pointed to an entry on Stanley Murdock's list. She spoke in a whisper. 'I know this man. He's a DS here.' There was a knock on the door and she shuffled some papers over the two lists before calling out, 'Come in.'

After handing over the answerphone to a uniformed constable, she waited until the door was closed and the footsteps had receded. She pointed again at the list. 'DS White. Been here for ever. I would have trusted him with my life. So what does this mean?'

'It means he was probably being blackmailed by Stanley Murdock but not by Professor Dobson.'

'Shit. That's three I can't trust.'

'Possibly four – that's where MI5 comes in. You've signed the Official Secrets Act?'

She nodded.

Ben moved closer to Vin and spoke in a voice just above a whisper. 'There's a man called Chris. He's MI5. He says you know his name. He knows about us.' Ben continued, 'I did some work for him on Turnbull's last case, Stanley Murdock's murder. Chris made sure your lot were sent off on wild goose chases. The reason for his involvement was...' Ben paused – this was an enormous secret he was divulging. And a secret once told couldn't be retrieved. 'Stanley Murdock was an agent in deep cover in Northern Ireland in the eighties. Chris thought his cover had been blown and it was a revenge killing. But it turned out to be a "domestic" of sorts.' He held up his hand as Vin seemed about to interrupt. 'Murdock was killed by his solicitor who also happened to be his daughter. Long, dirty story. I helped Chris find her and make sure there was no trial.'

This time she did interrupt. She looked horrified. 'You killed her?'

Ben chuckled. He'd been a killer once – but not now. He held up his hands in mock surrender. 'No. The woman who killed Stanley Murdock is now in a very expensive mental institution paid for by MI5. She has serious problems but I hear she's making good progress. Her mother had been gang-raped by Murdock and his friends when they were undergrads at Ethel's and she was the result. That was just one of his evil deeds. He'd gone rogue and the Service was delighted to be rid of him. It removed a problem.' He paused and sighed. 'They'll look after her.' Then he added with steel in his voice, 'I'll make sure they do.'

Vin looked thoughtful. She tapped her pen on her desk. 'I heard there was an MI5 connection. Before I came here. Haven't met this Chris but his name came across my desk while I was with the Met. And Dobson?'

'I'm sure the murders are connected but Murdock's killer is out of the frame for Dobson's. Professor Dobson was one of Chris's informants. Dobson knew Murdock. I believe that Murdock gave him this shorter list so Dobson could continue blackmailing the people he knew. But I think Dobson wasn't nearly as clever as Murdock and someone on this list killed him.'

'And the longer list.'

'I was supposed to bury that with Murdock. I kept it.'

'How do you know they're blackmail lists?' She looked from one list to the other. 'They're riddles – in some sort of code. I can see that they possibly make insinuations. Nothing more.'

Ben had to think quickly. The reason he knew was because, several months ago, Dr Clare had all but admitted to him that she and Professor Hallfield were being blackmailed. But he'd removed their names from the papers he'd given to Vin. Then he remembered his last meeting with Dobson. 'Dobson told me last time I met him. If you look, he's on the longer list but not the other one. Stanley Murdock had some kind of hold over him but I have no idea what it was.'

'Christ, Ben. We've been seeing each other for two months and I've learnt more about you in the last ten minutes than in all that time. I'll need time to get my head round this. You and me. You know.'

He did know. He'd only dated twice since Diane's death. The first time, he'd dipped his toe into the choppy waters of relationships with a very damaged woman. And she'd killed Stanley Murdock. He'd hoped then to meet someone uncomplicated. But he knew that the complications in his own past made him less than the ideal partner.

'I know – and I'm sorry. I couldn't tell you.'

'Deal with that later. Now, you said there was a possible fourth officer I can't trust?'

'Not sure where his loyalties lie. One of your officers is reporting to Chris, told him about us, I think. Chris says he's flaky. Drink. Says he'd rather deal with you. Called you "a canny woman". I'd say that's a big compliment from him.'

Vin held up her hand. 'Let me think.' She closed her eyes for a moment, then looked up at the wall clock. 'Nearly time I was giving that briefing. I want you to come with me and tell them about finding the body. Leave out this.' She waved the two papers. 'I'll present them with some names.'

'I've given you those lists but I know Chris has an interest. He'll need a head start. Can you keep the blackmail angle to yourself for the time being?'

As he said this, Vin looked doubtful, so he added, 'I needn't have brought them to you. We just need some time.' He clenched his hands. Putting himself into 'we' with Chris was not at all comfortable but he knew he would need help from both Vin and Chris. Dobson's dead face came to mind. Last summer, he'd asked for Ben's help and Ben had refused. The second time, he'd been too late. He needed to make reparations. And then there was Dr Clare…

As he pondered his perceived responsibilities, Vin went to her printer and did precisely what Ben had done earlier. After folding Murdock's list, so that DS White's entry was hidden, she copied it and handed the original back to Ben. 'OK. Take this away and hide it wherever you hid it before. Keep it safe, I may need it.' She put her copy in her drawer and locked it, then copied the shorter list which had only the six Dobson's victims on it and gave the original back to Ben. 'Ditto. But we'd have to interview all these people anyway.'

Ben smiled and his mind went back to his encounter earlier with the new Master at Ethel's. Fisher had described her as a woman who wouldn't wobble. Here was another. He hoped his girls would turn out like this.

'Ben – are you listening?'

'Sorry. What was that?'

'I'll make a point of talking to DS White. They call him Blanco. I want you to stay to the end of the briefing and watch my officers and tell me what you see.'

* * *

Two hours later, they made their way separately to The White Horse in Comberton, far enough from prying eyes to be safe. They sat in a corner hidden from all the entrances. After ordering, Vin got straight to the matter in hand.

'Well, what do you think?'

'Before we get on to that, no-one queried why I was there. Surely that's unusual?'

'Yeah. When I left you outside, I sort of told them that you had a history of solving murders and that you had to wait for your answerphone anyway. And that you had a cast-iron alibi.'

'And they took it?'

'Generally they don't like outsiders muscling in. But I didn't brook any argument and I'm in charge. And, if you look confident, you can get away with murder.'

Ben wondered about the aptness of this description, but realised it was probably true. 'Right. Your people. I don't think you need to worry about Blanco. He's late fifties, yes?' Vin nodded. 'I'd say he's low level and not ambitious. The insinuations on Murdock's list suggest he had an affair, possibly years ago and not connected with the job. He wasn't on Dobson's list so his blackmailer is long dead and buried. He could be eased towards retirement and he'd probably go quietly. Or you could just keep him ticking over. Your call.'

'That's reassuring. Anything else?'

'Yeah. You've got problems with those two at the back – the ones who came with you this morning. They the ones who keep you in the dark?'

Again she nodded.

'I could see they're working against you. But did you notice? They don't have a following. The others don't like them. Especially the young ones.'

'I know. They call them "The Apostles". No idea why.'

'You could either separate them and surround them with youngsters or isolate them together. I'd do the first. Not let them work together.'

'That's helpful.'

Before she could say more, Ben added, 'And I know who your MI5 mole is. He was put in as Family Liaison Officer for the Murdock family. That hefty fellow who kept spreading his legs. He went and sat next to Pam. Didn't take long for her to move.'

'God, yes. Another bloody too-confident male. The women call him Rambo. So your Chris says there's a possible booze problem. Good to know.'

As Ben listened to Vin, he felt happy with his lot; grateful that, in his family business, they were all pulling in the same direction. Katy was shaping up nicely. His uncle Mo was starting to

31

take life a bit easier now that Michael had joined the firm. He was pretty sure they wouldn't have Michael Murdock for long. When his inheritance from his Uncle Stanley came through, Michael would have several million pounds at his disposal, and working for an undertaker might not have the same appeal. Then he thought of Sarah and wondered how she was coping in this environment, so different from his own.

'So it's still difficult for a woman in the police. Do I have to worry about Sarah?'

Vin smiled. 'No way. Your daughter's doing fine. She's shaping up into a good officer. There are still elements in the Force that we could do without but the culture is changing – not quickly enough – but changing. And you certainly don't have to worry while I'm her boss. I look after my young officers. They're our future.'

'Good. That's a relief. Now getting back to the present. Dobson.'

She interrupted before he could say more. 'One more thing. Did you see any reaction when I read out the names from Dobson's list?'

Before he answered he thought he'd try a spot of fishing. 'Clever that – the way you read out the names without telling them why. Just the cover that they were the closest people to Dobson. You suspect some of your officers – but who and what of – care to tell me?'

The very slight intake of breath told him he'd hit home. But she shook her head. 'You really don't expect me to answer that, do you?' And that just confirmed his suspicion.

He tried again. 'Come on – you can tell me something. Whet my appetite.'

'OK. Just this. The Met thinks there's a link between Cambridge and Operation Yewtree. You know about Yewtree?'

'Only the Savile connection. I saw that TV programme. It was diabolical that he got away with it for so long. I'm assuming the ripples will spread a long way.'

'Yep. Even into my force.'

Ben looked aghast. 'You suspect your officers of paedophilia?'

'Who knows? But collusion is a possibility we're considering. Now I've said way too much so please be circumspect in what you say and do.'

'Right. Yes. Thanks for confiding in me. Reactions to your list – both your Apostles were looking down so I couldn't see their faces. Blanco was just that – blanco. I don't even think he took it in. Rambo was interesting. He sat up and took notice. But it might just be that he wants something to report to Chris.' He looked round just to make sure that there was no-one in earshot. 'And talking of Chris. He's arranging for me to bury Dobson so I can see what I can find out. Says the College people might talk to me as I'm one of them. He's right; I've got a better chance than your lot. Academics – they'll clam up – close ranks.' He looked away for a moment, dredging up an unwanted memory of one of his last meetings with Dobson. He remembered Dobson saying, 'Whatever happens in College stays in College.' So, even for him, a supposed insider, getting information could be difficult.

Vin looked expectantly at Ben. He looked back, eyebrows raised, mimicking her look. She laughed. 'You intrigue me. I'm not at all sure why you're working for this Chris.' She tapped her finger on the back of his hand. 'I think it's because it suits your purposes. I'd lay a bet you're mainly working for yourself. And I don't know why. Am I near the truth?'

'Spot on. And I'm not going to tell you why. Not yet anyway.'

'OK. Deal, but I want to ask you a favour. You see, I don't understand those College people either. I think my lot are hard enough to manage. God knows how you'd manage academics, they take independence to extremes. I want you to work for me too. Unofficial. Unpaid. Tell me what you find.'

'No problem. Suits me. And I hope you'll be able to share some more info with me.'

She inclined her head. 'Some things. Not sure how much yet – but if it helps to solve this murder – that's the aim.'

Ben grimaced. 'First thing I've got to do is see the Master and get an invite to High Table and drinks at the Master's Lodge. Make sure they remember that I'm one of them. I'll have to get a new hood and gown.' He grinned. 'Heh! Do I get expenses?' She shook her head and mouthed 'Sorry'. He laughed. 'You're a meaner boss than Chris. Don't worry. I'll get it from him.'

# Chapter 6

It had been easier than he'd expected to get himself an invitation to a seat at High Table. He'd never tried before so it came as a surprise to him that any alumnus could just book a place. He didn't know how Chris had wangled it but the Master had asked him if he was available to bury Professor Dobson. He would need to discuss arrangements with her. Next he'd gone to Ryder and Amies to get the correct hood and gown. Who would have thought that there would be a special maths hood, a special maths gown – a special hood and gown for every conceivable degree. No wonder they were so pricey. Anyway, now he had the right kit for dinner in Hall. And he would send the substantial bill to Chris.

* * *

'God, this looks preposterous. They even had to tell me how the hood should lie. Don't remember all this stupidity when I was an undergrad.'

'Dad, you look sooo distinguished. Love the colours – that red really suits you. Pity it's at the back. What do you think, Uncle Mo?'

Maurice was looking nostalgic. 'I remember when you was first wearing one of them. Your mum was so proud. And your graduation; she loved that. All that finger pulling, never did understand what that was about.' He laughed. 'Weird place, that university of yours. And now you're off to find out who killed that bastard Dobson.'

'Fraid so – hope so. And it's not my university. I went there, I left and, until I had to deliver that letter to Dobson, I'd never looked back. Now I've got to try to fit in, and dressing up is part of the game.'

Katy chimed in. 'Well, I think you look great. Anything we can do to help?'

'Well, now you mention it, there's this.' Ben riffled through the pile of papers on top of his desk. 'You can look through this list. It came from Dobson's study. It's similar to that list from Stanley Murdock; it's shorter, but with longer descriptions, more info but more convoluted. See what you make of it. I'll tell you why later.'

Katy's eyes lit up. 'It's like clues. Love it! Look at this one. *"Professor Olaf Pedersen, July 2009 – Not his native huldufolk at the end of this rainbow. Tie and dye – that's his hobby."* What the hell does that mean? Can I ask Michael to help?'

'Sure, three brains should be better than two.'

'Dad, d'you reckon Dobson's murderer is among this lot?'

'Could be.'

'Brill! Bloody brilliant. Let's get him.' She looked appealingly at her father. 'And Dad, can I borrow the car tonight. Promise not to drink.'

Ben held out the keys and she reached up to kiss his cheek. 'Thanks, Dad. You're the best.'

He thought briefly, then came to a decision. 'How about we buy you a car? Birthday present.'

Katy grabbed him and hugged him. 'Thanks, Dad. You're not only the best. You're...' She paused for a moment. 'You're the bestest!'

\* \* \*

Ben stood in silence then turned a full circle twice. The light from the full moon was playing with the yellow stone making it seem iridescent in places. When he'd first arrived here, he'd loved this place: its peace, its beauty, its entry into another world. He'd met Diane here, he'd excelled at his studies, he'd gained a Blue, but then he'd realised that there was corruption here and had turned his back on it all. For more than twenty years he'd eschewed Ethel's and all it stood for. Then he'd been enticed back by murder, first by one victim – an unimaginably evil man, then by another – a man he despised. To say he was ambivalent was an understatement. But he would not let this College woo him for a second time. Of that he was sure.

On his way to the Master's Lodge, he took the opportunity to have a quiet word with Mr Fisher. He wanted Fisher's advice about the names on his list. He poked his head round the door of the Porters' Lodge and was greeted by a worried smile. 'Mr Burton, I was hoping for a word with you. Shall we take a walk round the garden?'

As they rounded the pond, Fisher took Ben's arm and guided him to a bench away from any listening ears. 'Mr Burton, I'm in a bit of a quandary. I don't know whether I should tell. It could be nothing, you see, and I don't want to get anyone into trouble.'

As Fisher dropped into silence, wringing his hands, Ben asked gently, 'What's troubling you? You know you can tell me. We've known each other for – must be thirty years. Tell me and I'll work out what needs to be done.'

'It's like this, see. You put it in my mind saying it could be one of us.' Fisher paused and Ben waited. Ben knew one or other of them would have to fill the void and it wasn't going to be him. Eventually, after more wringing of hands, Ben's patience was rewarded. 'It's probably nothing, not really, not that unusual for him.' Fisher took another deep breath and ploughed on. 'The day before he died, I heard him threatening someone. I could only catch a few words. They were round the corner in Front Court and the wind blew some snatches to me. I heard "reputation of the College" and "think of your wife". Then there was something strange; "they'll fake them anyway", then I couldn't hear any more.'

Ben ruminated, rolling the words around a couple of times, 'They'll fake them anyway? Fake them anyway? Any idea what that was about?'

'Not a clue, Mr Burton. Didn't make sense to me.'

'Did you see who it was?'

'Sorry, by the time I got round the corner there was no-one there. Front Court was empty.'

'But you're sure it was Dobson?'

'Oh yes. He's got… Sorry. He had a distinctive voice. And that laugh. You could recognise it anywhere. Heard him often enough, laying into them poor students of his. Sorry Mr Burton, shouldn't speak ill of the dead.'

Ben ignored the slight slip in College protocol. 'What about the other voice? Would you recognise that again?'

37

Fisher drew his brows together. 'It was a cultured voice, but you could tell he was angry. Hissing through his teeth, he was. I might do. But possibly not.'

'Have another think. Is there anything else you can remember about the conversation? Or the other man?'

'No, Mr Burton. But I'll have another go at it and get back to you if I remember anything.'

'Good. And thank you for telling me. I think the police will want to know. Shall I tell them or will you?'

'Oh, Mr Burton – could you? I'm sure it's not important but I feel much better for getting it off my chest.'

'No problem. Let me know if you think of anything else.'

As they walked together in the direction of the Master's Lodge, Ben asked, 'Maybe you can help me with something. That list I left with you had one name on it that I couldn't identify. It was a Dr A N Taylor. Dobson knew him but I can't place him. Could be a woman, of course. You know everyone worth knowing round here – this college and others – any ideas about this Taylor? I need to make contact.'

'Well, now you're asking. Name doesn't ring any bells. I'll ask around, shall I? One of the other Head Porters might know.'

They'd reached the door to the Master's Lodge. They ceremoniously shook hands. 'Have a good evening, sir. My, but it's good to have you back.' And Fisher turned and marched away.

# Chapter 7

Ben had decided that he would have to use pretext with the Master. It rankled that he would have to lie to this woman, but he had higher priorities. He'd told her that he particularly wanted introductions to Professors Pedersen and Walpole and Doctors Hendrick, Fursley and O'Connor, as he'd heard that they had known Professor Dobson the longest and might be useful in providing background for his funeral service. He'd asked her about the sixth name on Dobson's list – Dr A N Taylor – and she'd been certain that they had no Dr Taylor at Ethel's. She'd suggested that she could look back to see if one had been employed there in the past. Ben had told her not to worry – Mr Fisher could take on the task – and, if the elusive Dr Taylor were to be employed in any college, Fisher would find him or her.

Helpfully, the Master had invited Ben and his five suspects, along with several others, to join her for a drink before the formal dinner. Ben had been agreeably surprised to find that this Master served, not sherry, but a very palatable sparkling wine. As the first of his five academics arrived, the Master introduced him to Ben.

'Dr Hendrick, come. I'd like you to meet Mr Burton. He'll be organising the funeral of poor Professor Dobson. It seems that we, in College, are the nearest he had to family so the onus is on us to make his passing memorable for the right reasons. Mr Burton hopes that you might be able to fill in some background for him.'

First impressions showed a youngish man with very bad posture; someone who seemed to be worn down by the burdens he carried. Hendrick looked apprehensive, as well he might. Ben quickly opened the conversation. 'Thanks. I really do need help. I knew him years ago, was one of his students way back when, but I lost touch. What I would like to do is come and have a chat with you. Would that be OK?'

It was obvious to Ben that that was not OK. Hendrick bristled. 'Look, I really didn't know him well. Sure, we've been in the same college for years, but I've really got nothing to tell you. So, if you'll excuse me...'

He was about to turn away when Ben said, 'Dr Hendrick, you're being far too modest. The police have released some of Dobson's papers to me and you are mentioned.'

Hendrick stopped abruptly and stepped back towards Ben. 'And pray tell me, why would the police do that?'

'It's odd, I know, but I'm standing in for his executor until a will is found. It happens sometimes.' Ben had no idea whether it happened or not, but relied on the fact that Hendrick would be equally ignorant. He was.

'So all his papers will come to you?'

'If there's no will and no next-of-kin, then yes. Why? Is there anything I should know about? Something you were working on together?'

Hendrick's face contorted and, at first, Ben took this look as one of distaste. Observing more closely, he reinterpreted the man's expression as fear. Surely, now his blackmailer was dead, fear would only be appropriate if the fearful one still had something to hide.

Before Hendrick could answer, the Master touched Ben's arm. 'I've explained to the other dons you mentioned that you need their help.' She half-turned and Ben saw she had been followed by a gaggle of black-robed academics. She introduced then one by one. He noted that only one was a woman, Dr Fursley. Ben idly wondered if this reflected the gender split of College fellows or was it just that men were more blackmailable than women. Fursley, Hendrick and O'Connor were much younger than the other two. Ben reckoned those three must be his age. No, younger, somewhere in their thirties or forties? Pedersen looked to be a little older, mid-fifties? And Walpole looked to be of pensionable age and was leaning heavily on a stick. Ben wondered if he, too, had been shuffled off to a pleasant sinecure in College.

Before Ben could even acknowledge them, Hendrick spoke to the group. 'Mr Burton is Dobson's executor and he'll get all Dobson's papers.'

Interesting, thought Ben. Hendrick's rattled – that's not surprising. But frightened? In Ben's considered opinion, he had precisely the look of a head-lit rabbit. And his speech suggested to Ben that he knew that some of the others in this group were also Dobson's victims. Ben quickly surveyed them. The black robes

40

made them look austere, but none of them looked like a murderer. But then, who does?

Ben spoke. 'Not entirely true. But it does seem likely that they will come to me eventually. The police tell me they've found nothing about any family among his effects here or at his house in Trumpington. And, as yet, no will has surfaced. So, at present, I'm organising his burial and the police have decided it would be helpful for me to act as temporary executor. It makes life easier for them. In due course, all his collaborative work will go to those of you who were working with him. So, if you let me know what your interest is, I'll try to expedite matters.' Ben knew at least one of these utterances to be a lie but he needed to keep them guessing, and be open to contact from him.

Dr Fursley asked in a quiet voice, 'His house in Trumpington? Are the police guarding that too?'

'I don't think so. They've done a thorough search and found nothing. They're a bit stretched so it seems unlikely. It could technically be considered a crime scene, but no crime happened there so they've excluded it.' He had no idea if this was true, but, again, it seemed plausible. He found himself surprised and disconcerted by the ease with which these lies were emanating from his lips. He continued, 'It seems that you five have known Professor Dobson for a long time, even if, as Dr Hendrick says, you did not know him well. I'd like your help to ensure that this funeral reflects well on the College, as the nearest thing to a family that Professor Dobson seems to have had.'

It was Professor Walpole who replied. He rapped his stick on the ground ensuring the attention of the younger members of the group. 'Nasty business. Got to limit damage to the College.' He pointed a long bony finger at Ben. 'I know you. Looked you up. Senior Wrangler and a boxing Blue. Brought prestige to the College. Was sorry to learn about your wife and your injury. Must have been hard for you. Anyway, good to be working with someone who understands us.'

Ben wondered how Walpole had known that he was going to be involved. Maybe the Master had told him. And why had Walpole researched his background? He would have to talk to Chris.

One of the group moved forward and shook Ben firmly by the hand. Ben felt pressure on his knuckle and, covering his surprise, returned it. Best to be thought to be a real insider. The man smiled. 'Good to have one of us involved. You mentioned the police. We have good relations with the police but we are quite in the dark as to progress on the dreadful murder of poor Graham. I hope you can provide us with news while we help to ensure that his funeral brings credit to the College.'

Ben wondered which 'we' Pedersen was referring to, the College or his handshake society. 'I'll do my best.' Ben looked questioningly at the other man. He couldn't bring himself to use Dobson's first name, 'I'll be burying Professor Dobson and dealing with his paperwork but I know no more than you do about the direction of police enquiries.'

'But I thought…' Then Pedersen checked himself. 'Sorry, thinking of someone else.'

Ben smiled inwardly and wondered which member of Vin's team was leaking to Pedersen. He'd have to tell her about the connection. He thought that handshakes would probably be involved.

Ben asked him, 'Are there any of Professor Dobson's papers you were particularly interested in? Perhaps you were working together at the time of his death?'

'Nothing in particular.' Pedersen waved a hand towards the rest of the room. 'We all had dealings with him. He was on the College Council so we all lobbied him.'

'Not that it did much good,' was O'Connor's mumbled response.

Ben smiled. 'I will need your help. I'd like to come to talk to all of you to make sure we do our best for Professor Dobson, and the College, of course. I hope you'll all be able to add to my knowledge of his life.'

Professor Walpole seemed to take that as a hint that it was time to move. He took out a pocket watch and looked at it. 'Good show, Burton. Keep in touch. Nearly time for dinner, I think.' And he ushered the rest of the group away.

Ben was left to talk to the Master. 'I'm intrigued. How did he know that I was a student here?'

'Oh, that was me. Mr Fisher told me about you. I thought they'd be more likely to talk to you if they knew you were one of them, and one of our brightest and best.' She looked Ben in the eye. 'The entire university – but particularly this college – is under scrutiny. We need to restore our reputation as quickly as possible. I'll do everything I can to ensure that this funeral reflects well on us. So, whatever you need, let me know and I'll do all I can to help.'

Ben had begun to admire this woman so he felt he had to be honest with her. 'You realise there may be further revelations about the College before this murder is behind you.'

'Yes, Mr Burton, I do. I'm preparing myself for a very bad time. This university has been here for 800 years. I've been here for only a few months but, already, I love it. So, we'll do our best. Now, let's go in to dinner.'

\* \* \*

'So, how was it, Dad?' Katy looked into the scuffed bag that her father had thrown on a chair. 'That's not your gown, is it?' She waved an admonitory finger at him. 'Shame on you!' She retrieved the hood and gown, shook them out and laid them carefully on a chair.

Maurice looked on, smiling. 'Well, how was it? Find out anything? Need a drink?'

'Hated it. Not much. And yes, I'd love one. How about you? Had a good evening?'

As Katy got out a glass for her father, Michael pointed to the paper in front of them. 'Been looking at that thing you gave us.'

Katy butted in. 'But first, tell us about your posho dinner in Hall.'

'Not much to tell. Met five of those people on your list there. One of them was rattled, the rest seemed just ordinary – including the one with the funny handshake. Obviously, the rumour machine has been in overdrive. As soon as I walked into the Great Hall, they all hushed and turned to look at me.' He smiled at the memory. 'It was like those films of synchronised flamingoes – all those heads turning in unison – following me from the door to High Table. The place is buzzing with speculation about the murder.

They want to see it as a burglary. Problem is that none of the usual things were stolen, but I suppose they don't know that.' He pointed to the list on the table. 'Anyway, I'll be seeing all those people again. Now tell me what you've come up with.'

Maurice looked at the other two. 'Who's going to start?'

'I will,' said Katy. 'Dr Clare – well, we know her.' She looked at her father. 'I love her. She's done a great job on you. You're more together than you've ever been. And now she's doing wonders with Josephine. We worked out why she was on this list. She's obviously having an affair with Professor Hallfield here.' She pointed to another entry. 'We think these two tie up nicely. Are we right?'

Ben was impressed. 'Wow! Yes. How did you get to that?'

'The same word came up in both of his snidey comments. They were the only two with mill in them. One was "going through the mill" and the other "along Mill Lane". So we reckon that they were meeting at the hotel at Quy Mill.'

'Blimey. How did you get the hotel? It's nowhere near Mill Lane.'

'That was a real leap – not totally sure we went the right way – but we think we did. We all know Stanley was totes obnox – but totes clever too – so we looked at those two entries again and one had "cow" in it and the other had "island"'. She turned to her great-uncle. 'And Uncle Mo knew that Quy was once called Cow Island.' She looked enquiringly at her father. 'So, are we right?'

'Brilliant – yes. Don't know about Quy Mill but way back she as good as admitted to me that they were having an affair. He's married with children.'

Michael joined in. 'She told you?'

'No, not in so many words, but he more or less confirmed it. He was one of my lecturers last year on my criminology course. I was the only mature student and we're about the same age so after lectures we often went for a drink. He never mentioned it was Dr Clare he was seeing but I found out that they knew each other well. We mostly talked about family and criminals.'

Michael laughed. 'And my uncle was both.'

Ben still wondered how Michael could be so normal having served a seven-year sentence courtesy of his wicked uncle. He nodded. 'Yep, your Uncle Stanley was an out and out bastard, but at least he did the decent thing and provided for you after giving you all that grief. Auction's next month. Any idea what you'll do with the money?'

Michael shook his head. 'I've got a financial adviser lined up. But I'm in no hurry. I'll see how much I've got before making any decisions. That OK with you?'

Ben didn't like to think of Michael leaving them. Notwithstanding Katy's infatuation, and the worry that gave him, Ben saw Michael as a trusted colleague. But Katy was only eighteen. It was the age gap – ten years, which was so difficult for Ben to accommodate. Or was it that Michael had been in prison? Ben sincerely hoped that his reluctance for them to form a liaison was not based on that. Michael had certainly been a boon to the business, bringing both new ideas and strong arms. He excelled at all aspects of the job and would be difficult to replace. But when he inherited his millions, Ben was sure he'd want to spread his wings. A bridge to cross for the future.

He pointed again to the list. 'Two down, six to go. So, what of the other people? Anything else to report?'

Mo waved the paper over his head. 'Yep – I can tell you that the man who thought these up was seriously deranged. Begging your pardon Michael, but your uncle was a nutter with a devious mind.' He flicked the paper. 'Who would make up this convoluted drivel?'

Katy squeezed Maurice's arm. 'Uncle Mo, you're wonderful. I'd do it. I love it. It's like you have these doors and you have to find the key to open them. And then you find another door, but it might be a window or a brick wall. Tell you what, I'll get you to play Monkey Island. Then you'll understand. You might even turn into a gamer.'

Maurice had time to utter a harrumph before Katy started on the next. 'Dr G. Fursley. It says *"June 2005. Playing the good man in Scotland set the cat alight."*'

Katy pointed to Michael. 'Tell him what you think.' She turned to her father. 'Michael got the end of this one.'

Ben looked at his daughter orchestrating this session and decided that perhaps he was being over-protective. She seemed to be more than capable of taking care of herself. Michael nodded and replied, 'Yeah, in Ireland, "cat alights" was what we called

45

Catholics. My uncle would've known that. But we couldn't get the first half.'

'That's a good start though. She's the only woman in the Ethel's group. May need to put that into our calculations. So, something to do with a Catholic woman. Can you note that, Katy.' Ben pointed to the last name on the list. 'I don't know this one. Dr A. N. Taylor, he or she is not from Ethel's. I've got Ethel's Head Porter on the case to try to find him or her in Cambridge. Katy, can you trawl through the other colleges too. And Anglia Ruskin. It's a common name so that could take time. Better get onto it soon.' Ben looked at his watch. 'But not tonight. We've got a cremation tomorrow. So I, for one, am going to bed.' He turned in the doorway and spoke to Katy. 'Thought you were going out. Wanted to borrow the car?'

'Did, but this was far more interesting.'

Ben wondered if it was the blackmail clues or sitting next to Michael, but he decided to keep his counsel.

Michael and Maurice stood up in unison. 'Better get our beauty sleep, eh lad.' And they went into the night leaving Katy still puzzling over the list of names and clues.

# Chapter 8

Ben arrived at the Priory in plenty of time for his appointment. Dr Clare had sounded surprised when he'd phoned, and even more surprised when he'd told her that it was neither about his treatment nor Josephine Finlay's. Earlier that morning, he'd led the cremation of a great-grandfather. It had gone smoothly leaving a very satisfied family and that pleased him. He was feeling content.

As he waited in the plush reception area, he was transported back into his journey through PTSD, leading to the relative tranquillity he enjoyed today. He hadn't had a flashback dream in the months since he'd started his course of treatment with Dr Clare. And he was learning to control his hyper-vigilance; to let go of those he loved and allow them to take their own risks. It was hard but he was seeing measurable progress. It had taken sixteen years but now, at long last, he felt his recovery was certain.

He jumped as a quiet voice spoke at his elbow, 'Mr Burton, deep in thought, I see. Sorry, didn't mean to startle you. You've intrigued me. Not here about yourself or Ms Finlay. Let's go to my office and we'll see what I can do for you.'

As they arrived at her office, Ben pointed to the sign on the door. 'Dr Alison Clare, Forensic Psychologist. I wondered, when I first knew you, why a forensic psychologist should be working here. But then I realised. You have clients like Josephine.'

Her answer was a non-committal, 'Um.'

As soon as Dr Clare had closed the door behind him, Ben started on his tale. 'Actually, I'm hoping I can do something for you. And I'm afraid that it will be me who startles you this time.' He waited until she had sat down before continuing. He removed two sheets of paper from his pocket. He had carefully folded them to reveal just her name and that of Professor Hallfield. He held them carefully so she could not see what was written on them, except for the names. 'One of these papers was found in the possession of a Professor Dobson at St Etheldreda's College.' No reaction. 'The other was in the effects of Stanley Murdock.'

She jumped at the sound of that name. He could see the colour drain from her face and her body sag in the chair. He waited while she recovered her composure and held out the offending messages so she could see the two names and the clues beside them. Tears began to overspill and slip slowly down her cheeks. Ben handed her a clean white handkerchief. 'Don't worry. No-one outside my family has seen these and I will keep them safe until they can be destroyed.' Ben realised that he wasn't being entirely honest and couldn't be until he had ascertained that she and Professor Hallfield were innocent in relation to the murder of Professor Dobson.

He smiled gently. 'Let me start at the beginning. Then I'd like some information from you so that I can help you.' She nodded in dumb agreement. He continued. 'When I started treatment with you, I mentioned that I'd been a student in Professor Hallfield's blackmail class. I saw the effect it had on you and said I would help you if you ever needed it. Remember?' Again she nodded. 'I believe that Murdock was blackmailing Professor Hallfield because you were having an affair. I know Hallfield is married and has children. I believe you meet at Quy Mill?'

'Oh!' Her sharp intake of breath showed that Katy had been right. For a brief moment he allowed himself to revel in the fact that his daughter was indeed a very clever girl. Dr Clare looked stricken. 'How do you know?'

'Mostly guesswork.' He held out the two lists again. 'This list belonged to Stanley Murdock and this one, Professor Dobson. Now what can you tell me about Professor Dobson?'

'Nothing. I've never heard of him.' She glanced again at the exposed entries on each list. She looked intently at the coded messages. 'I'm not sure I could work it out and I'm one of the subjects.' She looked straight at Ben and spat out her next words. 'I knew Murdock. Disgusting hateful man. I was so relieved when I heard he was dead.' Then she spoke in a calmer tone. 'But I have no idea who Professor Dobson is.'

Ben spoke in a hushed tone. 'Tell me about the blackmail.'

'The blackmail. It was dreadful. Murdock didn't say anything out loud. He just insinuated that he'd tell Peter's wife. She's not a well woman, so we couldn't take that chance. Murdock said he had proof: photos, hotel receipts. We thought we'd been so careful.' She looked sorrowfully at Ben. 'But obviously not careful enough. He didn't ask for money, just favours, introductions, information from Peter about aspects of the law. And he kept on and on and on. No threats that you could call threats but the threat was always there. Then, when he died, we breathed a huge sigh of relief. It was over.'

Ben smiled sadly. 'I know about Peter's wife. He told me a while ago, motor neurone disease, I believe. Not easy for either of you. And the blackmail finished with Murdock's death?'

'Yes. You'll have to verify this with Peter; I know that. But, since that man's death, we've had no further demands.'

'I'll talk to Peter.'

Ben thought for a moment. No need to tell her of Dobson's death. She'd learn soon enough. Either Dobson had been unable to crack Murdock's code, or he'd decided that the reward from these two was not worth the effort of applying whatever levers he had. Or he hadn't seen the proof. That was a possibility. The proof, the photos, receipts, whatever else Stanley Murdock had held, hadn't been found when Murdock was killed. So where were they? Did Dobson have them? He had blithely told the Ethel people that nothing incriminating had been found. It seemed the right thing to do at the time. But he would have to make sure. He must check with Vin to see if any proof of blackmail had been found in Dobson's possession. If it had, and it incriminated Dr Alison Clare and Professor Peter Hallfield, then his efforts to protect them would have been in vain.

Dr Clare continued. 'I know I shouldn't say this, but Josephine did us a great favour when she killed that evil man. Of course, whatever her background, I'd have given her the best treatment I could. But, every session I have with her, I could hug her.'

Ben wanted to move away from the depressing subject of blackmail. 'I'll talk to Peter and sort things out.'

She smiled at him and his heart went out to her. 'Thank you. I hope you can be the one to close this off entirely and bring an end to our suffering.'

Embarrassed, he quickly changed the subject. 'Let's talk about Josephine. How's she doing?'

Dr Clare immediately became professional. 'I've been meaning to speak to you about her. I know she still refuses to see you, but she has named you as next of kin, so you will need to be involved soon. She's doing really well. We think she'll soon be ready for a visit outside – next few months probably.'

'She's still seeing her mother?'

'Yes, regularly. That relationship is progressing well. I'm very pleased. It will be an enormous help in assisting her recovery. They have thirty years to undo but they're getting there. And it's partly because they're talking so freely to each other that I'm thinking of a visit outside.'

'Shouldn't her mother take over as next of kin? After all, she is really.'

'No. I think that would be a very bad idea. Agnes has her own problems and the two of them are still building trust. Josephine feels guilty because she thinks she's hurt you badly. But she trusts you implicitly. You saved her life and she's grateful. Agnes speaks well of you too. I don't think we should rock that boat. Is that OK with you?'

Ben wondered just what Josephine and Agnes had been saying. 'Yes, that's fine by me. Is there anything else I should be doing?'

'Not yet but I think that, eventually, Josephine might want to see you. What do you think of that?'

'I don't know,' was his honest answer.

\* \* \*

As soon as he arrived home, Ben phoned his office to make sure everything was in order there. He told them he was going to talk to the pathologist and would be back later. He reckoned he'd just have time to try to see Peter Hallfield before going to the mortuary. When he arrived, unannounced, Hallfield gave his tutorial group a task to perform and ushered Ben into an empty room. Having ascertained that Hallfield and Dobson were in different departments and different colleges, but that Hallfield had heard about the murder through the university grapevine, Ben asked how well he'd known Dobson. Hallfield laughed mirthlessly. 'Of course I know why you're asking. Alison phoned me as soon as you'd left; told me about your two lists. Listen Ben, he never approached me. I met him once at a drinks do at my college. Must be two, three years ago. Immediately recognised his type. Didn't like what I saw so didn't pursue the acquaintance. Nor did he. I doubt that he'd remember me. I wasn't useful, you see. That was it.'

'And you haven't seen or heard from him since?'

Hallfield shook his head. 'Not till I heard he'd been murdered. Then Alison phoned.' He sighed a heavy sigh and his eyes glistened. 'Looks like it will all come out now. I'll have to tell my wife. She's not got long and I'd rather it came from me.'

Ben couldn't allow additional suffering to a dying woman – not if he could prevent it. He grabbed the other man's arm and spoke with urgency. 'Peter! Listen! Don't do anything yet. Wait till you hear from me. Can you do that?' Hallfield looked questioningly at Ben. Ben gently squeezed his arm and continued, 'No-one outside my family has seen those entries in the lists. I owe Alison a lot and I'll do anything I can to keep your names out of this. I've shared Murdock's and Dobson's lists with the police but without yours and Alison's names. The blackmail evidence hasn't come to light, and if it doesn't, no-one will ever know. But, if it does, I'm afraid it will be out of my hands. I'll get back to you soon to let you know if Murdock's photos and receipts have been found. Can you hold off for now?'

Hallfield nodded and Ben was touched by the sadness in his voice. 'It's terrible, I know. I stopped loving my wife years ago. But, when we found out she had this terrible disease, I knew I couldn't leave her.' He paused and looked out of the window at the sky. He seemed to talking to himself. 'It's funny. We never know what we're capable of. We can be saints, but we can all kill when we become desperate.' As Hallfield returned to his tutorial group, Ben was left wondering who Peter Hallfield had been talking about.

# Chapter 9

The mortuary held no terrors for Ben. His terrors, he knew, were all in his mind. The reality of death was with him every day and he couldn't remember the last time he had spewed at the smells it produced. As he breathed in, the background smell of bleach assaulted his nostrils – a home from home really.

Jim Spire greeted him warmly then pointed to Dobson's corpse. 'Interesting body. Skinny but his liver was a mess. Hippocampus shrunken. I'd say he drank much more than was good for him. Might have had some memory lapses, but could have lasted a good few years if his throat hadn't been cut.' He smiled. 'How's it going with that young man you've taken on? Good lad. Had a grand conversation with him when he came to collect that "unexplained" last week. Listening to his voice made me feel nostalgic for the auld country. Maybe I'll retire there.'

Ben was surprised. Jim had lived in Cambridge all his adult life. 'But you've been here forty years. Why go back?'

'Dreams, my friend. Dreams and nostalgia. Maybe it'll just be a holiday. When I left, we couldn't cross the border. Now I can go back to Connemara, then visit the Giants Causeway, see some leprechauns, drink real Guinness and come home to Cambridge. That should settle me.' Jim Spire sighed then tapped Dobson's body. 'Now this man here. Vicious attack. See these little nicks just by his ear. Pre mortem. The killer stood behind him. Held him across the chest with both arms pinioned. Wouldn't have taken much force. Not much to the poor bugger.'

Ben interrupted. 'Could a woman have done it?'

'Possibly. Have to be a tall woman – about five-ten – possibly a bit shorter. And strong. But women these days work out, so things I'd have staked my career on thirty years ago don't hold good these days. Yes, a tall woman with strong arms could have done it. Right-handed. Now, cause of death. Carotids and jugulars cut. Would have died from loss of blood. But then, post mortem, not one, but three stab wounds to the chest. That killer was seriously annoyed with your man here.'

'Would you say "frenzied"?'

'No. Much more calculated and controlled. The three stab wounds are close together and were done with force. Each one chipped a rib. The perpetrator's clothes and shoes would have had blood on them. Lots of it. No blood in the study so this murderer didn't flee the scene. I think he or she must have taken off their clothes in the murder room.'

'So does that mean the study was done over before the murder?'

'I'd say so.'

Ben smiled. 'And the murderers left the scene in their underwear?'

'Now, I didn't say that. Could be the accomplice helped out there. The other chap stayed over by the far wall. Way outside spatter range. Had a chat with the CSI people.'

'And?'

'You know me. Tried to pump them for information. Got a tight-lipped woman. One thing I managed to get was, and I quote, "someone with bloody great size elevens compromised the scene with muddy footprints". Know who that was?' He grinned at Ben. 'But that led to the sizes on the two other sets of prints, the ones that went into the murder room. Killer probably size nine – popular size – other one indeterminate but not small. And I had to be my most persuasive to find out they were shoes not trainers – stout shoes, and both sets would have had blood on their soles. So the police should be looking for two people – probably men – walking round the College half dressed and carrying their shoes.'

Ben smiled. 'Sounds like an everyday story of College folk – undergrads anyway. Seriously though, makes it seem likely to have been an inside job.'

'That's just what I thought.'

'So, when can I have this fellow to take home.'

'Should be soon. The second pm is scheduled for today.'

'Second?'

'Yup. Mine's for the CPS. There'll be another one – independent of mine – for the defence for when it comes to trial. Have to be seen to be fair.'

Ben drove away from the mortuary, his mind churning with the information he'd acquired. But there was something that Jim had said that rang a bell deep inside his brain. He had the feeling that it wasn't to do with the victim or his killers. It was way more off-beam and it stubbornly refused to do more than clank away in the back of his brain. He shook his head to try to dislodge it. Nothing. No doubt it would surface in its own good time.

# Chapter 10

Mo, Ben, Michael and Katy were taking a break from their mundane tasks. Washing bodies had to be done with decorum and compassion but, as Katy had said, that didn't make it interesting. Katy counted on her fingers. 'We've got Pedersen, Walpole, Hendrick, O'Connor and Fursley from Ethel's and this other one, Dr Taylor, who we don't know but Dobson did. Let's look at the clues again. Then there's Dr Clare and her man – but we've ruled them out.' She waved the two lists. 'See, if you look at these – I think old Stanley was giving Dobson a leg-up to help him carry on milking these poor buggers.'

Ben bit his lip. He was making a conscious effort not to remonstrate with Katy about swearing. Part of his 'letting go', but it didn't come easy.

Katy pointed to Dobson's list. 'He wasn't going to make it easy for him though.' She laid out the two lists on the table and pointed to Dr Clare's name. 'I hope it works out OK for her and her man. I bet he's lovely cos she wouldn't settle for just any old prole. He'd have to be special.'

Ben sighed. He'd found out from Vin that the police had found nothing at Dobson's rooms in College or in his house in Trumpington; nothing that could be deemed blackmail evidence. He knew he'd have to search the house himself and he didn't relish sorting through Dobson's things. And, of course, it would help if he knew precisely what he was looking for. Pictures of a happy couple, hotel receipts – yes – plus other things unknown. He knew that Vin had her own problems with the search: not knowing what she was looking for and worse still, not knowing which of her team she could trust. She'd been wary of giving him the key to the house in Trumpington, but had relented when he said he would keep her informed of any evidence he found. He'd do what he could to help her.

He smiled as Katy took control. She proceeded to read from Dobson's list. 'I'll read them all out and you see if you get anything. Let's go for ladies first.' She pointed at the men surrounding her. 'See, I can say "ladies", but you can't. That's lib for you – whoever told you life was fair? Anyway we have, *Dr G. Fursley. June 2005. Playing the good man in Scotland set the cat alight.* Michael got the end of that one – but we still can't get the Scottish connection. Anything you can add?'

Ben shook his head so Katy continued. 'Next, we have, *Professor O. Pedersen, July 2009. Not his native huldufolk at the end of this rainbow. Tie and dye – that's his hobby.* Any idea about that?' When Ben and Maurice shook their heads, she continued. 'Then, *Professor H. Walpole, October 1961.*' She looked at her father. '1961 – that's forevs ago. You weren't even born and Uncle Mo was just a kid. This Walpole must be ancient.'

Maurice tutted while Ben tapped into his phone. 'He's got a Wiki entry. Born 1942 so he'd be nineteen in 61 – and at Trinity. What does the rest say?'

'*Better to be under the bed than in it, especially when dealing with him who's not the sharpest.*'

'Well, that's easy,' said Maurice. He waved a finger at Katy. 'See there's advantages to being very old and extremely wise. He's obviously a commie and he knew Anthony Blunt. Reds under the bed and the fifth man. All at Trinity. What's he teach?'

Ben scrolled down, then laughed. 'Emeritus Professor of Slavonic Studies. Russian, Polish, Ukranian etc.' His thoughts turned to Chris saying, 'The Ruskies get every-bloody-where.' They did then and, it seemed, they did now. He'd have to talk to Chris.

Katy had gone onto the next on the list. '*Dr J. Hendrick, May 1991, Charles Rennie opened his doors for a second time – saved by the Three.* The three what?'

'Stooges,' said Maurice.

'The what?'

'Never mind, lassie. Way before your time.'

Ben raised his finger. 'Got the first half. Charles Rennie Mackintosh, Scottish architect. Opened his mackintosh. We know what that means.'

'A flasher,' yelled Katy. 'Our Dr Hendrick is a perv.'

Ben bit his lip again. Maurice joined in. 'Indecency. He was how old then?'

Ben thought for a moment. 'I'd say late teens maybe.'

Mo clapped his hands. 'Yeah, course. Way back then, it was usual for a first indecency charge to be a caution, specially if he was young. Say he was drunk and there was no children present, they'd be telling him he was a very naughty boy. Put the fear of God in him and tell him never to do it again. But a second occurrence would mean trouble. Becoming a serial offender? Then they'd become interested. It'd be on record. Bound to.' He turned to Ben. 'You could ask your lady friend.'

'Yes, Dad. Can you do that tomorrow?'

Ben smiled and replied in a servile manner. 'Yes, M'lady.'

Katy grinned. 'Next, *Dr J. P. O'Connor, April 1997, should have been first in line. Your call Graham. And a good one.* Graham – that's Dobson isn't it?'

'Yes. Wonder what his "call" was? This one's different. It's the only one that refers to Dobson directly. Any ideas?'

After the shaking of heads, Katy tapped the paper in her hand. 'And last but not least, Dr A N Taylor. Real posho this one. Got two initials. Not at Ethel's, so must be at another college. I've started looking but no joy yet. Anyone else got a clue?' Before they could answer she read out the last entry on the list. '*Dr A. N. Taylor – 2011 – they played the violin together for years but he's lost his bog-light, so now he's a target.*'

Mo waved his hands in the air. 'That Stanley, I just don't understand him. He was one twisted weirdo. We know that. But why did he write all these clues? What did it get him? He knew the answers so who were they for?'

Ben answered. 'I think I know. He was a control freak. We know what he did to his children – controlled their lives in their entirety. They're recovering now, with the help of a counsellor. He's textbook for this new coercive control thing. We also know he was extremely clever and decidedly devious. Look what he did to his nephew. Let him take a seven-year gaol rap.' He shook his head as he continued, 'He passed all these on to his friend, Dobson; presumably to allow him to carry on the blackmail. But only if he could decipher the clues. It's a sort of control from beyond the grave, still pulling strings. Stanley Murdock spent his whole life pulling other people's strings. He was a puppet-master in chief. Why should he stop when he died? He managed to avoid being murdered by one of his nasty Northern Ireland associates and he managed to avoid being murdered by one of the people he was blackmailing here. Someone else did that job. Dobson, it seems, was clever enough to decipher some of these clues but not clever enough to see what danger he was getting into.'

'Ah!' said Mo. 'I get it. We're going hell-for-leather at doing what got Dobson killed.'

'Yes,' said Katy and Ben in unison.

# Chapter 11

He'd had to work hard to persuade Vin that he needed to look through Dobson's house in Trumpington. The deciding factor had been that his prior knowledge of the victim might just bring up something that the police had overlooked. Vin had confessed that the police search had turned up nothing and she had agreed to search the records for anything on James Hendrick in or around 1991 in return for anything he found out about the victim.

Now that he stood outside Dobson's house with its uncared-for air, he wondered about the man who had lived there; a man who'd had acquaintances, co-conspirators, enemies, but no friends and, seemingly, no family. A man disliked by one and all. It had been Dobson's petty spitefulness and dishonesty that had irked Ben – but did he deserve an end like that? Of course not. Ben took a huge in-breath and stepped up to the front door. He listened. Small scuffling sounds were coming from within. An empty house, a man dead, an ideal target for burglars. He carefully inserted the key in the mortice lock. It wasn't locked. Then he unlocked the Yale. He turned the knob and the door opened with the slightest of creaks. He waited and listened. The scratching sounds continued. They were coming from a room further down the hall on the left. Ben eased the front door closed behind him, locked the mortice, then pocketed the key. Then he padded down the hall.

He recognised the single burglar as Dr O'Connor. O'Connor was rifling through the contents of Dobson's desk. Ben watched from the doorway, secure in the knowledge that O'Connor was oblivious to his presence and that, if it came to a scuffle, he would have no trouble in overpowering this small man. Eventually, O'Connor found what he must have been looking for. He gave a small yelp of satisfaction as he extracted a sheaf of papers from a file. He searched through, took out three sheets of paper, then took a lighter from his pocket.

Before O'Connor could destroy the papers, Ben leapt forward and wrested them from him. Without looking to see who his assailant was, O'Connor ran out of the study and bolted for the front door. Finding it locked, he shook it hard, then banged on it with closed fists. Finally, he turned and slid slowly down the door until he was seated on the tiled floor. Then he started to cry.

Ben squatted till his face was on a level with O'Connor's. Being careful to keep the evidential sheets away from the unfortunate man, he reached into his pocket and extracted a clean white handkerchief. He handed it to O'Connor. As the crying man wiped his eyes and blew his nose, Ben said quietly, 'Why don't you tell me about it?'

O'Connor looked up and nodded mutely. Ben helped him to his feet and with a firm hold on his arm, motioned him towards the room they had just left. Ben closed the door behind them and ensured that he stayed between O'Connor and the door. He was not sure how O'Connor had gained entry and there might still be a viable exit at the back of the house. He did not want this bird to fly. While he had him in a vulnerable position, this would be the most likely time to get to the truth. He waved the papers in his hand. 'Tell me why these are so important to you.'

To Ben's consternation, huge tears again began to roll down O'Connor's cheeks. He waited while the man composed himself. 'They could end my career. That's how important they are.'

While keeping a wary eye on his captive, Ben scanned the papers. A copy of a degree certificate, another copy of the same certificate and a hand-written letter in Dobson's scrawl. 'So?'

'I needed to get them back. Dobson was the one who appointed me. He knew I'd lied to get the job, so he had a hold over me. This was my one opportunity to bury the evidence. And I've blown it.' Then more tears came.

Ben looked again at the two certificates. Almost identical, but on examination he could see that they differed in just one respect. One stated that John Patrick O'Connor had achieved a First Class honours degree in Maths with Physics from Trinity College, Dublin; the other that his degree class had been a Lower Second. 'I see. You got a 2.2 and claimed a first?'

John Patrick O'Connor nodded. 'Dobson checked with Dublin and...' He paused. 'We came to an agreement. He'd sanction my appointment and hide the false document if I agreed to back him up if he needed it.'

'And did you have to?'

'No. It never came up. But I decided early on that I wanted to leave here and make a fresh start. I told him I was going to apply to London with my real degree. He blocked it. Said he'd inform London and the university here.' A bitter look crossed his face. 'He held me captive.'

'So you killed him?'

A look of horror crossed O'Connor's face. 'God, no. I hated him but not enough to kill him. My life isn't bad. I gained a doctorate here and I've got a reputation in my field. I'm into some ground-breaking research, number-crunching for the medics. I no longer want to leave. I just wanted to destroy the evidence that brought me here and get on with my life.'

'Did you ever come across an acquaintance of Dobson's called Stanley Murdock?'

'God, yes. Lots of times. He often brought him to formal dinners. Didn't like him. Christ! He's the one that got murdered a while back. Oh God! Are the murders connected?'

'No idea. But let's leave it to the police to find that out. We don't need to look for the culprit. OK?'

O'Connor nodded again and laughed morosely. 'I'm not very good with violence, as you've probably guessed.' He pointed to the papers still in Ben's hand. 'I suppose the game's up. You'll be passing those to the police and then it will all come out.'

Ben was formulating a plan. No way could he believe that this gibbering heap had been involved in such a brutal murder. But he had to keep his options open. 'Not at all. I'm going to hold on to them for the time being. I'll keep them safe. But, listen. I'm not like Dobson. I won't hold you to anything.' He paused to let this sink in then repeated it. 'As I said, I'm not like Dobson. But I could do with your help. If you do find out anything that could help solve this murder, perhaps you could share it with me. And then, when the killer is found, you'll have your papers back. I'll even provide the lighter. OK?'

O'Connor nodded again. 'I've got no option, have I? I've got to trust you. But, can I just plead with you? I'm involved in some ground-breaking research. If I have to leave here, some crucial advances in gene therapy will stall. They'll be set back at least five years. It could cost lives. I want to stay and see it through.'

As he led O'Connor to the front door, Ben asked, 'By the way. How did you get in?'

'I broke in through the back. Climbed the fence, then smashed the window pane in the door. The back door key was in the lock so I just turned it.'

So much for the police securing the house, thought Ben.

He saw Dr O'Connor off the premises and then began his own perusal of the property. He needed to find Dobson's will or the name of his solicitor or an executor or even a relative. Plus he was looking for any evidence which might lead him nearer to his killer. He put on his latex gloves, then started his search upstairs, but there was little in any of the bedrooms. They were so clean and neat and empty of any sign of habitation that it almost looked as though no-one had lived there. He reached up inside the chimneys but found nothing but old soot. He changed his gloves then looked inside the chests of drawers. He felt inside all the cabinets to see if Dobson had repeated his veneer trick. Nothing.

Nothing in the bathroom cabinet. He expected that the police might have looked, but he searched behind the bath panel and in the cistern. He pulled down the attic ladder, again nothing. He went up to check but the attic was completely empty. Back downstairs, he decided to leave the study till last. The kitchen and sitting room were equally bare and Ben was almost beginning to feel sorry for this solitary man. He knew from Vin that the police had taken nothing away from this house, so if there was a clue here – apart from the papers of Dr O'Connor's which he already had – it must be in the study. A thorough search there again turned up nothing of note: no will, no solicitor, no obvious blackmail evidence and nothing to point him towards the perpetrator.

Time to go. A last look round the hall and his eyes lighted on the small door to the under-stairs cupboard. Might as well be totally thorough. The door creaked open and, at first, the cupboard appeared to be empty. He had to stoop to get in. He switched on the light. A naked bulb shed a sharp light into all the corners. The two shelves were thick with dust and held not even a mark to show that anything had resided there. Then, he shone his torch into the crannies. He was about to give up when he made out a solitary wooden box which slotted neatly under the lowest stair tread. It was wedged in so as to be virtually invisible; Dobson's second clever hiding place. On his hands and knees, and with perseverance, Ben managed to ease it out. He crawled backwards into the hall then blew the dust off the box. He retreated to the study. He opened the box carefully so as not to smudge any fingermarks and began to look through the photos within. His eyes opened wide, he gasped for air then stepped back in horror. He felt his way to a chair and sat down heavily. It took him some minutes to recover from the extreme turbulence his body was experiencing. When he had stopped sweating and his breathing had slowed, he felt able to continue. With trembling hands, he reached again for the box. It was full of old photographs and they were all of him, his wife and his two daughters. There were a few of Katy and Sarah as children, some of him and Diane, but as he examined them more closely, he realised that only Diane appeared in every single one.

# Chapter 12

On leaving Dobson's house, he phoned Vin and left a message telling her that the house had been broken into, so needed securing again, and that he needed to come to see her. He'd not been able to face looking at those photos again so that box was now safely stowed in his bedside cupboard. He knew that these, together with Diane's other effects – also unlooked-at and unsorted – would have to be looked through. He'd managed to push them to the back of his consciousness for sixteen years. One day he would have to face them all. That day seemed to be hurtling towards him. And he knew he wasn't ready.

\* \* \*

Vin had shuffled some meetings and Ben was now seated outside her office. He was in a quandary as to what to tell her. He really wanted to get information but not to give anything away in return, especially about the box of photos he'd found. He had to sort those in his own head first. He'd decided not to look through them until he'd talked it through with Dr Clare.

For sixteen years, he'd been trying to block out the mess in his head that Diane's death had caused. But, yet again, just as he felt he was turning a corner, fate had determinedly shoved it right back to centre stage. This time and every time, it enveloped him in the swamping guilt that she had died while he had lived.

'Hi, come in. What's the hurry?' He turned at Vin's voice. It brought him back to the reality of the present and for that he was grateful. With an effort, he pushed his memories back into that closed space inside his brain that kept him reasonably safe from the harm they always caused.

'Need some info. And to give you back these.' He handed over Dobson's keys. He cringed at the thought that, yet again, he was lying to Vin. 'I didn't find anything to help you. Your people did a good job. Now, what I really need to know from you is, did you find anything in police records against those people on

Dobson's list? I'm going back to talk to them tomorrow and it would help if I knew what you know.'

'Nothing. And we couldn't find anything untoward in Dobson's College rooms or his house. We've done a background check on all the listed Etheldreda people. Nothing. Haven't yet pinpointed who the other one is. Dr A. N. Taylor. It's a really common name but the details we have don't check with anything on our systems.'

'The Ethel's people. What? Not even a caution for any of them?'

Vin shrugged. 'They're all your average, middle-class, law-abiding citizens without even a teenage blemish to their names. So that really doesn't help us with your blackmail angle. We're at a standstill with your list.'

Ben didn't want to finger Hendrick – whom he believed should have had something on record for his second incident of flashing. 'You're sure? Nothing anywhere?'

'Nope. Clean as a whistle all of them. Upright citizens all. We've been trying to solve those riddles beside each one. Can't get anywhere. Maybe we should do more crosswords? We're now working on the premise that it isn't a blackmail list at all – just a silly academic exercise – which leaves us with no suspects at all.'

Ben knew it was a blackmail list. He had proof that Professor Hallfield, Dr Clare and Dr O'Connor had been 'leaned on' by Murdock or Dobson. He also believed that those three were unlikely to have killed Dobson. He still had Pedersen, Walpole, Hendrick and Fursley – and the elusive Dr Taylor – to examine in more detail.

He asked, 'This Dr Taylor? He or she isn't from Ethel's. You've looked to see if they're at another college?'

'Yep, nothing. Not at any of the Cambridge colleges nor at Anglia Ruskin. We've widened it to other universities and are waiting, but nothing yet. But on that other matter...'

As he looked more closely at Vin's face and demeanour, he could see tension around her eyes and mouth. She looked exhausted. He'd been too wrapped up in his sleuthing endeavours to notice the obvious strain she was under. He said gently, 'Why don't you sit down and tell me about it?'

She sat and looked squarely at him. 'My Apostles, DS Bennett and DS Burnham. Not the B's I'd use for them. I've done what you suggested. Separated them so they don't work together. They're not happy bunnies, and they still stand together at the back in briefings exuding malevolence.'

Ben was about to interrupt but Vin held up her hand. 'Hear me out. I need a sounding board. I know those two are trying to undermine me and I want to know why. I was sent here because there's evidence of Cambridge links with Yewtree and they know that. I keep wondering, do they know something about the paedos I've been sent here to catch? Something they're not telling me.'

'That's a serious accusation. Any evidence?'

'No, not a shred. It's just that I don't trust them one iota. Could be that they undermine me because they just want me to fail. Anyway, that's the least of my worries. It's taken a back seat with this murder.' She started counting on her fingers. 'I've got a murder investigation with no progress, a link to a previous unsolved murder which I believe was closed off prematurely. On top of that, I've got a paedo ring and officers I can't trust.'

Ben looked directly at Vin and gave her a sympathetic smile. 'What do you want from me?'

'Honesty. And someone I can talk to.'

'Honesty, um, difficult. I'm being honest with you when I say that there are things I can't tell you now but I will as soon as I can. What I can tell you is that I won't do anything to undermine you and will do everything in my power to help you. And whatever you tell me will be between you and me – unless you say otherwise. Is that enough?'

She smiled. 'It'll do.'

Ben leaned down and kissed her on the forehead then extracted a notebook from his pocket. He wrote something on it, tore off the sheet and gave it to Vin. He scribbled over the top page of the notebook making any impressions indecipherable then tore off that sheet, screwed it up and put it in his pocket. He pointed to the page in Vin's hand. 'This is Chris's email address. He wants to talk to you and he might be able to help you, especially with the closed murder investigation. But beware. He's a slippery customer. I'd say he's more trustworthy than your Apostles – but he's got his own agenda – and it's not the same as yours.'

'Thanks Ben. We make good colleagues. I really appreciate your help, and that makes this even harder.'

Ben held up his hand. 'Don't worry. I know. I was thinking the same. While this goes on, we have to stop seeing each other.'

She grasped his hand and said urgently, 'But only until this investigation is over.'

'Yes,' he said, but he didn't really believe her.

# Chapter 13

On this grey day, the yellow stone of St Etheldreda's College had taken on the sheen of dead ochre. Ben stood and looked up at the empty windows, glancing at the three black oblongs that had housed Dobson, then averting his eyes from them. For thirty years he'd ignored this building, this life – but fate had brought it back into his ambit and Ben knew that it would be easy to be pulled back into its alternative reality. He had to admit that the façade still looked imposingly imperial. His job was to find out what lay beyond the fronts, both corporate and personal, that lay behind that façade. He stepped into the Porters' Lodge to be met by the smiling face of Mr Fisher.

'Morning Mr Burton. I see you've appointments with Prof Pedersen, Dr Hendrick, Prof Walpole and Dr Fursley. I've got a note from Dr O'Connor – says he'd like to see you while you're here if you've got a mo. And the Master would like you to lunch with her after you've finished. That OK?'

'That's fine. Busy morning. Tell me, have you remembered any more about that row you overheard the day before Dobson's murder?' Ben saw Fisher's reaction to the word 'murder', a look of anguish followed by a shake of the head.

'See, we're a bit squeamish here, Mr Burton.' He screwed up his face and shook his head again. 'We're calling it "Professor Dobson's unfortunate demise". Makes it easier for us. But, as it happens, I have remembered something. It might be nothing, of course. You know, they were in Front Court and there's all those pillars. I was coming by the Old Library and, thinking back, I could swear I heard breathing. So I think someone else overheard the quarrel. But they'd all disappeared by the time I got through to Front Court so I still don't know who he was quarrelling with or who was listening in. I 'spect the listener heard more than me. He was nearer.'

'Sure it was a "he"?'

'Pretty sure. I heard heavy footsteps going up the staircase. Could've been a heavy-footed woman, of course.'

'Can you tell me again what it was you heard Dobson say? Think about it – something more might come back.'

Fisher scratched his head. 'They was having a good old slanging match, but sotto voce. Now, let me think.'

Ben smiled inwardly at the mixture of town and gown description as he waited for Fisher to continue.

'Yes, there was that bit about the College and his wife. Seeming to say whatever it was would cause both of them grief. See, I could only hear Dobson. He had that carrying voice, even when he was whispering. I could tell the other one was furious – sort of hissing – but I couldn't make out a word. Then Dobson said something about faking. Sounded like, "They'll fake them anyway." I can only think it was to do with some research they were doing. Maybe the other one had faked some results, or maybe Dobson wanted him to and he wouldn't. That fits better.' Mr Fisher straightened his jacket and stood tall. 'Not the sort of thing we want to see here. We've got a reputation to uphold.'

Ben didn't respond but he was not at all sure about that explanation. Dobson had been a mathematician. Ben too, in his youth, had been a mathematician, and he knew it was difficult in that discipline to fake anything. It was much more likely in areas where research subjects were routinely used. He'd already looked up the academic background of the people on Dobson's list. Pedersen's was Asian and Middle Eastern Studies, Walpole, Slavonic Studies, Hendrick, Maths, O'Connor, Maths and Computer Science and Fursley, Sociology. But Fursley was a woman, small and slight. Could she have been the listener or the watcher at the murder scene? Unlikely but possible. This brought the uncomfortable thought that both Dr Clare and Professor Hallfield were in disciplines that fitted into the category of 'more easily faked': hers was psychology, his criminology. But he was in a different college and she was, he thought, just a visiting lecturer. Neither, it seemed, would affect the reputation of this college.

Ben had set up his series of meetings with a plan in mind. He had decided his preferred times and order of interview and no-one had demurred. He'd chosen to see them separately, one straight after the other to reduce the possibility of collusion. He'd also decided to wait till the end of each interview to go for the jugular. And, of course, he had to remember that he was just the undertaker, looking for information to help the funeral go smoothly.

He wanted to talk to Professor Walpole first. He had the longest history and might have some useful information. And Walpole had made it his business to research Ben's background. Walpole was an enigma and Ben was intrigued. Fisher directed Ben to Walpole's rooms. They were, thankfully, well away from Dobson's staircase, which was still out of bounds. He wondered how the other residents of that stair were coping with being kept out of their rooms.

He now knew that Professor Walpole had been at Ethel's for more than fifty years and had been an Emeritus Professor for the last ten. From his time as an undergraduate, Ben could remember encountering ancient men tottering from their rooms to the Great Hall for meals. He'd always kept his distance, not wanting to be tottered into or grabbed as a substitute for a walking stick. As he approached Professor Walpole's rooms, he hoped that Walpole was not a totterer.

His knock was greeted with 'Enter,' in tones far too stentorian for a totterer. The rooms were somewhat as Ben had anticipated, but far worse. Every flat surface, including the floor, was covered with papers and books. There was one path through the tangle from the door to the desk and another from the desk to a plump pair of settees. Obviously, people didn't, couldn't, go straight to the seating area. He was greeted from somewhere behind the large desk but could not see the owner of the voice. A head popped up.

'Ah. Mr Burton. Come in. Come in. I'm just looking for a paper I wrote in 1999. Should be in this pile somewhere.' He waved a paper aloft. 'Bingo! Got it.'

The head, followed by a large body, was hefted, with the help of the desk, into a standing position.

Ben surveyed the desk. A volcano of papers covered its entirety. He pointed to the floor. 'Do you know where everything is?'

'More or less. And these days I can recycle my arguments because no-one remembers what I wrote last time. Neat, yes?'

Ben was impressed but perplexed. 'But Russia's changed with Putin, hasn't it?'

'Not a bit, dear boy. Same old, same old.' He looked hard at Ben. 'You're thinking, but Walpole's a Commie.' Walpole laughed. 'I am. I am. No secret about that. But the Soviet and Russian hierarchies are not. Capitalist to the core, and in it for their own ends. I found that out years ago.' He paused and pointed to the settees. 'I'm sorry. I could talk about Russia all day but you have a funeral to prepare. Sit down, dear boy, and we'll talk about poor old Dobson.'

Without a pause, he continued, 'An unfortunate soul. A truly unhappy man. Couldn't make friends, heartily disliked by all. But of course you know that.' Walpole raised one bushy eyebrow. 'You were one of his more spectacular students, I gather. How much contact did you have with him?'

'He was my supervisor.'

'You know he was MI5? Bet he tried to recruit you.' Walpole chuckled and looked sideways at Ben. 'He tried and failed. Would have been a blow for him. He'd want to impress his masters in Whitehall. Am I right?'

'Spot on.'

Walpole smiled broadly. 'Haven't lost it completely. Used to be able to sum people up and know how to use it.'

Going for the jugular earlier than he'd anticipated, Ben put in quickly, 'Was that when you were working alongside Blunt?'

Walpole slapped his thigh and laughed loudly. 'Hah! Knew you were clever. Not many people know about that bit of my nefarious past. Care to tell me how you found out?'

'No, I'll keep that to myself. But Dobson knew. Was he blackmailing you?'

'Tried to. Tried to get me to do something for him. Years ago. Nabbed me in the library. Told him where to go. Didn't come back.'

'But he could have had you outed as a Russian spy.'

Walpole leaned back, rubbed his corpulent stomach and laughed loudly. 'Well, that's where you're wrong. Shouldn't tell you this, but I'm old and rickety and I won't last long. And I don't want to take my secrets to the grave.' He paused a moment as if considering what to say next. 'Not like poor Dobson.' Then he continued, 'How d'you think they got on to Philby and the rest? When I found out that the Soviet machine was more corrupt than ours, I turned. The sixth man has never been found. Never really looked for. It was me, dear boy. I'm the sixth man and I'm being protected. So you see, poor old Dobson never had a chance. We going to say all that at the funeral?'

Ben smiled at the thought. 'Possibly not. I think we'd better stick to non-nefarious deeds.'

Then Walpole surprised him yet again. 'You're working for Chris. Terrible young man but good at his job.'

Ben began to feel uncomfortable under the stare from those rheumy eyes. 'Why would you think I know this Chris?'

'My dear boy, I'm at the age where I can't move much, can't do much. But I can watch from the sidelines and see what's going on. Dobson introduced you to Chris at one of the old Master's ghastly sherry-bashes. I watched you both and Chris went away looking satisfied. Q.E.D. Chris got you. Dobson got you. Much later than he thought he would. But he got you.'

This was not going at all the way Ben had anticipated. He wondered how much this old man knew about Dobson, about MI5 and about him. And, more importantly, how much of that knowledge he would divulge. He moved completely from his prepared questions. 'Yes, I suppose he did. So, do you know who killed him?'

The old man smiled. 'Now that's the killer question.' He laughed at his own joke. Then he paused and continued in a ruminative voice. 'Unlike the rest of the College, which is in denial, I think it was one of us. Terrible thought but there it is. I can't imagine what Dobson had done, or found out, to deserve to be silenced. I think he leaned on someone and that someone had a secret so incriminating that he leaned back – hard.' He wiped his eyes and Ben could see that Walpole was considerably moved by his thoughts. Ben wondered if it was the thought of Dobson's death or having a killer for a colleague. He had to try to find out.

'You think one of your colleagues is a murderer. What are you going to do about it?'

Walpole shrugged his shoulders and slumped down in his seat. To Ben, he looked utterly defeated. 'What can I do? I don't know which one it is. I have no proof. I don't even have evidence.

But I have been watching the people in this college for over forty years and I know that there are some terrible secrets here.' Ben wondered if one of the terrible secrets that Walpole was referring to was the gang-rape by four undergraduates which had resulted in the birth of Josephine Finlay – now locked away for the murder of her father, Stanley Murdock, one of those four.

Professor Walpole sat up straight. 'I love this college. It has been my home and my refuge for most of my life and I don't want to see its name dragged through the mud. So I'll just soldier on. I think I'll have to leave it to you to find out which of us is the guilty one. Come to me if you think I can help. I still have friends in high and low places. Of course, the low ones are the ones to go to. They know more than they let on. And they'll tell if you catch them right – less to lose, I suppose.' He looked into the distance then pointed a bony finger at Ben. 'You know what they say about clams? Not true. Get 'em at the right time of day, when the rock pool is still and quiet, and they'll open up beautifully. Just have to gauge it right.' Then he sat up and slapped his knee. 'Now, the funeral. I believe that no family has been found?' He looked questioningly at Ben, who nodded. Walpole continued, 'So the College has to put on the show. And we'll put on a good show, no doubt about that. We'll all be his friends, for the duration anyway. I'll help where I can.'

It seemed to Ben that he had got as much as he could for the moment, and more than he had bargained for. Walpole had shut off the murder and was moving on to funeral arrangements. Ben took out his notebook. 'We need people who've known him for some time to speak at the ceremony. Would you be willing to do that?'

'Yes. It's for the good of the College, you understand. Damage limitation. I can say good things about our esteemed Professor. Hard to dredge up something good. But I will. I'll send it to you beforehand. See what you think.'

Walpole waved the papers he was still holding. 'You'll need to get Hendrick to say something about his Maths research. And the Master will need to say a few words. Poor girl, only just got here and this happens.'

Ben had to hide a grin at the Master being referred to as a 'girl'. He guessed she was nearing fifty and wondered how old she'd have to be to progress in Walpole's eyes to being a 'lady'.

73

'Two more questions if I may?

'Go ahead, dear boy.'

'Do you know a Dr A N Taylor?'

Walpole thought for a moment then shook his head. 'Doesn't ring a bell. No, I can't help you there.'

'And do you know of any research conducted within the College where there are allegations of faking the results?'

'Ouch! Now that would be serious. In academic circles, it would probably have more long-lasting implications than the murder of a professor. If you have evidence, I'd appreciate it if you could bring it to us. We deal with this sort of thing very severely.'

'I can tell you the little I know. The day before Dobson's murder, he was heard to say something along the lines of "They'll fake them anyway". It happened in Front Court but I have no idea who he was talking to.'

'It was overheard by a member of College?'

'Yes, but, at present, that member is unwilling to come forward.'

'But trustworthy?'

'Absolutely.'

'Hmm. Nasty. Fake them anyway. I'll have to take this straight to the Master.' As he said this, Walpole was swapping his worn-out slippers for a pair of worn-out brogues. He looked up at Ben. 'Keep this under your hat, will you?'

Ben was left with the feeling that this was far more important to Walpole than the murder of a hated colleague. The reputation of the College was at stake and the College machinery would soon be in full swing to uncover any dodgy research. Whether that would uncover a murderer remained to be seen.

\* \* \*

On his way to Dr Fursley's rooms, Ben ruminated about the conversation he'd just had. Walpole seemed straightforward and was certainly plausible but, set against that, he'd been a spy all his life and that included spying for Russia. Ben knew that, for such people, the truth could become elastic. He knew, because he'd joined them and was feeling less than comfortable that, for him too, prevarication was becoming a habit. In particular, he was lying to his family – or, at least keeping things from them – and that made him feel decidedly uncomfortable. And he was lying to Vin. He turned his thoughts away from his attempts at verisimilitude and back to his suspects. He knew that, for all of them, he must keep an open mind. He was certain that Walpole wouldn't have had the strength to kill Dobson – but he certainly could have been the watcher – the accomplice.

His first impression of Dr Fursley was of a very worried woman. She greeted him with a faltering voice, her hand trembled as she shook his and she looked close to tears. She ushered him into her study. He looked round the room as he approached her desk. The bookcases and shelves suggested that a normally tidy mind lived here, but the slap-dash pile of papers slipping off the side of her desk and the contents of her handbag upended, suggested recent turmoil. The only personal item was a picture of herself and her groom on their wedding day. The woman in front of him bore little resemblance to the happy person looking out from that picture.

She asked if he wanted tea. He refused with a smile and gently asked her if it was OK to talk.

'Yes. I'm afraid I'm in a bit of a stew at the moment, but I'll do what I can to help.'

'Can I help at all with the stew?'

'No, sorry. It's a personal matter.' She took a deep breath and asked, with a voice still unsteady, 'What do you want of me?'

To Ben, this seemed a strange way of framing the question but it showed him just how vulnerable she was feeling. He spoke gently and low. 'I'd like to ask you just a few questions about Professor Dobson so that we can put together a funeral that the College can be proud of. Can you do that?'

'No. I didn't know him that well. Different disciplines and I've just come back from prolonged sick leave, so I'm afraid I'm not going to be much help. Ask what you have to.'

Ben was immediately solicitous. 'I'm sorry. I didn't know that you'd been ill. I hope you've fully recovered.'

Her reply was poignant. 'I'll never fully recover.' And then she added as if to herself, 'My own fault and I'll have to live with it.' She turned to Ben. 'Professor Dobson was a repugnant man and I had as little to do with him as possible. I'll keep quiet so the

College can bury him with due ceremony but this college is better off without him. You can't say that at his funeral, can you?'

'I'm afraid not. Do you not have any good word to say for him? Anything I can add to a list of qualities that can be shared?'

'No – he preyed on the vulnerable and that, I find despicable.'

Ben had to tread carefully here. 'And you have been vulnerable?'

At this she shot him an anguished look. 'You have no idea of the hurt that man has caused me. When I was at my lowest ebb – he was there – wanting me to betray my principles. I hated him when he was alive and I hate him still.'

Ben knew he too was preying on her vulnerabilities but there were two questions he needed answers to. He started with the one he considered to be the easier. 'I'm trying to find a Dr A N Taylor. Do you know him or her?'

She stumbled back as if she'd been punched. She turned away and said quietly, 'No, I don't know that name.'

Ben knew she was lying. 'You sure?'

'Perfectly. I don't know him.'

Ben decided he'd got all that he could from that question so he asked his final one, 'Did you kill Professor Dobson?'

She let out a bitter laugh. 'No, I didn't – but I wish I had! Now I think you'd better leave.'

'Yes. Of course. But before I go, I can see that you are troubled. I don't know what help you've been getting but, I too have troubles and I go to Dr Clare. She's helped me a lot.' He found her details on his phone and wrote them down. He handed the scrap of paper to Dr Fursley. 'I hope you feel better soon. And if I can help in any way, please let me know.' Then he left.

* * *

As he walked through Front Court to his next appointment, Ben's thoughts moved from the troubled woman he had just left to his own troubles. It had been a long time since his mental health problems had caused him as much agitation as the woman he had just left. He'd come through that and had left it behind. With Dr Clare's help, he was moving towards becoming a whole person again. He had no idea of the basis of Dr Fursley's unhappiness, but he could see that she was suffering, and she now had the option to call on the woman he considered to have been his saviour. Her choice.

In the meeting with Dr Fursley, he'd learnt something useful about the elusive Dr Taylor. Like Professor Walpole, Fursley could possibly still be in the frame as the accomplice, but he thought she would probably not have had the strength to overpower and kill Dobson. Added to that, she had small feet.

* * *

Dr Hendrick opened the door so promptly that Ben supposed he must have been standing just inside waiting for him. He ushered him in and pointed to a chair in front of a big desk. The desk was scrupulously tidy with the obligatory photo of wife and two young children in pole position. Hendrick proceeded to pace the room. Before Ben could question him, he blurted out, 'Please don't ask me to do anything. I can't help you.'

Ben held up his hands. 'I was hoping that you might say something at the funeral about his place in the Maths world. I believe he has been part of some ground-breaking research?'

'Ask O'Connor. He worked with him more than I did. To be honest, I shared a college and a discipline with him but our paths rarely crossed. He was older and much more senior than me. We didn't have much in common.' He abruptly stopped his pacing and sat behind his desk. Then he stood up and paced some more before continuing, 'So, if you'll excuse me. I have a great deal of work to do. I've taken on some of Professor Dobson's students and I'm a bit overloaded.'

Ben knew he had little time to find out anything more. He took his time rising from his chair. As he did so, he made sure he could see Hendrick's face as he said, 'One question please. Was he blackmailing you?'

Hendrick's face turned scarlet. His hand shook as he pointed to the door. 'Get out! Get out! How dare you suggest such a thing. Go!'

Ben felt he had no alternative than to move towards the door. 'I'm sorry. It's just that I'd heard that Professor Dobson was reputed to lean on people to get his way and I wondered if that had happened to you. I'm sorry to have troubled you.'

* * *

As Ben hurried along to Pedersen's rooms, he turned over in his mind what he'd got from that little exchange. Hendrick was obviously lying and, in addition to that, Ben could see he was frightened. What was he so scared of? Ben couldn't hazard a guess. He took his mind back to his other two encounters that morning and visualised their desks. He'd need to talk to Vin and Chris. That much was certain.

Pedersen greeted him at the door with the same handshake and again Ben felt required to reciprocate. Pedersen ushered him in and asked if he'd like coffee. 'Black please. No sugar.'

Pedersen pointed to a pair of Scandinavian style chairs. 'Have a seat. In the comfy chairs.'

As he passed Pedersen's desk, Ben glanced over it. Neat, clear, with obvious work going on. Nothing remarkable. Nothing personal. Ben looked round. The lack of personal touches was mirrored in the rest of the room. There was nothing here to show who this man was. While Pedersen poured coffee, Ben opened the conversation. 'Your chairs are a bit different from the usual here. Nice.'

'It's my background. My father was Danish. Now, how can I help you?'

A cool customer, thought Ben, as he took a cup of coffee from a very steady hand. 'I need to have some background information to make sure this funeral casts a positive light on Professor Dobson and hence the College.'

'Sure. Let's see. I've known him about fifteen years. You've spoken to Henry Walpole?' Ben nodded as Pedersen continued. 'He'll know more than the rest of us. More recently, my dealings with Dobson were mainly in his role as Bursar.' He laughed. 'Suited to that role. Didn't splash the cash. He was mean in that way too.' He looked thoughtful. 'The only thing I can add, in the past, we shared an interest in photography. We even shared a darkroom in College. Don't need that any more, of course. If I recall rightly, it's now a broom cupboard.'

'Thanks – that's interesting. It gives a more rounded picture. Would you be willing to say a few words at the funeral?'

'Happy to. I'm sure I can say something suitable. But I won't put myself forward if there are others more qualified. Just let me know if you want something from me.'

Ben was forming the opinion that this man was rather more worldly-wise than his other suspects. It didn't make him a murderer but...

He decided he'd have to tread carefully. 'Thanks. I appreciate that.' He leaned in towards Pedersen. 'This is outside my brief, I know, but I was one of Professor Dobson's students twenty years ago. He had the habit then of leaning on people more than was justified, almost to the point of blackmail. I'd be interested to know if he was still the same, or had time mellowed him?'

Pedersen's face hardened briefly and then he smiled. 'A side of him that we won't show to the world, I think. I'm sure the College can rely on us all to make sure his less savoury characteristics go with him into the earth. Now, here's a thought. As an alumnus, you can come to formal hall regularly. But if you want an invitation to the Master's drinks, do let me know. I'd be delighted to have you as my guest.'

'Thank you. I might take you up on that. One last question, if I may?'

'Fire away.'

'I'm trying to find another academic. A Dr A N Taylor. Do you know how I might find him?'

Pedersen looked down, stroking his beard. He pulled at it for a good while, then looked up and shook his head. 'Not at this university, but I expect you've looked here already. Not someone in my discipline elsewhere, not that I've heard of anyway. Can I ask why you're looking for this person?'

Either Pedersen was an accomplished liar or he really didn't know the elusive Dr Taylor. Ben was finding, to his discomfort, that he too was becoming an accomplished liar. 'Nothing really. Professor Dobson was organised, up to a point. He had a list of people to contact in the event of his death, but he didn't include any contact details. I can only assume they were all people he'd worked with in the past and the only one I've not been able to find is this Dr Taylor.'

'I'm sorry. I can't help you. I'll keep a lookout and let you know if I come across anyone by that name. Now, how about I prepare a little speech for the funeral and let you have a copy. Then you can decide if it's what you want included. Is that OK?'

Ben had to be content for the moment. He'd gleaned little useful information. He nodded and left. Here was someone who could be the murderer or the accomplice or be completely innocent. A cool customer indeed.

*  *  *

He looked at his watch. Just time for a quick visit to Dr O'Connor before lunch with the Master. He hurried to O'Connor's rooms. When the door was opened, he could see that O'Connor was agitated.

'Come in. Come in. So glad to see you. I really need to talk to you.'

Ben walked into a room with not a thing out of place. He wished his home could be this tidy. On second thoughts, that would mean he was living alone.

'What's the problem?'

'The problem. They've offered me Dobson's Chair. That's the problem. And I don't know what to do.'

Ben's first thoughts were of the furniture in Dobson's rooms. Then he twigged. 'A professorship?'

O'Connor nodded vigorously. 'In Mathematics and Physics in Medical Science. It's going to be an enormous field. There will be a huge expansion at the Addenbrookes site. They'll be building an enormous Biomedical Campus, state of the art. Cambridge will be a world leader in medical research. I want to be part of it. Saving lives. That's what I want my maths to do.'

'And your problem is that I hold two degree certificates which you think could scupper this appointment.'

'I don't think. I know. Academic integrity is fiercely guarded here. They deal harshly with people who falsify qualifications. I'd be out on my ear without a reference.'

'What do you want me to do?'

O'Connor sighed. 'I want you to trust me. I want you to give me back those two certificates and let me get on with my life. I know it's a lot to ask but it's the only thing I've ever done wrong. I've earned my place here. They wouldn't consider me for a Chair if I hadn't.'

'What about Dobson's murder? He had a hold over you and you gain by his death, a motive, I'd say.'

O'Connor began to look even more agitated. He marched up and down, wringing his hands. Then he swept his fingers through his hair, and finally he put his hands firmly into his pockets. He turned and looked beseechingly at Ben. 'I don't know anything about that. They're saying his murder was brutal. I couldn't do that. Please, I need your help.'

Ben thought for a moment. 'The last thing I want to do is to stop any medical research so this is what I can do. I told you I wouldn't share the information I have about you. That means I'm already perverting the course of justice. I'll keep to my bargain until Dobson's killers are found, then...'

He was interrupted. 'Killers? You mean there were two, three? How many? My God, the poor man.' Dr O'Connor sat down and put his head in his hands. 'What a mess. What had he got himself into?' Then he looked up at Ben. 'What can I do to help?'

Ben was thinking fast. Should he trust this man? Should he use this offer of help? 'You can keep your eyes and ears open and bring me any bit of information that you think might be helpful in bringing his killers to justice. Bring it to me, not the police. Understand?'

O'Connor looked doubtful. 'I asked you to trust me. But why should I trust you?'

'Because I'm one of you. I have the interests of the College at heart. And I want you to succeed in your discipline. That's why.'

O'Connor ran his hands through his hair again, then seemed to come to a decision. 'I suppose I've got no option. I have to trust you. I'll say yes to the Chair and hope like Hell that you keep your side of the bargain.'

'I will,' said Ben and they solemnly shook hands – a normal handshake this time and much more to Ben's taste.

*  *  *

Ben's head was full of jostling thoughts after his morning of meetings and lunch with the Master. The lunch had been the least interesting part except for one element. They'd made good inroads into the organisation of the funeral and all the main decisions were now taken. They'd talked of Ben's long – and not close – association with the College, and the Master's short and very close one. He'd learnt that the Master had undertaken a first degree while bringing up three children as a single mother, she'd gone on to further study and had juggled all those commitments, launching those three children onto socially useful careers. And that had unexpectedly brought thoughts of Diane. He wondered what his wife had given up when he'd been stationed in Belfast. He'd tried to dissuade her but she had insisted on moving there with him and had concentrated on bringing up their two girls safely in that unhealthy environment. She'd put all thoughts of a career on hold. It must have been a huge wrench for her to leave England to be at his side. And she'd been killed for her pains.

# Chapter 14

*Keep calm – he's just fishing. I'm sure he knows nothing. Don't worry – I've got a plan to neutralise him. And friends to carry it out. Destroy this – and don't email me again. It can be traced.*

# Chapter 15

'Hi Dad. How's it going?' Katy picked up a celery stick and started crunching it. She waved it towards her father. 'Newest thing for losing weight. Got to eat tons. And it's boring. Hey, saw Josephine yesterday. She's real thin. I sort of asked if she wanted to see you but then this nun arrived so she didn't answer. Anyway, they're going to let her out soon – just a visit to her mum's house so she might see you then.'

Ben wondered if he wanted to see Josephine. Probably not. It would be a move backwards and he so wanted to continue his forward trajectory.

Katy clicked her fingers in front of his face. 'Listen, Dad! Michael's had a breakthrough with one of your clues.' Ben looked at his younger daughter and sighed. He could see it in her eyes that she still had what he hoped was just a crush on Michael. He smiled at her. He was trying so hard to be objective and, as Dr Clare had told him, to stop trying to protect Katy from the mistakes that come from making choices. His brain told him that we all learn from our mistakes but his heart still wanted to wrap her up against the dangers of the world. Sarah had been easier; she took after him in so many ways. He wondered when Sarah would feel comfortable enough to share her news with him. Soon, he hoped. But Katy was more of a worry. She reminded him so much of her mother. He sighed.

'What's he found?'

Katy called through to Michael, then said to her father, 'He can tell you himself.'

Michael appeared, closely followed by Mo. And that did make Ben smile. Mo could be relied upon to pop up whenever anything important – or even unimportant – was being said. Ben had long suspected that his Uncle Mo kept one ear peeled for information, no matter what he was doing. It had probably made him a good copper in his time.

'Yeah – I had a breakthrough with Dr Fursley. The Catholic bit was easy but the Scottish connection bugged me. Then, ping,

Scottish connection, Scottish play. Even in Belfast we had to do Shakespeare in school so I went to the library and looked through the GCSE revision version – you know – with notes. The good man in Scotland – MacDuff.'

'So? What's this McDuff fella got to do with it?' interjected Mo.

'Of course!' said Ben. 'MacDuff was from his mother's womb untimely ripp'd.'

'Yesss!' yelled Michael and Katy together, high fiving each other.

'So?' said Mo again. 'C'mon. I ain't much of a scholar and I avoid Shakespeare like the plague. So tell me!'

Ben answered. 'I saw a happy photo on her desk today. Her wedding day with two beaming faces. I recognised the building. It was Westminster Cathedral. I think she's a good Catholic girl who married a good Catholic boy but somewhere along the line she's had an abortion.'

Katy looked sadly at her father. 'And, I suppose, the good Catholic boy doesn't know.' She waved a finger at them all. 'And that bastard Dobson and that bigger bastard Murdock held this over her.' She slumped and looked close to tears then she rallied. 'Both murdered and good riddance.' Then the tears appeared again. 'I do so hope it wasn't her.'

# Chapter 16

The phone-call had been peremptory. A minion had made it plain that this was a summons to Parkside as there had been further developments. He'd arrived and had been ushered into an interview room. That worried him. Yes, he'd removed evidence from the murder scene but then he'd shared that evidence – most of it anyway – with Vin. She couldn't know that he'd kept back the names of two people that she would see as suspects, so he was at a loss to know what had caused this change in attitude.

The door opened and the Apostles sauntered in. That was odd because Vin had said she was separating them. They loomed over him and he knew immediately what their purpose was. Their demeanour was designed to intimidate him. As the two detectives lumbered into the seats opposite, Ben took off his jacket, using the movement as cover for pressing 'record' on his dictaphone. He stood up and held out his hand. He spoke heartily. 'DS Bennett, DS Burnham, good to see you again. What can I do for you?' When neither officer reciprocated, he withdrew his hand and sat down.

Bennett thrust a sheet of paper towards him. 'Recognise this?' It was one of his pamphlets explaining the process of embalming. He kept an array of them in his front office.

'Yes. It's from my funeral office.'

'Recognise the writing?'

Ben looked carefully at the message written in block capitals at the top of the sheet. His eyes widened as he began to understand the purpose of this interview. 'No. I don't.'

'Read it to us.'

'Keep away from me or you'll be sorry.'

'Want to know where we found it?'

Ben remained silent. Bennet shrugged and continued, 'It was in Professor Dobson's house in Trumpington. See, we had to go back there cos there'd been an attempted break-in and while we were there we had another look round. And this was staring us in the face.' He tapped the pamphlet. 'Don't know how they could've missed this. Should've sent experienced officers in the first place.'

Ben's mind was in overdrive. He needed some answers. 'Where exactly did you find it?'

'See, we think the first lot was too quick. They didn't look under the stairs. It was there – all on its lonesome – on a shelf. Now, what do you think those words mean?'

Ben again remained silent. Either they were just putting the frighteners on him or he was being fitted up. Whichever, he had to work out the best way of playing it. They weren't taping the interview so he imagined it was 'off the record'. That under-stairs cupboard had been empty when he'd left it so these two had planted evidence to incriminate him. Why?

Burnham, who'd been quiet up to that point, leaned across the table. Ben could smell his foetid breath as he whispered, 'And we've got something else on you. You'd think it was good news but for you it's another nail in your coffin. Get it – joke – nail in coffin.'

Ben leant back into his chair as Bennett slid another batch of papers out of his folder. He tapped them as he spoke. 'We had a visit from a solicitor this morning. Nice man. Very co-operative. A pillar of the community. He'd read about Dobson's dreadful demise in the paper, so he brought in his client's last will and testament.' He waved the document under Ben's nose. 'And guess who's the sole beneficiary?'

'DS Bennett, DS Burnham, you are several steps ahead of me. That's obvious. I have no idea who gains from Dobson's will.'

'You, my friend. It's you. You cop the lot.'

'What! I hardly knew the man. Let me see that.' Ben snatched the will from Bennett. It was short and to the point. It had been drawn up just over four months ago and left everything to Benedict Burton.

'You trying to say you didn't know about this?'

Ben countered with, 'You trying to say this is a genuine legal document?'

Bennett took a third paper out of his folder and handed it across for Ben to see. 'I have a letter here signed by the solicitor to say that Dobson instructed him in July to draw up this will and have his signature witnessed by two of his clerks. It's legit and it gives you a big, fat motive, don't you think?'

Before Ben had a chance to reply, Burnham pointed a finger at him. 'And here's another thing. We surely do have CCTV of your car out near Waterbeach at the verified time of death. But what we don't have is proof that you were in it. Looking serious, ain't it?'

Ben's brain was working fast. They were trying to fit him up for Dobson's murder and his prints were now on both the pamphlet and the will. Foolish. But it was obvious that Vin wasn't involved because they didn't know about his perfect alibi – being in Waterbeach, in bed with their DCI when the murder took place. They also didn't know that he'd searched Dobson's house just before their visit so was certain that they had planted the evidence.

The two Apostles heaved themselves from their chairs in perfect unison. Burnham leaned over Ben and pointed a fat finger at him. 'We know you did it but we can't prove it – yet! But we know some bad people – some very, very bad people – people who can do you and yours a lot of harm. Understand?'

He did understand. He'd had a similar threat from Belfast heavies just a few months ago. He looked at the two detectives and decided they might know some 'bad people' but he'd bet that they weren't on the same scale as the Belfast mob. He'd brazen it out.

So many questions in his head. Why were they fixing on him? Whose toes had he trodden on? Who was pulling their strings? Why weren't they taping the interview? How bad could these 'bad' people be? And the most intriguing, if this was real, was why had Dobson made him his sole beneficiary? The question he asked was none of these. He took a last look at the letter from the solicitor and memorised the name and address. He stood up slowly. Then he looked Bennett squarely in the eye. 'Are you going to arrest me then?'

\* \* \*

Ben hadn't been arrested although he had the feeling that, if the Apostles could have had their way, he'd be only a hair's breadth from the custody suite. His request for an urgent meeting with Vin away from Parkside had led to coffee in the pub in Comberton. When Vin arrived, Ben was sitting quietly in the same secluded table as last time.

She greeted him with, 'What's the rush? Have you made a breakthrough? Hope so. We're completely stuck.'

'No breakthrough, but something just as interesting.' He quickly related his session with her Apostles, their threats and the planting of evidence in Trumpington. He told her he had a tape of the interview, if ever she needed it. As he spoke, her eyes widened and continued to widen till he thought she might do herself a damage. He told her of the insinuation that someone else may have been driving his car so his alibi was shot. 'This leads me to the conclusion that they know nothing of our relationship. So, they're not getting at you. At first, I couldn't fathom why they were fixing on me. Then I twigged. I must be treading on some very tender toes at Ethel's. And these are toes that can kick your Apostles into action.'

She sighed. 'We'll have to tell them about us. That'll mean you'll be out of the investigation and they'll probably have to get someone else to bury Dobson. Shit!'

'Hold on. Not necessary. They didn't record anything and they didn't caution me. So they're just putting on the frighteners, on their own account. We could run with this. The recording of the interview, it's a bit fuzzy but clear enough to use as evidence and I made sure their names were mentioned. Could sniff out your problem officers, give you something on them and, you never know, it might turn up something big. I'm happy to let it be and see what happens.'

'You sure?' She held up her hand. 'No, let me think. If it is something big, it will get messy. Look what happened to Dobson. No, I can't let you do that. No way! I'll have to corroborate your alibi.'

'Whoa! Hang on there. You're forgetting Chris. He's keen to carry on and see where it leads.'

Ben could almost feel the icy draught seeping across the table towards him. Vin's face froze. 'You talked to him before you talked to me?'

'I'm sorry. I had to.' His gesture of submission underscored his words. 'Look Vin, this all started way before you and me and there are security implications that Chris needs tying up. It's out of our hands. We're going to have to let it run. MI5 are up to their mucky little necks in all this. They've got to see it through – and, if they have to, then so do we.'

At Vin's look of horror, he added, 'Your Apostles are working for themselves and we all need to find out why. You, me and MI5. Don't worry – I can look after myself and I can call on back-up if needed.' He wasn't sure that this was the case but hoped it would mollify her. It seemed to. She nodded slowly.

Now that she was reluctantly on-side, he felt he should add his last piece of information. 'Let's see what they do next. I wonder when they'll tell you that they had a visit from Dobson's solicitor today. It seems that I'm the sole beneficiary of Dobson's estate – so that does give me an excellent motive for murder.'

* * *

He'd arranged with Vin that she would send a uniformed constable to meet him at the address that he had memorised from the solicitor's letter. The solicitor's office proved to be in a large and modern office block with an imposing lobby to the north of the city. Vin had sent his daughter, Sarah, for which he was grateful. He approached the receptionist with his best smile, his uniformed PC just one step behind. 'I'm really sorry. I need to see Mr Clayforth urgently. It's very important – to me and to the police – so if you could ask him, I'd be extremely grateful.'

She looked at her screen. 'Do you have an appointment?'
'No, but it is an urgent police matter.'
'Can I take your name, sir?'
'Ben Burton. He'll know what it's about when you give him the name.'

She pressed a number, turned away from him and spoke into the phone. She turned back with an apologetic smile. 'I'm sorry, sir. Mr Clayforth is in meetings all day. And he says he doesn't think it appropriate to speak to you at the moment.'

'I don't think you told him I was accompanied by a police officer? Perhaps you'd better ring him again. We wouldn't want him to be seen to be wasting police time, would we?'

She spoke briefly again, this time mentioning the police. That brought the response that Mr Clayforth would be with them in five minutes.

While they waited, Ben reminded Sarah that she must refer to him as Mr Burton and that he wanted her to keep notes of what was said.

A voice from behind them boomed in hearty tones. 'So sorry for the misunderstanding, Mr Burton, Officer.' If Mr Clayforth was wondering why the uniformed officer had not introduced herself, he gave no inkling. 'Come through to my office.'

Once Ben and Sarah were firmly ensconced in comfortable chairs around a mahogany table, Clayforth picked up a file from his desk and came to join them. They refused the offer of coffee and Ben opened the conversation. 'Firstly, Mr Clayforth, you don't have to worry about propriety. I have a cast-iron alibi for the time of the murder. This officer can vouch for that.'

Sarah nodded. 'I can confirm that Mr Burton has been eliminated from our enquiries.'

Ben continued, 'And now, I need some answers. I am totally at a loss as to why Professor Dobson has made me his sole beneficiary. Can you shed any light on that?'

With a flourish, the solicitor withdrew an envelope from his file. 'Professor Dobson required that I give this to you in person. Apologies, I need some form of identification before I can hand it over.'

Ben produced his driving licence. 'Is this sufficient?' The solicitor proceeded to photocopy the licence and place the copy in his file. Then he handed the driving licence back, together with a slim envelope with Mr Benedict Burton written on the front in Dobson's spidery scrawl. After he had signed for it, Ben turned it over and saw that it was sealed. The solicitor was leaning forward, looking expectant. Ben put the envelope in his pocket. 'Thank you. I'll read that later.' He was pleased to see the solicitor sit back, looking disappointed. 'And the will? I assume I can have a copy?'

The next flourish saw a copy of the will produced and handed over. 'You'll see, Mr Burton, that the will was drawn up, signed and witnessed in this office just this summer. The terms show that you will eventually be the owner of three houses in Trumpington. Professor Dobson owned the house he lived in and those on either side, both rented out on long-term leases. He also left in my keeping, his share certificates, various government bonds and details of his current account and ISAs. As you can see, if you peruse the end of the will, he appointed me his sole executor. I would think that you will come into quite a considerable sum when all the formalities have been gone through.'

Ben looked bemused. 'Did he give you any inkling as to why he left it all to me, because I have no idea.'

'There may be an explanation in the letter. The one thing he mentioned was that he thought he owed you. Yes, I remember. He said it was from years back. I had imagined that you had lent him money way back when and this was repayment.' The solicitor again looked expectant.

Ben decided not to indulge his curiosity. 'Thank you, Mr Clayforth. I expect I'll hear from you in due course. Here's my card.' And he rose and held out his hand.

As soon as they were outside, Sarah said, 'Well, Dad. Did you lend him money?' At Ben's shaken head she added, 'So what, then? I'm gagging to know why that old goat thought he owed you.'

Ben turned the envelope over in his hands. 'I think I'll do this on my own.'

'Aw Dad – that's so mean.'

'I promise you, if there's anything to tell, I'll tell all of you together. But I need to do this on my own. Want to come to dinner tonight? You, me, Katy and Mo.'

'Can't do tonight. Going out with Pam and Michael. Hey, though, Dad. I'm turning into a right gooseberry there. They try not to get all lovey-dovey while I'm there but they just can't help it. A Police Sergeant and a convicted criminal, wonder how that will go down with her folks?'

Ben wondered how it would go down with Katy. But countering that was an overwhelming sense of relief that neither of his girls was involved with a relative of Stanley Murdock, even one as sane and sensible as Michael.

After he'd waved goodbye to Sarah, he phoned to see if he was needed at work. Then he sat in the car for a full five minutes, turning the letter over. He felt a sense of foreboding about the contents but couldn't say why. He decided it was like getting exam results. Life might change for ever after the envelope was opened.

He ripped it open and pulled out a single sheet of paper. On it were written just a few lines of scrawl.

*Benedict,*
*Please forgive me for allowing your most precious gift to be stolen from you. She was mine before she was yours. I loved her very much. They found out, and then she died. You blame Stanley Murdock but I blame myself.*
*Graham*

'What the…?' Ben could feel his scar start to throb, a sure sign that he needed to run; to run as fast as he could away from Cambridge, away from those two dead people, Stanley Murdock and Graham Dobson, away from the past which kept returning to torture him. He got out of his car and raced north through Impington and on towards Cottenham. The pavements were empty and he was unimpeded. He ran and ran, faster as he left the village and flat fenland engulfed him. Ten minutes later, when his breath had run out, he stopped. He sat on a wall and put his head in his hands.

With trembling fingers, he took out the letter and reread it. Now he could fathom why Dobson had kept all those photos of his wife. He'd been stalking her. *She was mine before she was yours.* Ben could make sense of an affair before he'd known her. It didn't make it any easier that it had been with Dobson. He could even see that, as a student, she could find an affair with a tutor exciting. He could feel the tide of jealousy trying to overwhelm him. He quietly pushed back that tide. But then that next sentence, *and then she died.* What was that? It didn't make sense. And he didn't blame Murdock. Chris had told him that Dobson had lied and UVF dissidents had planted the bomb that had killed Diane. He'd hated Dobson and he'd trusted Chris. Now, he wondered, who could he trust? He thought of calling Chris and shouting down the phone at him.

As he walked back to collect his car, he had time to think. The letter raised too many questions and gave him no answers. Did he care that his wife had had an affair with a man he had come to loathe. Of course he did. *They found out.* Who the Hell were 'they'? And why did her affair mean that she had to die? Dobson had always been a small cog in the wheels of state. Surely not important enough to kill for? And anyway, the bomb had been at the barracks so it had been meant for him and those other soldiers. It could not have been meant for her. It had to be the UVF. But the most urgent question for him was, what was he going to tell the family? He decided, just as he had when the heavies and then the Apostles had threatened them all, he would tell them nothing but he would have to be even more vigilant. Safer that way.

# Chapter 17

The Wren chapel was so small that it was easily filled by the few who mourned Dobson's death and the rest whose arms had, no doubt, been twisted to attend. Ben had watched from the back of the church as the great and good of the academic world had squeezed into the pews near the altar, their gowns and hoods resplendent in the shafts of sunlight. Flowers overflowed the altar and covered the coffin. Now, the organist, the same one as for Stanley Murdock's funeral, was belting out the final rousing hymn. The College choir were belting out the rousing hymn in synchrony. This had been a celebration of a past life. Praise to God had filled the chapel to the rafters. Praise of Dobson had been more muted but, nonetheless, had appeared fulsome and genuine. The chosen speakers had all done their bit. They had praised Graham Dobson's fine work as a mathematician, his attention to his students and his excellent work as College bursar ensuring that St Etheldreda's was set to prosper in the years to come. It had been left to the Master to make brief mention of his 'untimely death' and anyone not in the know would have assumed a heart attack or some such. A few local hacks had been allowed in to record the spectacle but those from the nationals had been left outside.

  Ben surveyed the assembly. Dobson's killers were almost certainly among them. All his College suspects were in attendance and all were looking composed. Dr Fursley had even approached him and thanked him for the introduction to Dr Clare. She smiled as she confided that she was beginning to feel more at ease with herself than she had for many years. It gave him some little discomfort to know that he now shared a therapist with one of his suspects, but he had to concede that Dr Fursley was looking a whole lot calmer than the last time he'd seen her. He wondered if the elusive Dr Taylor was here. Somehow he doubted it. Everyone present seemed to know everyone else. All seemed to be connected with the university in some capacity and no trace had been found of Dr Taylor within that institution. He watched Dr Fursley in particular as she was the only one who had shown by her response at interview that she knew Taylor. She spoke to no-one from outside Ethel's.

As the final hymn was nearing its conclusion and Ben was about to signal for the coffin to be carried out to the waiting hearse, he heard a voice close to his ear. 'Good send-off. We academics are such excellent liars.' Professor Walpole was standing alongside him leaning heavily on a stick. He continued, 'I see young Chris is here, hiding in the shadows as usual. Also an accomplished liar. Are you coming to the drinks do? I have some information that you might find useful. Talk to me over drinks. There will be a crowd. Free drinks draw academics like a magnet. All this crowd will be there plus those who couldn't be bothered to come to the chapel. The Great Hall will be heaving. Should be able to talk in peace, surrounded by the great and good.'

'I had hoped to come. Are you inviting me?'

'Of course, dear boy.' He pointed his stick at the coffin. 'What about the old boy in the box? What's happening to him?'

'The Master decided it should be family only at the crem. As there's no family, I'm sending him back to my place until late this afternoon. It was the only slot I could get today so my people will be the only followers there. Sad end to a sad man.' And all the while Ben was thinking, but he also loved my wife so we have that in common.

Walpole pointed his stick at Michael, who was busy preparing the coffin for removal, 'That Murdock's nephew? Good looking boy. Will he stay with you after he gets the money from his inheritance, d'you think?'

Ben looked round sharply. 'How the Hell do you know about that?'

The old man tapped the side of his nose. 'I keep my eyes and ears open. Oh, and I still have friends in very high and very low places, remember? That helps.'

# Chapter 18

He'd been summoned. Well, it felt like a summons. After refusing to see him for four months, Josephine had suddenly decided that she had to see him today. Dr Clare had explained, on the phone, that Josephine had regressed over the past day and was extremely agitated. She thought it would be helpful if he could accede to Josephine's request and visit immediately. So here he was, driving out to The Friary, not knowing what to expect.

To take his mind off the impending meeting, he turned over in his mind the conversations he'd had the previous day after the funeral. He had again asked all of his suspects about their knowledge of the elusive Dr Taylor and all had been keen to be helpful – or, at least, to appear so. He'd implied – but hadn't stated – that Taylor might be a beneficiary to Dobson's will so it was imperative that he be found. All had denied knowledge and all had suggested avenues he might explore in his search. When he'd asked Dr Fursley about her knowledge of Dr Taylor, she had again denied knowing him and Ben had again been certain she'd been lying. The others, he couldn't tell.

O'Connor had taken him to one side to tell him he had accepted the Chair and sincerely hoped Ben would keep to his side of the bargain. Ben had again assured him that his secret was safe until after the murderers had been found. He was going with his instincts but he knew that Vin would be furious if she found that he was withholding evidence germane to her murder case. He also knew that Chris would see the sense. Pedersen had invited him to membership of the Isaac Newton Lodge, as he knew Ben had been a student at Ethel's and thus a member of the University. Ben had made what he hoped was a non-committal reply along the lines of 'when this is all over'. Hendrick had been the most antagonistic, or perhaps just defensive. He'd responded that he'd been at Cambridge since his 18th birthday and had never even come across the name of the elusive Dr Taylor. He'd then abruptly hurried away before Ben could ask anything further, but it had left Ben thinking he would have to look further into Hendrick's background, in fact, into the work background of them all.

He'd arranged to meet Professor Walpole so they could have a conversation where 'there was no possibility that they could be overheard'. And he would visit him after this meeting with Josephine. He had no idea what Walpole wanted to tell him. But more worrying was that he had no idea what Josephine wanted or what he could say or do to help her.

\* \* \*

Dr Clare met him on the steps of The Friary. She looked worried and began without the usual greeting formalities. 'She was making such good progress and now she's suddenly regressed and has demanded to see you. So glad you could come straight away. She's decided she wants to see you in a private space. I'm sure – well, as sure as I can be – that she won't be violent. What do you say to that?'

'That's fine with me. She murdered Stanley by just leaving him to die. He had no marks of violence and she was never violent towards me.' Ben carefully repressed the memory of Josephine brandishing a knife in his direction as he had tried to save her from killing herself. 'As far as I know, she's never been violent, so I think I'm safe.'

It was a short walk to the room where Josephine awaited him and Dr Clare took the opportunity to tell him where the panic button was situated, and that she had arranged the room so that he would be seated near it. She motioned him to wait outside, knocked on the door and immediately opened it. She surveyed the room then invited him to enter. The nurse who was sitting next to Josephine rose, patted Josephine's hand and nodded to Dr Clare before leaving the room.

Dr Clare looked from Ben to Josephine. 'I'll leave you two together. I'll come back in ten minutes. Call me if there's anything you need.' And Dr Clare too left the room.

'Hello Josephine. You're looking well.' Ben said.

No preamble. Josephine launched into her speech without looking at him. 'I don't know what to do. You're the only one I can trust. The only one who can help.' Ben was jolted by the similarity to Dobson's last message to him.

'What do you want me to do?'

Josephine looked up and quickly averted her gaze. She pulled a handkerchief from her pocket and held it in front of her mouth. Ben recognised it as one of his. She sobbed into it. He leaned towards her. She put out a restraining hand. 'Don't touch me. Please, don't touch me. I couldn't bear it. Please just listen. I don't want to cause you any more pain but I need your help.' She gulped then continued. 'There's a nun. She's very old. She comes to visit me and I love her. Yesterday, she told me that a paedophile she knows from her time abroad has surfaced in Cambridge. She was so shocked that she had to share it with someone. I told her to go to the police but she says he's important and they wouldn't believe her. She told me she's frightened and then she wouldn't tell me any more. She says it's to protect me.' Josephine turned and looked at Ben. 'I didn't know what to do. I'm so worried about her and I'm scared too.'

Ben answered briskly. 'For a start, you are well protected. No-one can get to you here. OK?' She nodded.

'Next,' he said, 'Tell me the name of the nun and where I can find her. I'll sort this out.'

\* \* \*

He left The Friary having ascertained that Josephine was feeling calmer after handing responsibility for Sister Theresa to him. He noted from the address of the convent that it was to the north of Ely, so he would have to leave that visit till the next day as he had a visit to Professor Walpole planned. As it happened, he was to manage neither visit in the time-scale he'd anticipated.

# Chapter 19

As he drove away, his thoughts were on Josephine. He wondered why he still felt responsible for her. She'd killed a man. An evil man, of that there was no doubt. She might well have killed Ben too, if he hadn't disarmed her. But she was still vulnerable, still disturbed.

He first noticed the white van when he turned off the main road onto a smaller one which provided a short-cut to Cambridge. The van turned too. It was keeping a discreet distance so he thought no more about it until he reached the next cross-roads and decided, on the spur of the moment, to visit his usual farm shop. This would take him away from Cambridge again. He turned left and the van followed. It was far enough away for it to be difficult to read the number plate. He deciphered it and memorised it. When he turned into the farm entrance, the van continued on the road. He left a voicemail for Vin with the registration number and details of his route and continued to shop.

As soon as he left the farm, the van joined him again. This time it sat on his bumper and hooted loud and long. There was no room for it to pass so he accelerated. The van did too. He tried to make out the face of the driver but both the driver and passenger were wearing balaclavas. That was when Ben began to be seriously worried. As he was considering his options, the van speeded up and rammed him. He fought for control and managed to keep the car on the road. He was approaching a bend and had to slow down. He was rammed again – this time with more force and his car now ignored the bend and continued through a hedge and bumped over stony ground at the field edge until it came to rest in a field of wheat. Ben just had time to punch 999 into his phone, get connected and hide the phone under his seat before looking in his mirror and seeing two enormous men in balaclavas approaching his car. One was carrying a crowbar.

He locked the car doors knowing it would only stave off the inevitable. He turned the key in the ignition, hoping it would start. Nothing. He tried again – still nothing. He shouted towards the hidden phone in the hope that the 999 handler could hear him. What weapons did he have? He looked round: a torch, umbrella, spare shoes – no match for a crowbar. His first thought was that he should, in future, carry a weapon in the car; his second was that he might not, in future, be in need of a weapon or even a car. Then the realisation that he would be abandoning his girls. He wondered if there was, indeed, a Heaven. He hoped so.

The men walked round to the front of the car, raised the crowbar and smashed the windscreen. The noise was deafening as glass showered down on Ben. The one without the weapon snarled, 'Outa the car or we'll pull ya through the screen.' Ben obeyed, all the time looking at his surroundings for deliverance and at his attackers for clues to their identity, just in case he survived.

As he left the car, Ben lunged at the crowbar carrier. In a swift movement, the other one grabbed him from behind, pinning his arms behind him. He could see through the balaclava that crowbar man was grinning. He had a missing front tooth. Crowbar man spat on the ground and said, 'We just bin told to beat the guts outa ya but you ain't to be killed. Pity. And before we start – we've bin told to tell ya. Keep your snitch outa business that ain't yours.' And with that, he dropped the crowbar and started alternately punching and kicking Ben. The pain was so intense that, in less than a minute, Ben had passed out.

\* \* \*

When Ben woke, he found himself in a hospital bed with both his daughters holding his hands. His uncle Mo was standing at the end of the bed. Ben realised he must be alive because every bit of him hurt: his head, his ribs, his stomach. He must be on strong painkillers, but still he ached.

He tried to speak. Nothing came. He felt around inside his mouth with his tongue. Remarkably, all his teeth seemed to be in place. He tried again but his jaws wouldn't open properly. He squeezed his daughters' hands. They returned the pressure. Sarah was composed but he saw a tear escape and trickle down Katy's cheek. She quickly brushed it away. A woman in a white coat approached the bed. 'Ah, good. You're awake.' She looked down at her notes. 'Well, the good news is that they knew what they were doing. Maximum short-term pain with minimum long-term damage. Your liver, kidneys, internal organs all intact. They avoided your head and testes – I'm sure you're pleased to hear that. Gave your legs a good kicking. Don't try to speak. Plenty of time for that later. Best to have another sleep if you can.' And, with that, she walked away.

Ben couldn't bring himself to be pleased about anything – except that he was alive and his family was safe and well. His fault. He hadn't taken the Apostles' warning seriously, a major miscalculation on his part. With that thought, he drifted back into a dreamless sleep.

\* \* \*

When he woke again, it was dark and there was a uniformed officer sitting by his bed. The officer was asleep. Ben tried to sit up. He lay back down as sharp pains spread through his entire body, even down to his hands and feet. His associated grunts woke the officer. 'You OK, sir? Do you want me to call a nurse?'

Ben shook his head slowly. He realised that every move would have to be in slow motion. He enunciated his words carefully, as even the effort of talking was painful. 'Did they catch them?'

'No sir, sorry. DCI Wainwright got your message about the same time as the emergency services. They tracked your position and got to you pretty quickly. But they'd gone by then.'

Ben gathered his strength to ask another question. 'The van?'

'Reported stolen the night before and found burnt out near Cottenham. Painter and decorator, been planning to get a new one anyway so he's not unhappy.'

Then the one that he'd been dreading. 'My family?'

'All fine. Got a family liaison officer in your house now. DCI Wainwright insisted.'

Ben relaxed.

\* \* \*

The next time he woke, Vin was sitting by his bed reading a book. If it hadn't hurt to do so, he might have smiled. It was a police procedural murder-mystery.

'Hello,' he croaked.

She put the book down. 'Bloody Hell, Ben. What were you doing? You could have been killed.'

He shook his head slowly. Moving was painful. Even talking was painful. 'No, they said they'd been told not to kill me. They'd been sent to teach me not to stick my nose in.' He managed a small smile. 'But thank you for rescuing me.'

'You're safe in here. There's a police watch. They're keeping you in another day, then God knows what will happen. I can't help you.'

He couldn't fathom that one; his brain felt like it was in the clouds, separate from his body and just out of reach. With an effort, he gathered his neurons into some sort of order. 'I must have rattled some cages at the funeral. Asked about Dr Taylor. Still no leads?'

'No, and your bloody Chris is poking his nose in. Says I'm not to interfere. Says he had you before I did so he has precedence. Bloody Services. They always have precedence! Anyway, clues as to the perpetrators. What can you tell me?'

Ben's head was aching with a pulsating ferocity and he was beginning to feel sleepy again. His speech became slurred. 'Yesh. One had a front tooth missing and a limp – left leg. Other, a tatt on his neck. Saw half. Looked holy.' And with that he fell asleep.

# Chapter 20

*You're not backing out now – forget that idea. You're in this up to your neck. He knows nothing. Keep your nerve. Do nothing. Let the architect take care of it.*

# Chapter 21

It was Sunday before they let Ben out. He'd been home from hospital for less than an hour when Katy came in with the news that 'Chris with the sexy voice' was in the hall and wanted to see him. 'He's real insistent but I said you're too ill to see anyone. He said to ask you, so I am, but I think you should make him wait.' She sighed. 'Big disappointment. He's not nearly as sexy as his voice on the phone. Who is he, anyway?'

'He's someone who might be able to find out who did this to me. So I'd better see him. Ask him in. And be nice to him.'

He heard Katy in the hallway. 'My Dad says you can see him and I've got to be nice to you. But just you make sure you don't make him worse. Or you'll have me and my family to deal with, and we've got muscle.' Katy stomped into the room followed by Chris. He looked more chastened than Ben had ever seen him.

'God, you look rough,' was his opener. Chris pointed a thumb at Katy. 'Should have had this young lady with you.'

Katy cut in. 'We're women these days.' She poked him in the chest. 'Ladies went out with the ark. You should know that. Do you want a cup of tea?'

It was the first time Ben had seen this cock-sure young man seeming less than comfortable. Ben beamed at his daughter. It hurt but it was worth it. 'We'd both like one. Thank you.'

As Katy left the room, Chris complained, 'She didn't ask me how I like it.'

'That's my Katy. Doesn't do to get on the wrong side of her. Now, what can I do for you?'

'More what I can do for you. D'you want a minder?'

'No. Not for me, but I am worried about the rest of the family. You've seen Vin? Did she tell you about her Apostles? They threatened me and my family. I want them taken out of the equation.'

'Any proof they were behind this?'

'No.'

'No problem. We'll sort it.'

'I did record the interview where they threatened me.'

'Well, why didn't you say so before! Gissit here.'

Ben played back the tape. Katy stomped back in with two mugs of tea and was in time to hear a growling voice say 'We know you did it but we can't prove it – yet! But we know some bad people – some very, very bad people – people who can do you and yours a lot of harm. Understand?'

Katy stared at her father's dictaphone. 'What the fuck is that?' Then she turned to her father. 'And don't tell me not to swear. How come you didn't tell us about this?'

'I'm sorry. I didn't take it seriously. I should have.'

'So that's why we've got a cop sitting in our kitchen, drinking tea. And why Uncle Mo's sitting with her reminiscing about the Force and what it was like in the olden days.' She stopped. 'What about Sarah. She OK?'

'Vin's looking after her.'

'And who's that slimeball on the tape?'

'A police officer who will be in custody just as soon as I get this to Vin.'

Chris spoke up. 'You got a copy?'

'Of course.' Ben could see, in his mind, his copy disc nestling in his fireproof box with the blackmail lists and the mysterious key he had omitted to bury with Stanley Murdock. For additional security he'd hidden the box on a shelf he'd erected in the chimney aperture in his bedroom.

'Gimme that gubbins and I'll copy it. Get it back to you in an hour. Who are these two morons on the tape?'

'DS Bennett and DS Burnham? Work for Vin – trying to destabilise her.'

'Got any idea who the heavies are?'

'I gave a bit of a description to Vin. The police have a good idea who they are. They just need to pull them in.'

'Hope the woodentops know what they're doing. How long till you're fit again? We need those bloody clues busted. We know about Walpole. Been one of ours forever. Our people got the abortion woman but that's all. Bloody Murdock was a devious bastard. One of our best till he started working for himself. Finest bloody brains in the country and we can't crack his bloody clues.'

Katy couldn't keep quiet. 'Well, we've done better than that.'

Before she could say more, there was a ring on the doorbell. Chris said, 'Got a back way? Don't want to be seen.' As he left, he added, 'Walpole sends his regards. Hopes you're better soon and then he'd like to see you.'

As Chris left by the French windows, clutching Ben's dictaphone, his parting words were, 'Get this back to you pronto.' Ben hoped so. He could hear Katy talking at the front door. She came back with a big box. 'Mary says to tell you she's only two doors away if you need anything. She said not to disturb you and she's cooked a casserole and a cake. News around here is that you were mugged.'

'That was nice of her.'

'Oh, come on, Dad. You know she fancies you like you're Clooney or something.' She sniffed in the aroma emanating from the box. 'You could do worse if this casserole is anything to go by. And if we're all to be stuck in here till they catch those bastards, we're going to need good food. And we might as well solve those bloody clues. Don't look like that, Dad. I'm only quoting that policeman, your friend Chris.'

'He's not police and he's not my friend.'

'Ha! Gotcha! So, he's not police. I could tell that. I bet he's MI5? Yes?'

Ben didn't answer but asked a question of his own. 'How come you took against him? There were evil vibes coming off you in waves.'

She started counting on her fingers. 'First, it was the way he looked me over when I opened the door. You know, that male entitlement look, like I was some bimbo. Second, he stood too close in the hall. Third, he wasn't at all concerned about you being beaten up. Just wanted to know when you'd be fit again. Fourth, he was too cocky by half. Can't stand men like that. Fifth, he wore too much aftershave. yuk!' She went on to her other hand. 'Sixth, he didn't live up to his voice on the phone.'

Ben laughed then doubled up clutching his stomach. He waved a hand. 'OK. You can stop there.' At the look on Katy's face he added, 'Yes, I'm fine. Just remind me not to laugh for a day or two.'

'So am I right about his provenance?'

'I think I'm supposed to say "no comment" here.'

'Aha! So I am right. But I'm not to tell anyone. Right too?'

'Right.' Ben smiled. At least that was beginning to hurt less. His daughter was growing into an impressive young woman. He was beginning to think that it was him, not Katy, who needed protection.

The doorbell rang again and Katy ushered in Sarah, Pam and Michael bearing grapes and chocolate biscuits. Sarah kissed her father gingerly and immediately told him that the grapes were for him, the biscuits for themselves.

\* \* \*

Katy organised them around the dining table. She even dragged in the police liaison woman. Ben took Katy to one side and told her not to say the names, as it was all conjecture at the moment. The real reason, for Ben, was that they had a stranger in their midst, a police officer who would be on the lookout for evidence – any evidence – and Ben needed to control the evidence flow. They all introduced themselves to Louise, the Family Liaison Officer/Protection Officer. Katy took charge.

'See, we're stuck in here so we may as well do something useful. What we need to do is think outside every box there ever was to try to work out what all these people's secrets are. But, as Dad says, we mustn't name them cos it's all conjecture.' She pointed to her copy. 'These clues were written by a devious bastard who was also Mensa-plus in the cleverness stakes. We've got to be Mensa-plus-plus. But there are seven of us. And we've got wine!'

Katy held aloft a bottle of Villa Maria and Ben's mind went back to the first time he'd shared a drink with Josephine. Then she'd been a mysterious and beautiful solicitor. But a solicitor who had already murdered the man who had written these clues. He was transported back to that other time in his life, the time between his wife's death and the arrival of Stanley Murdock on his slab. Sixteen years. He'd brought up his two daughters. He'd recovered, to some extent, both physically and mentally from the bomb that had taken Diane and had almost taken him as well. The Stanley episode had definitely been a setback in his recovery, but he hadn't had 'the dream' since starting his sessions with Dr Clare, and he was working towards the point where he would lose that feeling of guilt at being the target of the bomb but not the one who had died. Immediately, he felt a different pang of guilt. He hadn't yet contacted Josephine's nun. But at least Walpole knew that he hadn't forgotten him.

'Dad, you're not listening.'

'Sorry, love. What were you saying?'

'I've told them how we solved the clues for Dr C and her lover, with Mill being in both and Quy once being called Cow Island. Then I explained how *"playing the good man in Scotland set the cat alight"* took us to Macduff and her abortion even though she's Catholic.'

Pam cut in. 'You lot are so clever. I don't think I'll be able to add anything.'

Mo waved a finger at her. 'Don't you underestimate yourself. It's amazing what a bit of local knowledge can do.' He puffed out his chest. 'I'm the one that got Cow Island. And we got Prof W being a commie because I'm old and I remember the Cambridge spies. Burgess and his lot, they legged it to Moscow. So we've all got something and between us we might solve them all.'

Katy grinned at her great-uncle. 'We're a team – so let's get to it. I'll read out all the rest so you can get them all in your heads. I'll start with the ones we've half got. That OK?' They all nodded.

'Here goes, *Dr J. H, May 1991, Charles Rennie opened his doors for a second time – saved by the Three.* See, we've got the Charles Rennie – Mackintosh – a flasher. But saved by the three, any thoughts?'

Pam looked tentative, then put up her hand as though in a classroom. They all laughed, including Pam. 'In the police a "code three" response means use lights and siren – it's an emergency. Could that be anything?'

Katy was hastily writing notes. 'Great. Anything else, anyone?'

Ben smiled at Pam. 'That sounds good. We'll have to follow it up.' From Ben's position, he could see that Michael had squeezed Pam's hand under the table when she'd ventured her answer, and had kept hold of it afterwards. Interesting pairing; a convicted criminal and a Police Sergeant. He looked at them and each had a secret smile on their lips. He looked at Michael and gave him a surreptitious thumbs up. Michael and Pam both grinned back.

'Next,' said Katy, '*Professor O. P, July 2009 – Not his native hulduholk at the end of this rainbow. Tie and dye – that's his hobby.* We've got nowhere with this except I looked up huldufolk.'

She stopped as the Police Liaison Officer fled the room and they could hear her retching in the kitchen. Sarah followed her. The rest of the group sat in stunned silence until Katy said, 'God, I hope we haven't poisoned her.'

Ben called out, 'Need any help?' to which there was a negative reply.

After a few minutes, the two women came back, both looking grey. Sarah answered for them both. 'It might not be this but Louise thinks it's snuff movies. She did a bit in the Met years ago with Obscene Publications and that's what some of the officers called them. Tie and dye. If it is, this is seriously deep shit we've waded into.'

Michael looked aghast. 'Christ! When I was in Highpoint, there was someone in for distributing snuff movies. Yer man got a real rough time.' He looked towards Ben. 'Kickings worse than you got. The straight-up killers sure don't like it. Screws were always somewhere else when it happened.'

Louise had recovered enough to speak. 'Sorry for throwing up out there. Brought it back. PTSD. I only lasted a couple of months. Couldn't handle it, still can't.' She took a deep breath. 'The old hands had to keep sane so they joked about it. Only way to survive long-term. They used the term "tie and dye". Brought it back. Sorry.'

While she'd been talking, Ben had been scribbling on a piece of paper. He handed it to Louise. 'I'm so sorry that we've caused you pain. Here's a phone number. I have PTSD. She's done wonders for me. She might be able to help.'

'Thanks. Appreciate it. I've had counselling but, as you can see, I'm still not over it. It's still an issue.'

Katy smiled at her. 'You OK to carry on? You don't have to, you know.'

'Fine – I'll be fine now.'

'You sure?'

Louise nodded so Katy continued, 'OK Next. *Dr M. O'C, April 1997, should have been first in line. Your call Graham. And a good one.* We think Graham is Professor Dobson.'

Ben turned to Louise. 'Dobson's the one who's just been murdered.'

'I know. DCI Wainwright told me all the background before I came here.'

Ben wondered what, and how much, their protection officer had been told of the complexities of this situation. Not all, he was sure. He continued. 'I know this one. He falsified his degree credentials to get a job here. Dobson found out but gave him the job anyway.'

'That's nice,' said Mo. 'I thought Dobson was a complete shite – pardon my French – but it seems he had a good side.'

'Sorry Mo. He used it to keep a hold over this man. So not so nice.'

'Oh!'

Katy waved her paper again. 'And last – the one that no-one can find. *Dr A. N. T – 2011 – they played the violin together for years but he's lost his bog-light, so now he's a target.* I've been puzzling about this but can't make anything of it! I Googled bog-light and got will-o-the-wisp. You know, that methane thing you get in marshes. But it could just be he was sitting having a crap and it went dark.'

This time it was Michael who waved his arm around, then both arms. 'I've got something. My uncle wrote this and he spent a good few years in Ireland – yes? Well, we have bogs aplenty there. There's an Irish folk tale about Stingy Jack. He has to wander the country, to this day, carrying a hollowed lantern. He's Jack-o-lantern – and the bog-light is named after him.'

The cogs in Ben's brain were turning. His mind was still in a fog from his beating but there was an Irish connection forming. He said nothing. This was not to be said aloud. Chris had said 'the Ruskies get every-bloody-where'. Ben was beginning to wonder if the Irish were doing likewise.

# Chapter 22

He was counting the days. He had three more to endure before the family would let him out of the house. He'd been feeling like a caged tiger but the world, it seemed, had moved on without him. And, at least, he'd not had to rely on Katy's cooking so he was well fed. The regular meals from his neighbour, Mary, had been a bonus and he was definitely going to have to ask her for some recipes. But when he'd seen her, recipes had been the last thing on his mind.

Mary must have been their neighbour for five years at least. He'd helped her with small DIY jobs, dripping tap, that sort of thing. And they'd chatted about this and that. He'd known very little about her, except, he now knew that she was a very good cook. He'd asked Katy to invite her for a drink with them and had smiled inwardly at Katy's lame excuse to leave the two of them alone together.

Their conversation had not been about 'this and that' but had instead been surprisingly informative. Ben now knew that, for the past five years, Mary had been the University Librarian. And he'd found that before that, she had been Librarian at Ethel's and she knew all his suspects there. She had been refreshingly forthcoming about life in College.

'I love Henry Walpole. D'you know, he proposed to me once. Said he loved me and couldn't live without me. All lies, of course. I was to be a cover for his other life, but I was flattered that he'd chosen me.'

'Other life?'

'Well, Henry's gay, of course, and a spy. The first is common knowledge, the spying not so much.'

Ben asked nonchalantly, 'Spy? How do you know that?'

'Ah! That was easy! By being invisible. Librarians are like waiters. People don't see us. It's amazing what we get to know. Lots of conversations take place in libraries; whispered conversations where people don't want to be overheard. Most are boring, people's affairs and other mundane secrets but sometimes we learn something interesting.'

'And...'

'Years ago, the library was empty except for me. I was filling a bottom shelf so I was invisible to them. I heard Henry talking to Dobson. Henry was so angry. Tearing Dobson off a strip. I think that's why he forgot to keep his voice down. It was all about some undercover agent in Belfast. So then I knew that they were both involved.'

Ben was suddenly worried for the continued health of this woman. 'So who have you told?'

She laughed. 'I'm not stupid. Only you.' She looked sideways at him. 'That's because I think you're involved too.'

Ben felt a sudden tightening in his chest. He decided not to prevaricate. He somehow knew it wouldn't work. 'Am I that obvious?'

'No. Don't worry. I still go and have long conversations with Henry. He's a lovely old man but he's getting a little indiscreet, with me anyway. I think he's feeling his age and wants to make sure that things don't go pear-shaped when he dies. You know, trying to tie up loose ends. He's got something on his mind that he wants to talk to you about. I'm damned sure it's got nothing to do with esoteric Russian history.' She looked sideways at him. 'And I'm pretty sure you're not gay, so that only leaves one option. Am I right?'

Ben nodded. 'You are one very clever woman.'

\* \* \*

And now, the day of his release had come, and he had a spring in his step, despite his still-aching muscles. He was on his way, at last, to meet Henry Walpole and to find out what Walpole wanted to tell him. As he walked, he looked back on that encounter with Mary. Ben was delighted by the thought that he was surrounded by clever women. Lucky him, and especially lucky that they all seemed to be batting on his side. Soon he would be visiting a convent and would meet a whole gaggle of women, but first he had a meeting with Professor Walpole. After that, he would go to see Sister Theresa and try to calm her fears.

At first, the Mother Superior had not been at all keen on him visiting Sister Theresa – until he had said that he was a friend of

Josephine's and that he was worried about her. Then she'd told him that Sister Theresa was visiting Josephine that morning and he could come to see her that afternoon, and would it be possible for him to bring a female chaperone with him. Katy had readily agreed. She'd never been inside a convent and had decided that 'a female collective would be a cool place to visit.'

He'd heard from Vin that they were still looking for his attackers. The police had identified them from his description but they both seemed to have temporarily abandoned their places of abode. The surprise had been that Chris and two officers, that she assumed to be Military Police, had played the tape to Vin and had removed Bennett and Burnham – she knew not where – but they had not been seen for two days.

So now he was making his slow and still painful way to see Professor Walpole, who had confirmed that he had important information for him. Ben hoped it would bring him closer to finding Dobson's killer, and preferably without further assaults on him or his family.

The professor welcomed him in with, 'For someone who's been beaten to a pulp, you're not looking too bad, dear boy. Come in and take the weight off your feet. Coffee, tea?'

At Ben's refusal, he nodded sagely. 'Good call. Hopeless at both. They always look like dishwater and taste worse. Used to have a secretary to do all that – but cutbacks, dear fellow – you know how it is.' He closed the door behind them with a thud. 'Good solid doors these. Won't be overheard.' They weaved their way through the piles of papers and the professor pointed to a saggy leather armchair. Ben lowered himself gingerly and found the chair to be surprisingly comfortable. While the professor uncovered some papers from the mound on his desk, he continued, 'I survive mostly on gin these days. Queen Mother lived to a hundred and one so it must be good for you.' Ben had not uttered a word so far so had to smile when the professor added, 'Enough of the pleasantries. We need to crack on.'

He came and sat opposite Ben. 'Been doing some historical research on your behalf. It's turned up some things you won't want to hear.'

Ben looked across at the old man. They exchanged a look of sadness as Ben replied, 'Que sera, sera.'

'Good man! I used what influence I have to look back through files at HQ. This is all still on paper. Luckily it's not been digitised yet. But it takes time – had to blow off the dust. That's good news, means no-one's been looking at them recently. Anyway, wanted to see what they had on Dobson. Not much, I'm afraid. He was low level. His main contribution has always been for talent spotting here. Seems he was good at that. But then I came across the name of an associate that he had worked with over a number of years, one Stanley Murdock. Now he was a nasty piece of work. We were all glad when you popped him into the ground last summer. I'm afraid, even with my little bit of influence, I wasn't allowed to see his file. Must be full of contentious stuff that they don't want to get out. Now I come to the bit where I might cause you pain.

He paused, looking soulful, then continued, 'In amongst all the years of paperwork another name cropped up in relation to Dobson and Murdock. Brace yourself. It was Diane Burton nee Scott, your wife. I asked to see her file but they wouldn't confirm that there was one. I got the impression that, even if there were to be one, my clearance wasn't high enough to be allowed to see it.'

Ben could feel the ground shifting, and, as his world slid sideways, his brain latched onto one significant detail. It might mean nothing at all or it might mean that his life for the last sixteen years – or longer – had been a mirage, an illusion. 'They had her married name as well as her single name?'

'Yes.'

\* \* \*

As Ben left the building, he began to offer rational explanations. It meant nothing. Perhaps it was because she'd had a fling with Dobson. That would be it. They had kept her name on file because there was a connection with Dobson. And her married name because of a connection with him. He'd been in a different part of The Services, but he knew they shared intelligence when it suited them. His thoughts still churning in confusion, it took him a while to realise that his phone was ringing.

It was Katy. She got straight to the point. 'Dad, the convent's rung. That nun you were going to see – she's dead. She had a heart attack at The Friary a couple of hours ago. Bit of a bummer cos I really wanted to see inside a convent. Anyway, her doctor's signed the death cert and the main nun talked to Dr Clare, who suggested that we should collect her body and do the funeral. I'll pick you up on the way, shall I?' Without waiting for an answer, she added, 'Meet you behind The Tram Depot – ten minutes?'

He just had time to say, 'Yes,' before she added, 'See ya. Bye.'

In that ten minutes, Ben's mind had time to brood over his recent discoveries about his wife. Dobson had loved her, MI5 had a file on her, and that file had continued into the time of their marriage. And, while married to him, she'd died in a bomb explosion where he had been the target. Those were the facts of the case and he would have to come to terms with them. But those facts were not enough to give him the answers he needed. He would have to delve deeper and that would undoubtedly open old wounds.

# Chapter 23

Their body-van swung into Adam and Eve Street and Ben, despite his dark thoughts, was impressed by Katy's progress in learning to drive this beast of a vehicle. She was in a voluble mood so he had no time to ponder further about the knowledge he'd been exposed to that morning. As soon as he got in the van, Katy started talking. She wanted his opinion and told him it had taken her some time to pluck up the courage to talk to him. That put him on alert. But then she surprised him.

'See, I think I want to go to uni like you said I should. But then, that would leave you in the shit. And I can't do that. Uncle Mo said I had to talk to you.' She took one hand off the steering wheel and waved it as he opened his mouth to speak. 'Don't interrupt. I've been practising this for weeks. Mo's getting old and he's lovely with the oldies but, if we're being honest, not much use besides. Michael might stay, but he's going to be mega-rich so might just want to go travelling or something. Anyway, he'll marry Pam, so she might make him stay on, or she might go with him. I've got to decide soon and I don't know what to do.'

Ben spoke quickly before he had time to allow himself to worry. 'For someone who's so clever, you can be incredibly dense sometimes. Apply. Go. You deserve it. You're wasted here. I can employ people if I want to.'

'Aw, really? You sure?' And before he had time to reply, 'Thanks, Dad. You're ace. I was so scared to tell you cos I know you worry about us, but you don't have to.'

Ben had already moved on. 'What and where? You should aim high. With your A level results, you could go anywhere.'

'I think it will have to be maths – and I think here – or Warwick. They're the best. If it was Cambridge, I could live at home.'

'Oh, no you don't.' Ben forced a laugh. His brain was telling him he had to let her go. It was time. His heart would just have to follow in due course. 'To get the best out of uni, you've got to live in. Here or there, you'll be best in hall.'

'You sure, Dad? I don't want to abandon you. Tell you what, Vin could move in with you. Stop you rattling around in that big old house. Or Mary. She'd look after you. And if that doesn't work out, we could put you on some dating sites. You're not too old.'

That certainly made him feel old. But he supposed that forty-nine was ancient to an eighteen year old. She waved her hand again and Ben had a new worry. Was organising his life distracting her from driving? 'Concentrate on getting us to The Friary and we'll talk more this evening. OK? But I'm very pleased for you. It's a good decision.'

Katy prattled on for the rest of the journey and he was delighted to listen as it left him no time to think.

\* \* \*

Dr Clare met them at the entrance. She took them to a small room, explaining on the way, 'When we found her, we knew immediately that she was dead. We phoned the convent and they sent for her GP. He said he'd been seeing her for heart problems so he came along and signed the death certificate. It's all been very efficient. He wanted to use a local undertaker but I suggested to the convent that they call on you.'

'Thanks for that.'

'She was found slumped in a chair so, with her doctor's permission, we laid her out on a bed. I hope that's OK for you.'

Ben nodded. 'Much easier for us.'

He looked at the body laid out before them. This nun was of the old school. She wore a full habit with coif, wimple and veil. Her dress reached her ankles. He studied her face. Her expression was serene.

Ben's thoughts turned to Josephine. He asked Dr Clare, 'Does Josephine know?'

'Not yet.' She looked shamefaced. 'We've kept this very quiet. We don't want to alarm our more sensitive clients so no-one knows except me and the two orderlies who moved her body. They've been here for years and I trust them not to gossip.' She fiddled with the papers on her desk. 'I was rather hoping that you might break the news to her?'

'Now?'

'No. She's still recovering from her last episode. I think, leave it for a day. Tomorrow? We can keep this under wraps till then.'

Katy stepped forward to look at the body. She gave the nun's hand a gentle squeeze. 'Do we know how old she was?'

Dr Clare answered. 'The convent says eighty-nine. They'd been expecting this for some time but say that she had insisted on continuing her pastoral work. They want to lay her out at the convent.'

'Oh, good!' said Katy. Then she blushed. 'Sorry. I thought we'd be taking her straight to our place and going on from there. But I really want to see inside a convent.'

'Don't worry, Katy,' said Ben. 'We'll need to go to see the Reverend Mother to organise proceedings so you'll get your chance.'

\* \* \*

Katy pulled hard on the heavy chain and a bell clanged somewhere deep inside. The echoes died away to silence. She counted out loud to sixty and tried again. Same silence. She turned to her father, 'What do we do now? They're supposed to be expecting us.'

'Try again until we get an answer. It's an enclosed order so they must be in.'

Katy stamped her feet in her work shoes. 'Wish I had boots on.' She turned again towards the door. It creaked open and a tiny woman, dressed in grey, was smiling up at her. 'Welcome to you both – I'm Sister Mary Joseph and I've been given the pleasurable task of showing you through to see the Reverend Mother. Come in, come in out of the cold.'

The big door thudded shut behind them and Ben's eyes travelled upwards to the high ceiling. He shivered. To his mind, it was as cold inside as out. As they marched along the interminable corridor, their footsteps echoed and re-echoed from the polished floor, up the plain walls and across the arched ceiling. The nun's feet skittered; theirs seemed to be plodding in comparison. The sounds stopped as the nun halted beneath a huge crucifix. She bowed in front of it.

The sister beamed at them again and knocked once on a plain oak door. Without waiting for a response, she opened the door and motioned them inside. Ben wondered how they knew to open the door without invading the privacy of the occupant but then realised that privacy might not be an option here.

They entered an enormous room that was almost empty and scrupulously clean. A single plain desk stood in the centre. Ben thought of his office at home, cluttered and lived-in. The Reverend Mother rose and glided towards them. Ben was, at once, transported back to his primary school where he'd always thought that nuns ran on wheels. This one was certainly following the pattern.

'Thank you for coming so quickly. We do appreciate that your time is precious. We have so much more of it at our disposal here. Now, so as not to waste your time, I'll tell you briefly about dear Sister Theresa's death.'

Without taking a breath, she continued in a sonorous voice, 'This morning we all rose at five as usual. Sister Theresa was with us in the chapel until six. She was in fine voice. Such a loss. Such a loss.'

The Reverend Mother breathed a long, drawn-out sigh. Her face took on a look of deep regret. To Ben, this woman's reactions seemed to be contrived, as if acting a part. Her delivery sounded to him like a well-rehearsed speech. He wondered if she was as solicitous as she seemed. There was something about her that repelled him and he couldn't say what. Immediately, he remonstrated with himself for having such thoughts.

The Reverend Mother continued her soliloquy. 'After chapel we had breakfast then we all went to start on our tasks for the day. We work alone and in silence and Sister Theresa went off in the taxi as usual. Pardon me. It is nearly six o'clock and the Angelus bell will ring for prayer. Don't be alarmed – it's very loud.'

Ben's heart gave a leap. Even with the warning, the bell jangled his eardrums. It went on for at least a minute. The words of that poem leapt into his brain. *The curfew tolls the knell of parting day.* He shivered.

The Reverend Mother raised her head and continued as though there had been no interruption. 'Sister Mary Joseph was on duty so she took the telephone call.' She continued in her smooth voice. It neither rose nor fell. 'Such a shock. We thought we'd lay her out in her cell. Appropriate, we think. I'll get Sister Mary Joseph to show you.'

'Thank you. We'll prepare Sister Theresa's body. It will take about two days then we'll bring her here in a casket. In the meantime, I'll send you the details of costings. Does that suit?'

'I'm sure you realise we have very little money. I hope your fees will bear that in mind.'

Ben replied in the affirmative.

The Reverend Mother nodded in a peremptory manner, then picked up a bell from her desk and shook it vigorously. That too reminded Ben of school days. At the sound of the bell, the same small nun appeared at the door. She motioned for them to follow her and again, their feet echoed in the silence of the corridor. Ben decided that this building was beautiful in its way, but he would still be delighted to leave it when their task was done. They descended a stone staircase to a semi-basement where the gloomy remnants of the rays from a street light fought their way through windows set high in the walls.

They arrived at the cell door and studied the small room. If the Reverend Mother's room had been bare, this room was stark. It contained a bed, a bedside shelf and a bookshelf – with, Ben noted, nowhere to keep personal belongings. A newspaper, untidily folded, sat on the bedside shelf. Ben was intrigued. This was the first speck he'd seen out of place since they'd entered the convent. He pointed to it with a questioning look to Sister Mary Joseph, 'Do you all have your own newspaper?'

'Well done, young man. I just knew you were clever, and I'm always right about people. That is so odd. We've cut ourselves off from the world. We have no newspapers in here, nor do we watch television or listen to the radio. Her only time out is...' She paused and took a deep breath, 'Was, to visit those poor people at The Friary. We all talked about it at Recreation and we've come to the conclusion that she must have picked it up there.' With that she thrust the newspaper at Ben as though it were contaminated. 'Here, you take it and then we won't be tempted to read it.' He took it and put it in the inside pocket of his coat so as not to provide further temptation.

121

'We do hope she brought it in from outside. We are an enclosed order but it's not impossible to get in here. Only last week, Reverend Mother had to eject some teenagers who had climbed the wall for a dare. She put the fear of God into them, I can tell you. If Sister Theresa didn't pick it up at The Friary, it means we've had another intruder. Poor Sister Theresa's death has put us all in a quandary. We will all pray for her immortal soul.'

'Why a quandary?' asked Ben.

Suddenly, the nun's face closed in. 'Don't mind my blither. The Reverend Mother says I have an imagination and I'm not got to let it run away with me.'

'Can you tell me why Sister Theresa is to be laid out here? Surely your chapel would be more fitting.'

The nun looked both ways before responding. She motioned them to move closer then whispered, 'I shouldn't be telling you this but Reverend Mother says Sister Theresa's soul was in peril when she died so she's going to have to be shriven before she can go in the chapel. None of us knows why, but I do know she went to see Reverend Mother before she went out and they had a fearful row. That's probably why she had the heart attack. Too much excitement for her poor old heart. God rest her soul.'

\* \* \*

Once outside, they both took a long in-breath. 'Well, my lady, you wanted to see inside a convent. What d'you think?'

'Gross, yuk. Getting up at five! And not talking! And that Rev gave me the heebies. Her voice was so creepy; la, la, la, all on one note. Sent shivers up and down my spine. She was one strange woman.'

Ben felt better for knowing that he wasn't alone in finding the Reverend Mother off-putting. He replied, 'Well, obviously she's hiding something. She didn't tell us about the argument. Maybe she was just embarrassed that she'd had a row with a person who had died soon after. I get the impression they don't disagree much in there so it must have been serious.'

'D'you think it could be to do with the paedophile thing Sister Theresa told Josephine about?' Katy hit her forehead with the palm of her hand. 'But doh! She didn't tell Josephine who it was! And then she went and died. Sooo inconsiderate.'

'I'll have to go to The Friary to break the news to Josephine. Better go now before she hears from anyone else. Will you come with me? I think a bit of female solidarity would help.'

'Yep, can do. As long as it's not female solidarity of the convent kind.'

*  *  *

The meeting with Josephine had been difficult, and Katy had been a godsend. She had been able to hold Josephine as she'd wept silent tears. Josephine had looked so vulnerable that he and Katy had wept too. Dr Clare had given Josephine a mild sedative and sent them away suggesting they return the next day.

# Chapter 24

They arrived at The Friary the next morning to be greeted by two police cars and the door barred to them. A young constable ambled towards them. 'Sorry, Sir, Miss. Unless you have an urgent appointment, I'm afraid you can't go in. There's been an incident.'

Dr Clare came hurrying out, her hair flying. 'Constable, thank you. I've been trying to contact Mr Burton. He may be able to help with the situation.'

Katy grabbed his arm and looked up at him. 'God, I hope...'

'Let's wait and see. Alison will tell us.' And he realised, to his shame, that Josephine's death would release him from any feeling of obligation to her. He immediately pushed that thought firmly to the back of his mind.

They hurried in behind Dr Clare, who took them directly to her study. 'Josephine's disappeared. We've searched and we can't find her so now the police are searching the building. ' She gave a resigned shrug. 'Considering her background, we had to call the police.'

Ben asked, 'Do you think she could have left the building?'

'I'd have said not. We take very seriously the security of patients referred to us by the courts. She fitted into that category, so she was kept under surveillance.'

'When was she last seen?'

'The police are going through the CCTV at the moment but last human contact was when I left her last night. She had rallied and seemed to be coming to terms with her friend's death. I ordered another mild sedative to help her sleep.' Dr Clare wrung her hands. 'I should have realised. She was calm – too calm. I think she must have been formulating a plan. What plan, I don't know. But I know my phone's missing and I think she may have taken it.'

'Have you told the police about your phone?'

'Not yet. I've been too busy trying to minimise the impact on our other clients. News travels fast in an enclosed community.'

Ben was reminded of the convent. Gossip at Recreation would magnify any unusual incident. The same would undoubtedly happen here. 'Yes, a priority, I'm sure.' Ben was also formulating a plan. 'Can I ask a favour of you? Tell the police about your phone, but leave it for...' He looked at his watch. 'Leave it for an hour. Make that an hour and a half. Can you do that?'

'If you think it would help Josephine.'

'Believe me. I do.'

\* \* \*

'God, Dad, that was a quick exit. Where are we going?'

'Cherry Hinton, to her mother's house. If she hasn't come to us, she must have gone there. Agnes is her only relative. You drive while I phone Chris. He needs to know.' Ben took out his phone then put it away again. 'Second thoughts, I'll do that later.'

'What's he got to do with Josephine?'

'Long story and one you really don't need to know. Secret stuff and the fewer people who know the better.'

'Spoil sport!' But she said no more and within the hour they were parked outside Agnes Barrett's house in a small side-street in Cherry Hinton. Ben noticed that it was looking a lot smarter than the last time he'd been. The garden was being cared for and the windows were sparkling. The front door was newly painted. He rapped on the knocker then called through the letterbox. 'Agnes. It's me, Ben.'

The reply came as she opened the door. 'Well, of course it's you. You'd be the one to know where she's gone. I've been expecting you. Took your time. Anyways, come in out the cold.'

They followed Agnes into her small, neat sitting room. 'D'youse two want a cup of tea? There's a fresh pot.'

'Sorry, Agnes. This is urgent. Josephine's here, I take it?'

'Yes, of course. Where else is she to go? She wouldn't go to you. She thinks she owes you too much already and she hasn't got anyone else.' She went to the bottom of the stairs and called out, 'Jojo, it's Ben and that nice girl of his. You can come down. It's safe.'

Josephine emerged and smiled wanly. Ben immediately asked her, 'Dr Clare's phone. Have you used it here?'

'No. I just used it to call a taxi to get me here.'

'Where is it now?'

125

'I left it in the taxi. I didn't have any more use for it.'

'Good. That should keep them guessing for a while. Now,' he looked at his watch. 'I'm assuming you have a good reason for running. So we need to get you somewhere safe. We have precisely forty minutes to get out of here. Pack a bag each of you.'

As they stood looking puzzled, he added, 'I'm assuming you don't want them to take you back?'

'No. No! I'm really scared and I won't be safe there.' Then she added in a plaintive voice, 'For the first time in my life, I was feeling secure. I was conquering my demons. Now I think there's a demon out there who's taken my friend and will come to get me.'

'Then get packing! Do you want Katy to help you?'

\* \* \*

Once they were in the car and the house had been locked, barred and bolted, Ben asked, 'Can you tell me now why you ran?'

'Sister Theresa had found out about a paedophile. Then she died suddenly. It's obvious, isn't it? He killed her. He must have done it at The Friary, so I'm in danger there.'

Ben was beginning to feel foolish. How had he got into the position of abetting a runaway mental patient? He knew that her leaps of logic were improbable to say the least. He articulated his thoughts. 'Josephine, she died of a heart attack. Her doctor has confirmed it. She'd been seeing him for heart problems and her death was not unexpected. I'm sorry that you've lost your friend but it's just an unfortunate coincidence that she died now.'

'You're wrong. He killed her. I'm sure of it.' Ben glanced in the mirror and could see that Josephine was getting agitated.

Before he could speak, Katy butted in. 'How about this for a plan? We'll be preparing Sister Theresa's body for burial. How about Dad and I make sure there's been no foul play?'

Ben was sure that they couldn't, on their own, rule out murder. They didn't have the facilities, but he hoped that Josephine wouldn't know that.

But she did. 'You'd need a post-mortem for that.'

'I'll talk to Jim Spire. He's a pathologist. See what we can do. Now we need to get you somewhere safe. Josephine, who knows about your house in Hunstanton?'

'Only you and your family. It was my bolt-hole. I was never going to tell anyone and I only told you because...' She tailed off.

Ben continued the sentence for her. 'You only told me because you were planning to kill me. I know. But that's the point. No-one knows except us.' He kept quiet about Chris's involvement and it seemed that Josephine had been in such a state last time she'd been there that it hadn't registered that Chris also knew.

He added, 'You'll be safe there for a while. But I'm sure the police will check with Land Registry to see if you've got any other properties.'

Josephine gave a bark of a laugh. 'They'll have trouble. See, I wanted it to be secure. Somewhere safe from prying eyes, so I set up a company in the Virgin Islands in my former name and bought it with that. I have clients who do that all the time. Being a solicitor has its perks.'

Agnes had been sitting quietly in the back of the car next to Josephine. She took her daughter's hand. 'Clever girl! And I'm sure they'll find out if your friend was murdered. I think we should go and stay in Hunstanton until they've sorted it all out. Would you believe, I've never been there! What do you think of that? It would be a winter break by the sea. Then you can go back to finish your treatment. They say you're making good progress. We don't want to set you back.'

Katy added, 'And as soon as we've sorted this out, we'll have to put a stop to your holiday. What a bummer!'

'But the house will be in such a state. No-one's been there since the summer. And I don't know where the keys are!'

Ben replied, 'I've got the keys and I've been keeping an eye on it since you left. The keys are at the office so we can pick them up now and take you there straight away.' He had a sudden thought, remembering that Josephine had tried to throw herself off the cliffs there. How could they keep Josephine safe from herself for the few days it would take to refute her delusions? Inspiration struck. 'Would you like Mo to come and stay with you for a few days? I'm sure he'd love a holiday by the sea.' He wasn't at all sure that Mo would love it, but he was sure that he could be persuaded.

# Chapter 25

'Come on then, Katy. Let's get started on prepping Sister Theresa and putting Josephine's fears right back where they belong. As soon as we've got this sorted, we can get Josephine back into Alison Clare's capable hands.'

Katy put her mug in the sink and followed her father into their prep room. 'Sad, isn't it? It'll put her back, and she was doing so well. Every time me and Mo went to see her, she seemed a bit better. She was chatting about coming out for a visit to her mum's house. Thinking about life after The Friary. D'you think this murder thing is a new phobia, or part of her old trouble?'

'No idea. Dr Clare's the one to ask, and she probably wouldn't tell you.'

Katy sighed. 'It's too quiet without Mo. He's only been gone for less than a day and already I miss him. Bet he's keeping Josephine and Agnes amused. If you can spare me, I'd like to go and see them this afternoon. Do some shopping for them. That sort of thing.'

'Sure. Michael and I can cope.' As he spoke, they gently slid the body of Sister Theresa on to the prep table. He removed the cloth that covered her and checked the labels – even though he was sure he had the right cadaver. 'D'you want to do this and I'll take notes? We might need them to reassure Josephine that we've done everything necessary.'

'Yep. Thanks Dad. And you've asked Jim Spire to pop over when we've finished? Did you tell him what it was about?'

'No, I just said we had a body and we'd like him to take a quick look. Thought it best to cover all bases. If he adds his expertise, Josephine will have to be convinced.' He pointed to the body. 'Then I'll go back to the convent to pick up her fresh set of clothes. They've provided a clean set for her to be buried in but they want the old ones back.' Ben smiled. 'Unless you want to go back to the convent?'

Katy laughed. The sound bounced round the sterile walls. 'No way. Seen it, done it, and no, I don't want the t-shirt.' They carefully removed all the nun's clothes, folded them neatly and packed them up ready to return to the convent. Katy started to examine the body, washing it as she went. She carefully moved the dead nun's arms so she could wash the torso, then she washed both legs. Together they turned the body onto its side so her back could be washed. Katy talked as she worked. 'You told me about lividity way back when I started work. Shows well here. Does that mean she was definitely sitting down when she died?'

'Could do, but it does mean that she was sitting for a while after death. But you can ask Jim when he comes. Now, about your university application. I looked it up and you're too late to apply here. You could go for Warwick and see how it goes.'

Katy looked sheepish. 'I sort of filled it in and sent it off before I told you. Oh my God!' Katy stepped back, away from the body. She waved her arms wildly. 'Dad, you need to see this.' She pointed to a small puncture wound near the spine just below the shoulder-blade. Ben leaned in. It looked like a mosquito bite. 'Calm down, Katy. It's probably nothing. A bite or a sting.'

Katy looked at her father. 'Yeah, sorry Dad. Josephine's made me a bit paranoid. Must be catching. We'll show it to Dr Spire.' She thought for a moment. 'We could look at her habit and see if there's anything odd in the same place.'

Ben was sceptical but decided to humour his daughter. He was used to Katy's flights of fancy and they amused him. He brought over the parcel of the nun's clothes and carefully unwrapped them. He laid them out on a side bench. Together they examined each item. The white cotton vest showed a small speck of blood coinciding with the wound. Katy picked up the grey tunic and Ben the wimple. As Ben examined the stiff white wimple, he carefully placed it back on the table and told Katy to put her piece of clothing back down too. 'We need Jim straight away. Don't touch anything. Leave it just as it is.'

Twenty minutes later, Jim arrived. 'You said it was urgent so I've left a pm. Hope you're not having me on.'

Ben gave him a pair of latex gloves and took him to the prep room. They were closely followed by Katy. As they walked, Ben began to explain. 'The background; a nun dies at The Friary. She's eighty-nine. She's visiting a patient there. Her GP signs the death cert as a heart attack but the patient she's visiting is convinced she's been murdered. We're burying her so I said we'd look her over and ask you to do the same. We thought the patient was being paranoid.' He carefully turned the nun's body and pointed to the puncture wound. 'At first, I thought it was a mosquito bite but then I found this.'

Ben held up the white wimple. He pointed to a tiny circular hole in the stiff fabric. 'No mosquito could have done this.'

'Hmm.' As Jim examined the body, he hummed to himself. If it was meant to be a tune, it was so distorted as to be unrecognisable. Then he examined the wimple, the vest and the rest of the nun's clothes. He looked up at Ben. 'You informed the police? If not, I'd do so now.'

Katy had been hopping back and forth, foot to foot, while Jim had been carrying out his examination. She could obviously contain herself no longer. 'So it's murder? Oh, the poor poor woman. Did she suffer? I sooo hope not.'

Jim smiled. 'Oh, the impetuosity of youth, and the passion. Wonderful. How old you make me feel! The answer is – I'm not sure – so don't go leaping to any conclusions. Hear that?' Katy nodded and he continued. 'But there's enough here to make me suspicious. Looks like it could have been made by a hypodermic and that's not a place where you'd usually inject. And certainly not through clothes.'

\* \* \*

Vin had ordered a post mortem and taken all the nun's clothes so they had to twiddle their thumbs until some results came through. Ben needed to talk to Dr Clare but didn't know how much he should tell her. He had to reassure her that Josephine was safe. Just that. No details. Then there was Chris. A progress report, or lack of it, was overdue. Vin had told him that her team – together with specially trained 'appropriate adults' – were systematically interviewing all the in-patients at The Friary. The staff were being interviewed off-site.

What a mess. He'd been leant on by two bent cops, beaten up by two thugs still at large, hidden a mental patient and found that a nun had almost certainly been murdered. And all this on top of Dobson's murder that he was trying to solve. And yet, his mind kept turning back to Dobson's letter and the MI5 file on his wife. He knew he had to come to terms with an affair between his wife and Dobson. It had been over before they'd married. Or had it? Of course it had. She wouldn't have lied to him or even have lived a lie. Get over it, he told himself. Get on with what you have to do. But first, Vin had summoned him to meet her at Parkside, immediately. This was at the police station so that made it serious.

* * *

As soon as he arrived, he was ushered into her office. To his surprise, Chris was there, lounging in the only comfortable chair. 'Hello, stranger, you've certainly been busy,' was Chris's greeting.

'Enough,' said Vin, immediately taking charge. Chris grinned but made no attempt to interrupt. Vin continued, 'We have two murders which may, or may not, be connected.' She looked straight at Ben. 'Apart from you, the only thread that joins them is Stanley Murdock. Murdock's killer was present at the murder scene when this nun...' She looked at her notes, 'Sister Theresa, was killed. Josephine Finlay has now disappeared, so we have a killer on the run. She is, at this moment, our prime suspect. We've been to her mother's house, but neighbours say the mother left yesterday with three other people that they don't know. A neighbour described the car as...' Again she looked at her notes. 'A sort of grey colour and big. That tells us a lot! Apparently, the mother's a very private person, doesn't mix much so the neighbours couldn't give us a clue as to where she's gone.'

Ben decided not to intervene yet. He needed to know what the police knew, or thought they knew. Vin continued. 'We can't get anything about this Findlay woman from the staff at The Friary. They've all been warned about patient confidentiality. And they know they're all potential suspects so they're keeping tight-lipped anyway. I'm pretty sure the other patients don't know anything to help us. We have a suspect on the run; we believe she's killed twice. Ben, you know her and I need your help to find her.'

Ben thought it was time to put a few of his cards on the table. He held up his hands, palms forward in a conciliatory gesture. 'Hold on a minute. Yes, she killed Stanley Murdock and yes, she's gone missing. But I don't for one minute believe she murdered Sister Theresa.' Chris looked about to speak but Ben motioned for him to keep quiet. 'Before I was attacked, Josephine called me to see her. This was a first. She'd refused to see me before so I knew this must be important to her. She was in a state. Terrified. She told me that her nun had confided in her that she knew someone who was a paedophile.' Here he improvised. He couldn't let Vin know that he had spoken to Josephine when he had orchestrated her flight to her hiding place. 'She said that the nun was in fear of her life. I was going to go to see Sister Theresa but was attacked and laid up. I never got to see her. So when we received her body, I decided to check just to relieve my conscience about not visiting her. That's when I found the wound and called in Jim Spire.'

Ben took a deep breath. He'd always valued truth and was disconcerted by the ease with which he was lying to the police – and more importantly, to his lover – ex-lover for the time being – or possibly for ever. His next utterance was about to compound his deceit.

'Does either of you have any idea where she is?'

Ben immediately replied, 'No.' Chris did likewise.

Vin countered with, 'Pity. We could do with a short cut.' She turned to Ben. 'Well, be careful. We haven't managed to find your assailants yet.'

# Chapter 26

When they'd left the building, Chris suggested that they walk across Parker's Piece. In that open space, they would not be overheard. When they were in the middle of the green, Chris opened with, 'Where've you hidden her then? That place in Hunstanton? That's where I'd put her.'

Ben decided to counter one question with another. 'What makes you think I've hidden her?'

'Oh, come off it. It's got your stamp all over it. Knight in shining armour bowling up to help a damsel in distress. Plus knows more than he lets on. Plus feels guilty that he didn't believe her at first. I saw you when you had to lie. I'm trained to spot liars. Don't like doing it, do you? But, I'm impressed. You're getting good at it.'

Ben cringed. Chris, for all his wide-boy traits knew him too well. He countered with another question. 'OK then, how come you know I lied?'

'Easy. Been up to Hunstanton. Saw your Uncle Mo going shopping. And there were at least two other people in the house. That Josephine, she's one clever lady. I tried to find that house through the Land Registry. Owned by some company in the Virgin Islands. The plods won't find her there. And you, my friend, you got another car you can use until this gets sorted? One that's not big and grey?'

Ben laughed. 'Yeah, I'll put that one in the garage and use Mo's. I was going to tell you. I knew, if Josephine was right and it was murder, she'd be the prime suspect. I didn't believe her. Thought she was paranoid, more fool me. I just went along with it to calm her down so, yes, I'm feeling guilty. Sure, she had the opportunity but no, she hasn't means or motive. So, we're looking for a paedophile who can blag his way into a secure unit. Any ideas?' Chris shook his head.

They'd reached St Andrew's Street. Ben's thoughts turned to his real reason for wanting to talk to Chris. He desperately needed to find out why his wife had been mentioned with Service connections, both Dobson's and Murdock's. 'Grand Arcade for coffee? I've got some questions for you.'

*  *  *

They settled in the corner of the library café with a pair of black coffees. Ben found he didn't know how to open the subject of Diane. Chris didn't give him a chance to try. 'They've got the toxicology reports on that nun. Ram jam full of adrenaline. She was snuffed.'

Ben was immediately taken back to the scene with the Family Liaison Officer vomiting on recalling that they called snuff movies 'tie and dye'. He was in a murky world. He hoped he'd be able to exit it soon.

Chris was still talking. 'What have you got for me, then? Found out more about Dobson's life and death?'

'Life, yes. Death, not yet.' Before his courage failed, he blundered on. 'Tell me, what's the connection between Dobson, Murdock and my wife?'

Chris's jaw fell open. He quickly closed his mouth. Then he opened it again. It closed and opened one more time before he spoke. 'Didn't expect that one! Connection, yes, Dobson and Murdock. Your wife? None that I know of. Why? What've you found?'

Ben handed over the letter he'd been left by Dobson. Chris took some time reading it. Ben suspected he was stalling.

'Well?'

'News to me. I don't want to intrude, but it looks like an affair. Sorry.'

'And Murdock?'

Chris waved the letter before giving it back to Ben. 'Nothing in there about Murdock. Where'd you get that from?'

'Walpole.'

'Aw Jeez. Look, he's fucking ancient. Most days he goes around in his slippers. Doesn't even know what day it is. I don't know what sort of conspiracy theory he's dreamed up but, mate, it's all in his imagination. OK?'

Ben had been watching closely as Chris had been speaking. Sure, he looked confident, and there wasn't anything to show that he was lying, but Ben was sure that Chris was an accomplished liar. He had no proof that Chris had ever lied to him but now there was a niggling doubt. It centred on the word 'mate', and he didn't know why. But he knew where his next dialogue must be.

\* \* \*

Ben hurried to St Etheldreda's College. In his hurry, he very nearly bumped into Professor Walpole as Walpole shuffled round a corner of Front Court. He was balancing a precarious pile of papers on one arm and leaning on his stick with the other. Ben reached round and grabbed some of the papers as they lurched towards the ground. As he stooped, he looked down and had to smile. Walpole was wearing a pair of very old and very bald slippers.

'Ah, wonderful, dear boy. You can help me get this lot safely back to my room. Fearfully good new intel from a friend in Ukraine. Had to open it out front. Couldn't wait to have a look. It's hotting up out there. I keep putting in warnings about Putin, but they don't want to listen. Think I'm gaga.' He sighed. 'Anyway, you still trying to solve Dobson's murder? I think I may have something for you.'

They arrived at Walpole's door and he said, 'Open the door for me. There's a good fellow.'

'Isn't it locked?'

Walpole laughed. 'Better than a lock. Video surveillance. So I know who they are and what they've come for.'

'Caught anyone?'

Walpole looked wistful. 'Nary a one, there's the pity. They're not interested in Russia now. It's all Islamic terrorists. But just wait a few years. Wait till Putin overreaches just that bit too much, then they'll take notice.' He pointed to a small space on his volcano of a desk. 'Pop those down there, will you.'

Ben looked at the papers in his hand and looked at the space on the desk. Then he looked questioningly at Walpole.

'Shove the others over a bit. That's it. Now, let's see.' He sifted through some papers on the other side of his desk. 'Ah, yes.' He held up an envelope. 'Bit sensitive, this. We're clearing out Dobson's rooms. Taking time. There's so much to sort through.' Ben looked round the room they were in. A wry smile crossed his face as he tried to find a horizontal space that was empty. Apart from the chairs, there were none.

'Who's "we"?'

'We're doing it in pairs. Shows we don't trust each other, eh? O'Connor and Hendrick have drawn up a rota. Those two plus Dr Fursley, nice woman, fragile though, and then there's Pedersen and me.'

'And you've found?'

'Oh yes, the envelope. I was with Gillian.' Ben assumed this must be Dr Fursley. 'Anyway, she seems so much better recently. Said you'd been helpful. I didn't pry.' Walpole paused. Ben knew what he was waiting for but didn't enlighten him.

'The envelope?'

'Ah, yes. The envelope. Tricky this. Should give it to the police but I'm sure they'd come to the wrong conclusion about the College. And they're so leaky, it would come out in the Press. Can't allow that.' He paused.

'How come the police didn't find it?

Walpole tapped the side of his nose. 'They didn't find it because they don't understand people like Dobson. It was carefully rolled in the spine of a book.'

Dobson's third hiding place, thought Ben. And he wondered how many more there were.

'And what is in the envelope?'

'I'm the only one who's seen this. Managed to keep it from Gillian. Should have taken it to the Master but that poor girl has too much on her plate. And anyway, it wouldn't do to bring it to the surface. Not now. I couldn't decide what was for the best and then I came to the conclusion it should come to you. But before I give it to you, I need an undertaking.' Again he paused and Ben wondered if he was ever going to acquire that marvellous envelope with its dire consequences for the College.

'I need you to promise that this information will not be divulged to anyone, outside this college or in it.'

'You know I can't do that. It could be evidence in a murder enquiry.' Ben pushed to the back of his mind the fact that he had already withheld evidence from Dobson's house, the bogus degree certificate and all those photos of his dead wife. And the information about Dr Clare and her lover. His conscience pricked and he ignored it. He was doing a lot of that these days.

'If I tell you that it mentions your wife?'

Ben sat down heavily. 'You certainly know how to get under a man's defences. Show me. What have you got?'

Ben realised that his hands were shaking. He took the envelope. It was addressed to Stanley Murdock at an address in Belfast. It was not sealed and there was no stamp. He pulled out a single sheet. It was dated 1st October 1996 – sixteen years ago and just six days before his wife's death. He took a deep breath and started to read. It was in Dobson's untidy writing which made it difficult to read. Thankfully it was brief.

*Stanley*

*You are mistaken. Diane has no evidence and Ben doesn't suspect her or you. She told me yesterday. Relax – your secret is safe.*
*Graham*

Ben let both the letter and its envelope slide to the floor and sunk his head in his hands. 'What does that mean? She didn't know Murdock. I know she didn't. At least, I thought she didn't. Christ, I don't know what's going on. I'm beginning to think I didn't know my wife at all. And now I can't ask her because she's dead. They're all dead.' With that, he burst into shuddering sobs.

Professor Walpole rested a hand lightly on his shoulder. 'You see, I think she found out about the rape. Stanley – nasty little turd that he was – had raped a poor girl, a College servant.'

Ben was incredulous. He wiped his eyes then looked straight at Walpole. 'You know about the rape?'

'My dear boy, I've been about this college for nigh on sixty years. I was a spy. Of course I know about the rape. The hierarchy at the time hushed it up. The poor little girl was sent packing and the College has been paying her ever since to keep quiet.' He paused and pointed a bony finger at Ben. 'Wait a minute. You're not surprised. How do you know about it? This is a dark College secret. Even the Masters haven't been told. Are you clairvoyant?'

'No. Nothing that sinister. I know the woman who was the product of that rape. There was a daughter. She was the one who murdered Stanley.'

'Well, blow me down.' And, with that Walpole too slumped into a chair. 'I thought one of his nasty Irish connections had caught up with him. What happened to the girl, the daughter?'

'Until a few days ago, I'd have told you she was safe and getting treatment for her mental problems. Now she's on the run, in fear of her life.' He added, almost involuntarily, 'I'm hiding her.' As soon as it was out of his mouth, he wondered if he would regret that utterance.

'Good Lord Almighty. Anything I can do to help? I've always felt guilty that Murdock got away with it. Ask anything. I'll do what I can to help her.'

'Thank you. But I still don't understand how Diane knew. And why didn't she tell me?'

'Women. She was a woman. No sane man understands women. Probably trying to protect you. They do that sort of thing.'

Ben had to be content with that. But there was a little niggle in his mind about the wording. He looked again at the letter.

*Ben doesn't suspect her or you.* Why would he suspect her? The rape had nothing to do with Diane so, what had Diane done that he should suspect her? He had no answer to that.

# Chapter 27

Ben had no time to think further about his dead wife and her secrets. As soon as he left Walpole's rooms, his phone beeped. He saw it was a call from Dr Clare. He'd already informed her that Josephine was safe, so wondered what she could want. What she did want was for Ben to come and collect a letter. It was addressed to Josephine and was the only letter she had received in her time there. They'd had to collect it from the sorting office, as it was without any postage. Having paid the additional fee, they now wanted it to get to its rightful recipient. He phoned Katy to see if she could hold the fort. Then he called Mo to tell him he was on his way to Hunstanton with a letter for Josephine.

* * *

Traffic was bad so he had to concentrate. Since the van incident, he'd been vigilant and was soon sure he wasn't being followed. So that his phone wouldn't give away his location, he turned it off and removed the battery. Then he started to toss around in his mind what he had surmised from the snatches of information he'd gleaned about Diane. And still it didn't make sense. None of it made sense, least of all an affair with Dobson. How could she stoop so low?

    He remembered when they'd first met. There had been a party to celebrate passing first year exams. She'd been so confident, so intelligent, so incredible that he'd immediately been mesmerised. He'd always believed, and still did, that he'd been amazingly lucky and that she had felt the same. They'd had fourteen glorious years and then she'd been snatched from him. Now he was learning things about her that he really didn't want to know. His memories were being sullied and that left him feeling unclean.

    He realised he was gripping the steering wheel with an iron grasp. He was already passing Kings Lynn and had not remembered any of the journey so far. He pulled into a lay-by and took several deep breaths. He did his breathing exercises and felt his heart slow to normal. He sat and thought about his life. He had two beautiful daughters who still needed him sometimes. He had a business to run with responsibilities to his uncle and his staff. He had a murder to solve. Make that two murders. He needed to get a grip. He would try to bring forward his regular appointment with Dr Clare. She hadn't been on his to-do list but he realised that he still desperately needed her.

  He arrived at the bungalow on the cliff top. The sun was shining and the air was fresh. He looked across and saw that they had replaced the damaged railing that had allowed Josephine through to try to leap from the cliffs to take her own life. Now that he knew she was not paranoid; that the nun had indeed been murdered, he was more sanguine about leaving her here with her mother and Mo. He raised his hand to the knocker but before he could knock, Mo opened the door and whispered, 'Come in. They're in the garden – weeding. All wrapped up. Want to talk before going through?'

  'Could do. How's it been?'

  'Absolutely fine. They sit and chat most of the day. I do the shopping, they do the cooking. I won't let them go out without me.' Mo blushed. 'They're two lovely women. Must say, I'm getting very fond of them. We have a good laugh and they've been happy to have me tag along.'

  'Does Josephine want to see me? I can give the letter to you, if not.'

  'I asked her and she's sure she can cope. We've talked about you. Told her you're fine and she's not to worry. She's getting over thinking that she damaged you. I told her you had a woman friend. Hope that's OK?'

  'Anything. If it helps.'

  They went through to the back garden to see two very busy women pulling up enormous dead weeds. Agnes turned and beamed at Ben. 'Well, young man. How's it going with you? Want to help clear this wilderness? Or will I make you a nice strong cup of Irish tea? Your uncle, fine man that he is, found it for us.'

  'Tea would be great. Hello, Josephine.'

Agnes gathered them all and ushered them into the kitchen. 'It's grand to see you. And isn't Josephine looking well?'

Josephine grinned at her mother. 'Agnes, I can speak for myself, you know.'

In their brief time as a couple, Ben had never seen Josephine grin and had not, for a long time, seen her so confident. It delighted him and he sincerely hoped the improvements would continue. He had no idea what was in the letter he carried and was worried that it would cause a setback.

'Mo told me I had a letter. I can't think who it could be from. No-one knew I was in The Friary except you people.'

Ben handed her the letter and Josephine turned it over a few times. Agnes leaned across. 'That's criminal! What you have to pay if there's no stamp. They must all be gurriers at that bleddy Post Office.'

Ben had no idea what a gurrier was but he knew Agnes was not being complimentary. Meanwhile Josephine had opened the letter. She passed it to Ben. 'It's from Sister Theresa. You read it.'

Ben read aloud.

*Dear Josephine*
*I hope this gets to you because I don't know anyone else outside. We're not supposed to read the papers but I did and I saw his picture. I hadn't seen him for 20 years but I still recognised him. Oh yes. You don't forget those wicked men who defile children. Worse still, he's a doctor. And now he's been to the convent to treat Sister Mary-Joseph. I told Reverend Mother and she said I must be mistaken. I had a dreadful row with her this morning. She doesn't believe me and told me not to spread wicked lies. She said I must confess my sins or I'd face eternal damnation. But I'm not lying. She forbade me to come to see you any more. In case she stops me, and I don't manage to see you, I'm sending this to show you that I haven't abandoned you.*
*Your very good friend*
*Sr Theresa*

'And now she's murdered. May the Good Lord grant her eternal rest.' Agnes made the sign of the cross, closed her eyes and dipped her head. She silently mouthed some words, then raised her head again and said, brightly, 'Now! What are we to do?'

Ben turned to Josephine. 'Tell me what you can remember of your last conversation with Sister Theresa. How explicit was she about this doctor?'

Josephine's brow creased. She paused, looking into the distance. Agnes looked about to speak but Ben motioned her to stay silent. At last Josephine spoke. 'She said there was a man she'd known abroad somewhere, and she'd seen him again. She didn't know what to do. That's all I remember.'

'Was there anyone else around to overhear you?'

'We were in the day room so there would have been people all around. People come and go. I don't think there was anyone new. New people get noticed in there.'

'Did you give her any advice?'

'I said she should go to the police but she said that was impossible for her. So then I said she should talk it over with someone in authority. Someone who would know what to do.'

Ben felt anger stirring. He said through gritted teeth, 'So she went to see her Reverend Mother who didn't believe her.'

It seemed that Agnes had waited long enough. She stood up. 'We must catch this disgusting fella before he does any more harm. Ben, what's the plan?'

Even in these dire circumstances, Ben had to smile. The Agnes he'd first met would never have been this assertive. He answered her, 'I must take this to the police. And you must all stay here. Agnes, I'll get on to it straight away. I won't stay for that nice cup of Irish tea, thank you. Mo, will you see me out?'

On the way through to the front, he grasped Mo's arm. 'I'll take this info to Vin. If this doctor is the murderer, he could get it into his head to harm Josephine. I'll only tell Vin where she is if she can promise not to arrest her, so there may not be any police protection; we may have to do it ourselves. But first, we need to get the name of that doctor out of that bloody Reverend Mother.'

He decided not to phone Vin until he was back in the vicinity of Cambridge. Paranoid or not, calls could be traced. As soon as he was out of the house, he called Chris on the burner and updated him. As he was walking back to the car, his mind's eye saw the out-of-place newspaper in the nun's cell. He had chucked it

on to the chair in his bedroom. Thank God he hadn't thrown it out.
He phoned Gillian Fursley and asked if he could meet her.
Tomorrow, she'd said, in college. He had the beginnings of a plan.

## Chapter 28

*Pull yourself together. She was eighty-nine, for God's sake. You're in this right up to your neck so just keep your nerve. Or you could be next.*

# Chapter 29

His heart was pumping way too fast. He could feel the sweat trickling down his back. He opened his eyes wide and could see nothing. His first feeling was of relief. Relief that his nightmare was only in his head. Relief that it was his brain that was recreating the worst moment of his life and he only had to relive it in his dreams. Relief that his waking self could push this tragedy into the far recesses of his mind and close the door on it. But the sights, sounds and, worst of all, the smell of the explosion were still reverberating in his head. Devastation lay in a vast circle and the body of his wife lay ripped and bleeding at his feet. That last piece of shrapnel had winged its way towards him prior to burying itself in the frontal lobe of his brain. The relief did not last. Next came despair, realising yet again that everything he valued was lost.

He reached for the tissues beside his bed and began to mop his brow and then to wipe the tears that had started to flow. Since beginning his course of treatment with Dr Clare, he'd been dream-free. Why had it returned now? He had only to think for a moment to realise that the hint of revelations about Diane had begun to undermine his belief in their life together. In this highly charged state, he was vulnerable. In his rational moments, he could dismiss his doubts. He knew he would have to face them soon. But not yet. Not yet.

\* \* \*

His session with Dr Clare had been short but reassuring. He'd told her about his doubts about his marriage and the return of 'the dream'. She was insistent that this setback could be overcome. Such was his trust in her that he now believed that, with her help, he could get through it – whatever further difficulties might sidle out to subvert him. That was another reason to protect her from police interest – selfish, he knew – but why not? She, in turn, had told him that Vin and her officers had been thorough in their search of The Friary and had uncovered no problems with the drug regime and no missing drugs. So they were in the clear with regard to whatever had been used to inject Sister Theresa. She'd also told him that Vin was still convinced that Josephine, whether or not she was responsible for the nun's death, was dangerous and had to be caught. Ben wondered when Vin would tell him this herself. Or whether, indeed, she would ever share the knowledge with him that her prime suspect had neither motive nor means so had suddenly become totally unprime.

* * *

He raced to Ethel's and arrived at Dr Fursley's door at the appointed time for their meeting only to find a note that she was helping Dr Hendrick with clearing Dobson's rooms and would meet him there. It suddenly came to him that, as sole beneficiary of Dobson's will, someone should have asked his permission to clear Dobson's papers. On his way through Front Court, he put through a phone-call to Dobson's solicitor. It seemed that Clayforth knew nothing of this clearance and would hot-foot over to Ethel's to see what should be done. And what did Ben want him to do? Ben wanted him to keep quiet about who his client was and to make sure that he stopped any disposal until Ben's say-so.

Ben was greeted warmly by Dr Fursley and less so by Dr Hendrick. When he asked them what they were proposing to do with Dobson's things, Fursley replied that all his academic papers were being collated and the rest would be shredded and taken to the recycling centre. They didn't know what would happen to any personal belongings, but as Ben knew, there were not many belongings here or at the house in Trumpington. Apart from his academic work, it seemed that Dobson had left little imprint on the world he'd inhabited.

'Have any been shredded so far?'

Dr Fursley pointed to two black bin bags in the corner of the room. 'Not so far. We were going to do it all in one go, then take it to the dump.' She pointed to the heap still in the middle of the room. 'We've got some way to go, as you can see.'

Hendrick added, 'We have to clear the room for the new prof. We can't wait till a will is found, if one exists. Which I doubt.'

'Ah. I'm afraid that's where you're wrong. A solicitor has come forward with a recent will. I've phoned him and he's on his way over. He should have contacted the College. But, in my experience, solicitors can be notoriously slow. This one seems to be no exception. No doubt he'll start to earn his fee soon.'

Hendrick's eyes narrowed. 'Any idea who benefits? Should be a sizeable sum. He was always careful with money.'

Ben wasn't sure whether to tell them that he was the sole beneficiary. While he was deciding what to say, Hendrick continued, 'We're hoping he's left it to the College. A lot of Fellows do.'

Ben decided to keep his counsel. He had the uncomfortable feeling that the news would not be well received in this place. He realised that the main reason he was keeping quiet was because he had no desire to be coupled with Dobson in any way. 'I think the solicitor will advise that nothing should be disposed of until probate has been granted – or, at least until beneficiaries have been notified. Anyway, I didn't come to discuss Dobson's will but to ask Dr Fursley a favour. Can we talk when you've finished here?'

Before she could answer, Dobson's solicitor came steaming in followed by Mr Fisher. Fisher spoke first, 'Sorry gents, lady. Mr Clayforth here says we have to stop clearing till his client has decided what's to be done with all this lot.' Fisher looked despairingly at the mess still evident. 'We'll have to pack it up and store it. I'll get some bedders on to it straight away.' He turned to Clayforth. 'We need the rooms. So, if we store it all till the will is sorted, will that do?'

Clayforth turned towards Ben, who shrugged, hoping this would distance him from the decision. Clayforth nodded. 'That will suffice.'

'Well, Mr Burton,' said Dr Fursley. 'It seems that I'm no longer needed here so I am at your disposal.'

They walked back to Dr Fursley's rooms. As she made coffee, Ben watched. Her hands no longer shook and her voice, which had always before seemed strained, was calm. Ben spoke with urgency. 'Look, I need your help. I know you're a Catholic. A nun has been murdered and I think you might be able to help.'

At this she looked up sharply. 'What an odd thing to say. I have you to thank for putting me in touch with Dr Clare, so I am already in your debt. I'll do what I can. What do you want me to do?'

'You might be able to identify a man whose picture is in the local paper.'

'And this person – what has he done to deserve your attention?'

'The nun thought he was a paedophile.'

'And what makes you think I will know him. There are millions of Catholics in the world. It's not an exclusive club, you know; we don't all know each other. And we're not all nuns or paedophiles!'

'This is where it gets a bit tricky. And I believe I might cause you some pain.'

She looked him squarely in the eyes. 'Go on.'

He waited until she had sat down and had put her coffee cup on the table. 'I have a theory and I need your help to see if I'm right. When I came to see you the first time, you lied to me. You said you didn't know a Dr Taylor. I believe you do. I want to see if you can pick him out from the newspaper.'

She looked at him with head on one side and he realised that she was weighing him up; deciding what to tell him. She had obviously come to a decision, for she squared her shoulders and sat up straight. 'Before I met my husband, I was not a Catholic; I had no religion. When I was eighteen I met someone at university who I thought was "the one". It was ridiculous; I was so stupid. I became pregnant and he left me high and dry.' She paused then said at a rush, 'I had an abortion. Then John, my husband, came along and I fell completely in love with him. He was Catholic and I converted. I didn't tell him about my past. I've thought about it every day since with such regret. I even thought that our inability to conceive was the fault of the abortion.' She paused with one of the saddest looks that Ben had ever seen, then continued. 'Dr Clare has helped me to shed that guilt and I've told John about the abortion. He's been amazing. He says it's not him who has to forgive me. I have to forgive myself. I've been to confession and I feel as though a ton weight has been lifted from my shoulders. I'm telling you all this because the doctor who performed that abortion was a Dr Taylor.'

Ben could only imagine the grief and years of regret that Dr Fursley had suffered. He said the only thing he could possibly say. 'I'm so sorry.'

But Dr Fursley was businesslike. 'Now, show me the picture and I'll see if it's him.'

Ben suddenly felt foolish in the extreme, so foolish that he actually felt himself blushing. Of course! Some pieces fell Tetris-like into place. They'd all been so focussed on Dr Taylor being a doctor of philosophy at a university that they had completely neglected the more common title, that of a medical doctor. It was becoming clear to Ben that they had been looking in the wrong place entirely. Could Murdock's and Dobson's Dr A N Taylor be a medical doctor, the same doctor who had performed Dr Fursley's abortion? He handed her the paper. 'I don't know which picture it is but there's a group photo at Addenbrookes that might be the one. Can you look through the whole paper though, just to be thorough.'

He sat quietly while she worked through the paper scrutinising every photograph minutely. She included all sections, even the sports pages. Then she started at the front and went through them all again. She handed Ben back the newspaper. 'I'm certain that the Dr Taylor I know isn't here.'

Ben sighed. He wasn't really surprised but he was disappointed. It would have been a shortcut to finding Dr A N Taylor, the person he was now beginning to believe was implicated in both Dobson's murder and that of the nun, Sister Theresa.

# Chapter 30

They'd all gathered for supper at Ben's request, Ben, Katy and Sarah plus Michael and Pam. The only people missing who'd been at their last gathering were Mo, in Hunstanton, and the Police Liaison Officer. Police resources were such that the threat to Ben was now considered minor, even though his attackers had not yet been caught. Instead of police protection, he'd been advised to lock his doors and keep away from minor roads.

He'd called the family together to update them on progress and pick their brains further. There had been a collective intake of breath when he'd suggested that they'd all been victims of tunnel vision and that Dr Taylor could be a medical doctor. Katy had even banged her head on the table causing them all to flinch. He told them about Dr Fursley and that he was as sure as he could be that she was not implicated. He suggested that Prof Walpole was too rickety to have even been the watcher and that O'Connor had probably not been involved because he was so wussy that he wouldn't be able to cope with the aftermath, and he seemed to be coping well. That left their front runners as Pedersen, Hendrick and Taylor.

At this point Katy took over. 'Have we ruled out Dr Clare and her man? I think we should. She's almost like family.'

It seemed that Sarah wasn't going to let that one go without a response. 'And where do most murders occur? Inside the family, that's where. And she had motive for the first and means and opportunity for the second so, even though we love her for what she's done for Dad, we can't discount her completely.'

Pam clapped her hands in applause. 'Spoken like a true copper. You'll go far, my friend.'

Ben saw that Katy was about to retaliate, so intervened swiftly. 'We'll keep them on a back burner. Now, we do have...' But he got no further.

Sarah intervened again. 'We can't start. Uncle Mo isn't here yet. We've got to wait for him.'

Ben looked across at Katy. They were the only ones who knew where Mo was and they had decided that the fewer people who knew, the better. With Sarah's previous comments in mind, Ben decided this was not the best time to divulge that Mo was harbouring a fugitive from justice and that he, Mo and Katy were co-conspirators. Katy gave him a conspiratorial wink. Then she launched into the explanation that they'd already given to Michael, but with a few embellishments of her own. 'Uncle Mo was feeling a bit under the weather. You know, it's the anniversary of Auntie Gwennie's death so he was a bit sad. So Dad said he had to take a few days holiday and he's gone to the seaside with a couple of his mates. He's taken his bucket and spade...' At this point she wagged her finger like a teacher in telling-off mode. 'And we've warned him that there are bound to be predatory old women there, so he's not to have a holiday fling.' She giggled. 'Or worse still, bring an old harridan home with him.' She paused for a moment. 'Hey, what about that? S'pose he finds a nice old girl to spend his days with. Dad could be his best man.'

Sarah was suddenly solicitous. 'Shut up Kate. This sounds serious. Is he OK? It's not his heart or anything?'

Ben replied, 'No, he's as fit as a fiddle. Just needed a break.' He smiled at Katy, but inside he felt a little twist of worry in his gut. Katy had remembered the anniversary of Gwen's death and had used it to create a plausible cover story. Just the sort of thing he used to do in his old job. He sincerely hoped that Chris and his lot wouldn't realise just how clever his younger daughter was. If she went that way, he wouldn't be able to guarantee her safety. But, of course, he couldn't do that anyway. He shook himself back into the present as Katy finished her story, 'Michael and I have covered for him at work but I sooo miss his dreadful jokes.'

Ben became business-like. 'He'll be back soon. Let's move on. Front-runners, first one, *Dr J. Hendrick, May 1991, Charles Rennie opened his doors for a second time – saved by the Three.* We got the first half. Charles Rennie Mackintosh, Scottish architect. Opened his mackintosh, a flasher. Mo said that back then, he would have been given a serious talk the first time, but a second offence would ring alarm bells and it should be on record. I've asked Vin and none of these people has a criminal record, so he got away a second time. 'Saved by the Three'. Can we work out who the three were?'

'Well, in 1991, I wasn't born and Sarah only just, and Pam probably too. Michael was only six. So if it's something about then, we won't know. It's up to you Dad. You're the only oldie here.'

'Thanks Katy – kind of you to say so. OK. What comes in threes? Let's just brainstorm. I'll record it.'

They were all silent for a moment then the answers came in quick succession.

A musical trio, The Good the Bad and the Ugly, paper, stone, scissors, three men and a baby – oh no, that makes four, Liberty, Equality, Fraternity, the three Witches in Macbeth, (had to do that in school – wouldn't it be good if Shakespeare actually wrote in English – Katy! – sorry Dad) King Lear's Daughters (God that was such a drag – anyone else have to do that? Yeah – hated it. Sarah! Pam! – sorry Dad, sorry Ben), the three wise men, the three blind mice, the Three Deathly Hallows in Harry Potter (I'm just reading that – it's really good. Can I borrow it after you? Stop – it's a brainstorm – sorry Dad), The Three Faces of Eve, Three Mile Island, The Three Musketeers, Poverty, Chastity, Obedience (like those nuns have to do – bet that Reverend Mother doesn't keep to any of them – KATY – sorry Dad).

Ben held up his hands. 'Stop. This could go on for ever. We'll have to try to get into the mind of Stanley Murdock even though it's not the nicest place to be. We know he was devious, amoral and bullied his wife and children.' Ben nodded towards Michael, 'He stitched up his nephew, he blackmailed people, is that enough?'

Ben knew much more about Murdock's life. He knew that Stanley Murdock had been an agent of Her Majesty in Northern Ireland and had worked under cover, he knew that he had consorted with terrorists and he knew that Murdock had 'gone rogue' and had had to be recalled. Ben had been extremely careful not to reveal any of this in the attributes he had exposed to public view.

Pam spoke. 'Not a mind I'd like to inhabit. Glad I never met the bastard.' And Ben could see her give Michael's hand a squeeze.

Michael was thoughtful. 'I believe my wicked uncle would go for something lasting. And, as you know, he spent a long time in Ireland where religion is, let's say, a religion. Not like here. Over there, religion is in everything. Katy said about the nuns and that made me think. My uncle would go for something big. He'd go for the biggest three in religion, the Trinity – father, son and holy ghost. It'd just suit him to call on God – as an equal, of course.'

Sarah asked, 'If it was that three, would he say holy ghost or holy spirit? It might make a difference.'

'Definitely ghost.'

Ben added, 'Saved by God. Hendrick wouldn't be the first. I'll have to find out if he got religion in his youth. I think we should leave him with his God and move on.'

He picked up his list again. 'We have the doctor who may be a medical doctor. Dr Taylor. Anyone got an idea how to find him?' He held up his hands. 'And before Katy can attack me, the extract says "he" so I think we can safely assume Dr Taylor is a man.'

Katy beamed at him.

Sarah replied, 'It'll be harder than trawling the Universities. They list all their staff on their websites. You'll have to talk to all the GP surgeries and hospitals in Cambridge. If there's nothing, you'll have to go further afield and he could be anywhere.' She smiled at her little sister. 'Don't envy you. Let me know if I can help.'

Ben made a mental note to get Chris on to it. He would surely have avenues not open to Katy. He read out the entry for Dr Taylor. '*Dr A. N. Taylor – 2011 – they played the violin together for years but he's lost his bog-light, so now he's a target.* Any ideas?'

Pam was the first to speak. 'We thought it could be the Fens? Bog-light?'

Ben replied, 'Yes, methane. The peat gives off methane and sometimes it ignites. We've always called it "will-o-the-wisp".'

Michael took up the tale. 'There's this old tale about Stingy Jack and...'

Katy broke in. 'You told us that last time.' She pointed to the clock on the wall. 'We should move on.'

Ben's first thought was that Katy must be getting over her fixation with Michael. But that was quickly superseded by memories of last summer. His mind went back to a conversation with Alistair, one of Stanley Murdock's offspring. He'd told Ben that once, he'd been taken by his father to Belfast to meet a man called Jacko: a man that everyone around him was afraid of, a man who was certainly a terrorist. Surely, it was too far-fetched to think there was any connection. But Stanley had written these clues, and Stanley had been devious and very, very clever. And he'd spent all that time in Ireland. And he knew Jacko, a terrorist. *He'd lost his bog-light.* If his bog-light had been Jack-o-lantern, a terrorist – and that man was now dead, that might have been enough to bring Dr A N Taylor into Dobson's web. Something else to talk to Chris about.

Katy asked, 'Anything else?' But the assembled company had nothing to add.

'So, on to the last one. '*Professor O. Pedersen, July 2009 – Not his native huldufolk at the end of this rainbow. Tie and dye – that's his hobby.* Do we really think this is to do with "snuff" like that police officer said?'

Michael was usually quiet and reticent at these family gatherings, but this time he was fast and forceful in his response. 'Nonces got a really bad time in prison. The hard men picked on anyone they thought was vulnerable and nonces were their first target. They got beaten up regularly. At the time, I felt sorry for them. I thought they couldn't help it but if people die...'

Ben could see Pam squeeze Michael's hand under the table for a second time. Ben knew that, despite or maybe because of his time in prison, Michael was still one of life's innocents and he needed protecting. He'd had protection in prison because the 'hard men' had thought he was a terrorist and that there would be repercussions if he was hurt. Now it looked as though Pam was his guardian. Again he thought, a serving police officer and a convicted criminal, even one who was innocent and rich enough not to have to work, not easy. Silently, he wished them well.

Michael was still talking. 'I've been thinking about this and, sure to God, it worried me. See, in Ireland, there's leprechauns at the end of the rainbow – we call them "the little people". Then I looked up huldufolk and they're hidden people, sort of like elves. So I think it's children he's into. Hidden children.'

Of course, thought Ben. That was it! That's what had bugged him when he'd visited Jim Spire. The pathologist had mentioned leprechauns when he'd visited him at the mortuary.

Little people – leprechauns. Leprechauns aren't innocent but children are.

They all looked horrified. Katy spoke first. 'Oh my God! Could he be killing them? But surely we'd know if there were missing children. It'd be on the news.'

Sarah joined in. 'Where does he take his holidays? That's where he'll be doing it.'

Ben looked through the other information he'd written down about each of their blackmailees. 'He's a Professor of Asian and Middle Eastern Studies. God, that's a brilliant cover. What if he travels for work and...' He tailed off not knowing quite what to say. They all sat in stunned silence. Ben was the first to recover. He waved the paper in his hand. 'This proves nothing. We have no proof, only conjecture. I'll take our conjecture to Vin, pronto. The police need to know.'

Pam spoke. 'With Savile and Yewtree, it's big stuff at the mo. They'll take it seriously. It makes me sick to think of it. And I bet Murdock and Dobson knew about it and never reported it. The bastards.'

# Chapter 31

He'd been surprised that Vin had called him before he'd had a chance to contact her. He'd decided to update Chris first as he wanted information from him, lots of information. When he arrived at Parkside for his meeting at nine sharp, she'd been waiting at reception for him. She'd welcomed him with, 'Let's walk across Parker's Piece and grab a coffee.'

She went straight to the point as soon as they were out of earshot of the police station. 'My Apostles are back and they're still trying to pin the Dobson murder on you. They've set out a good case to me. You have motive, means and opportunity, and you found the body. There's the phone message, which they say you could have staged. And it's possible. The time of death has been confirmed as about the time of the phone call so, if you hadn't been in bed with me at the time of the murder, I'd be seeking to arrest you – or at least call you in for questioning.'

'Um. Looks bad. What do you want to do?'

'They want to put it to the team later today. I really can't put myself in their debt by just telling those two so I'm going to have to tell the whole team about us.'

'I'll have to talk to Chris. What time is the briefing?'

'I've put it off till six o'clock. I said it was the best time to get everybody together.'

'I'll be in touch before then. I was going to call you anyway. You mentioned Yewtree. I think I have a lead for you.' He handed over the notes he'd made about Professor Pedersen. 'We think he's going out to Asia for his hobby – but we have no proof. The officer you sent to babysit me says she thinks tie and dye means snuff.'

She quickly scanned the note. 'Christ, Ben. If this is true, and Dobson had deciphered the clue, it would be one helluva motive for murdering him. My team are investigating all the people on your list, been back and forth to your college and have come up with nothing on any of them. You know how it is when you're certain they've closed ranks and there doesn't seem any way of getting through.' She pointed to Ben's notes. 'I'll feed this into the Met immediately. Thanks.'

'Be careful though. He's a Mason.'

She looked sideways at him. 'God, we've got so many of them in the force. And with people I don't trust on my team, I have to be careful.'

'How are your Apostles? Unwell, I hope. I'm pretty sure they're the ones who organised my "little accident". We couldn't manage a link between them and Pedersen, could we?'

'Would be interesting. I won't do anything official, but I'll work on it. My hands are tied, internal politics. Bloody Masons get everywhere.'

Ben thought, they can join the Ruskies and the Irish then.

She continued, 'And you may have noticed that I'm a wee bit busy. Maybe you could see what you can find out? You and Chris? Oh, here's some news you'll be pleased about. There's been a report of missing adrenaline and morphine at a hospice in Ely. No break-in that they can identify. We're investigating it now.' She smiled broadly. 'Seems your Miss Finlay is in the clear. There is no way she could have got the adrenaline that killed that nun but someone else obviously did. We're tying this theft to the murder – morphine, we wouldn't consider a link but adrenaline, not the addict's drug of choice. We think that's where the murder weapon came from. I don't know where you've hidden Miss Josephine, but you can bring her out of hiding now.'

Ben laughed. 'You are one clever detective. I'll let her know. But I think she'd better stay where she is for the time being. Sister Theresa posted a letter to her before she died. She'd seen a picture in the paper and recognised a paedophile she knew years ago and he's a doctor.' For some reason that he couldn't articulate, he did not want to disclose to Vin that he had that newspaper in his possession.

Vin's smile disappeared. 'Have you got the letter? It's evidence. I need to have it.'

Before the police got involved, Ben wanted to talk again to the Reverend Mother and the small nun who had let them into the convent. 'I'll see if she still has it.' Then he added, 'Have you sent someone to the convent yet?'

'Not yet. Too much to do! She was killed at The Friary, no other nun was there and we had Josephine down as our prime suspect.'

'I'm going back tomorrow to liaise about her funeral. Is there anything I can do?' Ben cringed inwardly as he spoke. He knew that, yet again, he was being less than honest with Vin and this was causing him acute discomfort.

* * *

Ben was ushered into the convent by the same small nun. When he asked her about Sister Theresa, she was unusually tight-lipped. 'Reverend Mother says we're not to talk about dear Sister Theresa. She says there will be a police investigation and we're not to say anything that will reflect badly on the convent.'

Ben was reminded of the other institution that had recently seen one of its members murdered. Replace convent with college and you'd have Ethel's to a tee. The nun hurried along the echoing corridor as if needing to get away and they swiftly arrived at the Reverend Mother's door. The nun knocked and walked in and Ben followed. Ben had, at first, decided to bring Katy. But they were short-handed with Mo away and, when Katy had referred to the Reverend Mother as 'starchy-knickers', that had sealed it the other way. He'd left her beavering away, and ordering Michael around. She'd obviously got over that infatuation.

The Reverend Mother stood and glided towards him on those same invisible wheels. She dismissed the nun with a slight nod of her head. 'Mr Burton, welcome. But in such sorrowful circumstances. How could anyone do that to our wonderful Sister Theresa? I gather there will be a delay because of the post mortem. But that will mean that she can lie in state in the chapel after all.'

'But I thought she was to be laid out in her room?' Ben didn't like to call it a cell – though indeed that is what it was.

'A change of plan. Shall I take you to see the chapel?'

As they walked along several more echoing corridors, Ben said, as casually as he could, 'I've been to see Josephine Finlay. She's taken it very hard and I don't quite know how to help her. You know that she has mental problems. She seems to have some sort of delusion that she's partly responsible for Sister Theresa's death, although she had no way of acquiring the drug that killed her.' He looked sideways at the Reverend Mother. 'Can I ask for your help?'

'Of course. I'll do what I can but you know we are an enclosed order so I can't go to see your Miss Finlay. Sister Theresa had come from an open convent and wanted to continue her pastoral work, so she had a special dispensation from the Archbishop to go out.' She looked down, and to Ben's mind, she seemed to be trying to look demure but was failing utterly. 'We follow the Orders of our community and hope to serve the Divine Lord from within these walls.'

Ben felt nauseated by this false piety. He knew that this nun knew something. He wondered if she would tell him what it was. He replied quickly before she could change her mind. 'Oh, no, Reverend Mother, all I want is some advice from you. Miss Finlay seems to think that Sister Theresa was frightened of a doctor. No-one at The Friary can get to the bottom of it. Have you any idea where she got that from?'

Ben was reminded of the term Katy had used, as the Reverend Mother drew herself up to her full height before responding. 'All the doctors who visit here are local and have been vetted to ensure total propriety. I have no idea where Miss Finlay has got that idea from. Preposterous. I'm afraid I can't help you.'

But she didn't realise that she already had.

## Chapter 32

Chris was his usual ebullient self. He'd taken Ben to the furthest corner of the coffee shop in Waterstones and had brought over two black coffees and two slices of carrot cake. 'Love this cake, so oozy.' Ben hadn't touched his. 'Not want yours? Pass it over then.' Through a mouthful of cake, Chris began his tale. 'Sorted your alibi problem. Been in touch with your lovely Lavinia. We've come to an understanding. And this is genius; I'll give you a cast iron alibi and she'll liaise with me in future. Clever – eh? She's high enough up to be really useful and her dalliance with you remains a deep, dark secret so her reputation is untarnished. Win-win for your Vin.' Ben wasn't so sure but it was not his choice to make. Chris continued, 'And, since your link with the convent, I've got news of your Dr Taylor.' Now Ben was interested. He waited impatiently while Chris swallowed another mouthful of cake. His wait was worth it.

'See, you were looking for a Dr A N Taylor. I don't know if Stanley made a mistake. More likely, knowing what we know about Stanley, it was a misdirection. One of the newer doctors at the surgery used by the convent is a Dr Andrew Neville-Taylor. Looked up his background. After qualifying, spent a couple of years in Africa then moved to Northern Ireland. He was a GP there when our Stanley was about. Then he moved again, this time to Hong Kong. Been back in this area for three years. They usually send a female GP to the convent but last week there wasn't one available so Dr Neville-Taylor bowled up.'

'Did he know Stanley?'

'Haven't any evidence, but we're very interested now because there's the potential of a real-time connection in Ulster.'

'Right. There's a UVF man called Jacko. Know who he might be?'

'How the hell did you get to that?'

Although he knew that he was taking a punt, Ben said nonchalantly, 'Solved Stanley's clue. Easy.'

160

'Christ, Ben, you're into a big-time terrorist here. John-Joe McKinnon was one of the Shankill Butchers but he was too clever – or too feared – to be caught. Could never pin anything on him. No-one would testify. He was locally known as "Jacko". Dead now. Died last year. Died in his bed.'

Ben waved his hands to stop Chris from saying more. He was fast building a picture. Alistair Murdock had described a visit to Belfast with his father. The Jacko he'd been taken to meet in Belfast had accosted the seven-year-old Alistair much to Stanley's disgust. In Alistair's words, Jacko had been 'a kiddy-fiddler'. Lost his bog-light, played the violin together – bloody Hell, that nailed it. Dr Neville-Taylor was the paedophile; the one Sister Theresa was so frightened of. Had been one in Northern Ireland, and had been protected by Jacko. Until Jacko had died.

'Did you know Jacko was a paedo?'

Chris replied, 'There were rumours but never anything concrete.' He thought for a minute. Ben waited until Chris grinned. 'I get it, playing the violin, so our Dr Taylor is a nonce? Knew Jacko. My people will love this.'

'Did you know Stanley also knew Jacko, met him in a pub in Belfast at least once?'

'Shit, bloody shit. Where'd you get your info? We had no idea of that connection. You sure of that?'

Ben's face turned grave. He didn't want to expose Alistair Murdock to Chris's questioning. 'Third-hand account, but worth pursuing, I should think. OK. I've given you useful intel. Now I want a straight answer from you. What is the connection between my wife and Stanley Murdock?'

Now it was Chris's turn to look grave. He looked squarely at Ben and his face gave nothing away. 'Look Ben. I don't know anything about that.' He gave a small sigh. 'If there had been anything we'd have known about it. I've searched through and I can't find anything. So I can't help you with that one. Best forget it.'

Ben said nothing but he was certain that Chris was lying.

# Chapter 33

Ben breathed in the crisp clean air as he surveyed the cliff-top scene. Hunstanton was looking glorious in the winter sunshine. He peered across at the mended fence and sighed. It seemed a lifetime ago that he'd saved Josephine from jumping off those cliffs. It was barely three months and her progress towards full health had been remarkable. He needed to talk to Mo. He walked past the house and along the cliff path, knowing that he was putting off the moment when he would have to face up to his past, his present and his future. And he knew that whatever path he took, it would be hard. Was he brave enough to take the most difficult one, the one that could blow his world apart for a second time? He wasn't sure; he didn't think so. He turned back, marched up to the front door and pushed the bell hard.

As he went into the house, an overwhelming smell of fresh paint assaulted his nose. The downstairs rooms, which had been neglected and dowdy, were fresh and bright. He could hear chattering and laughter upstairs. Mo nodded his head towards the stairs. 'They're going great guns. They'll have done the whole house by next week. Don't know how I'll keep them amused then. Could get them tiling the bathroom maybe.' He called up the stairs. 'Hey, you noisy pair, Ben's come to see us.'

A voice came from on high. It was Agnes. 'Hallo, Ben. We'll be down in a minute. I'm gasping for a cup of tea. We'll make you one when we've finished this wall. Mo, would you be an angel and put the kettle on?'

Ben looked sideways at Mo. 'An angel, eh?' And, to his surprise, he saw Mo blush. He called up the stairs, 'I need a few minutes to talk to Mo, so don't hurry. I wouldn't want to be the ruination of your painting.' He followed his uncle into the kitchen.

Mo filled the kettle and switched it on. 'You said you wanted a word and you sounded odd. What is it?'

Now he'd come to the reason for his journey, Ben was reluctant to voice his fears. Maybe he should just keep them to himself and deal with them alone? That had been his way for all the years since Diane's death, and it had sort of worked. But now Dr Clare was helping him to open up. He was finding that this was all infinitely more complex than he'd anticipated and he was unsure that he could face the consequences of dealing with it. If he moved forward, he knew that more pain was on the way. He took a deep breath. 'I need some advice and you know me better than anyone. And you knew Diane. I've come by some information and I don't know what to do.' He raised his hand as Mo was about to speak. 'Diane had an affair with Dobson before I knew her. I'm jealous, of course I am, but that's not what's bothering me.' He took out the letter that Walpole had given him and handed it to Mo. 'Read this. Dobson wrote this just before Diane died. He was going to send it to Murdock but he never did.'

Mo peered at the untidy scrawl. 'Can't make it out. Read it to me.'

Ben's voice shook as he read, '*Stanley, you are mistaken. Diane has no evidence and Ben doesn't suspect her or you. She told me yesterday. Relax – your secret is safe. Graham*'

'Bloody awful writing. You sure it says that?' Mo collapsed into a chair and waited in silence while Ben took out a clean handkerchief and wiped his eyes.

'Absolutely. Mo, I need help. The world I thought I knew, the life I had with Diane, is disintegrating. And I don't know what to do.'

'Look, it's probably nothing at all. You told me your Service friends said that Dobson was unreliable. You, yourself said he was a lying bastard. I wouldn't trust what he said. I'd say, tear it up and forget it.'

'NO!'

Both men swivelled to face the door as Agnes burst in. 'No! You can't do that. You just can't. D'you hear me?' She wagged a finger at Mo and tutted. 'And you such a sensible man.'

Then she turned back to Ben. 'Don't let that sleeveen ruin your life. So, he raped me. But then I let him fester in my head for thirty years. I shut away what he'd done and I paid the price. I nearly lost my daughter because I wouldn't face the truth. Josephine tells me you're a good man, and you've saved her and me.' Agnes took hold of Ben's hand and squeezed it hard. 'Please listen to me. You're an undertaker. You bury people. Dead bodies stay under the ground, but lies don't. They wriggle up like nasty little snakes to bite you when you're not looking. Stanley Murdock was a wicked, wicked man and now he's dead and good riddance. But if you're going to be free of him, you're going to have to find the truth and deal with it.'

Josephine joined them in the kitchen. She smiled at her mother and turned to Ben. 'She's right, you know. We all have to face our demons.'

# Chapter 34

He was running. This was his usual route but the landmarks that he passed went by without a flicker of interest or even recognition. He ran through Sheep's Green and Lammas Land and along the river path towards Grantchester. The pound, pound, pound of his feet in that regular rhythm brought some relief to his tortured soul. And it gave him time and space to think. His thoughts were not welcome but they needed to be voiced. Diane had lied to him. Of that he was now certain, but how and why he could not tell. Dobson had lied to him, equally certainly, but he could not divine which among his utterances had been true and which false. And he was sure that Chris had lied to him, possibly in telling him that Dobson had lied. Henry Walpole seemed to be the one truth-teller, but could he trust him, for he too was mired in this life of espionage? And then he, himself, had lied to Vin. How was he to reach the truth amid this dislocation of fact from fiction? His life was becoming a tissue of lies and he knew he had to extricate himself from it or he would collapse under the weight of those untruths. Stanley Murdock had been a spy, a blackmailer and had undoubtedly been involved in other criminal activity, and he lay at the centre of this web of deceit. But he was dead, as were Diane and Dobson. He would have to rely on his own intuition and Chris and Walpole. He hoped it would be enough.

\* \* \*

Katy was bubbling over when he got back. He hadn't even had time to retreat to the shower before she accosted him. 'Dad, Dad, I've got it. The three that saved Hendrick. It's so bloody obvious. We are sooo stupid! He was at Trinity, right here under our noses. He came up to Trinity when he was nineteen. I've looked him up. And I've been looking at the Cambridge spies. They all came from Trinity before they buggered off to Moscow.' She wagged a finger at him. 'Don't look at me like that. Bloody and bugger are not swear words these days.' Ben held up his hands in mock surrender as his daughter continued, 'So I think they recruited him and that's why there's no record of his second flashy-flashy. What d'you think? Can you go and ask him?'

'I'll have a shower and do that right now.' He would go to see Hendrick because it meant he would be doing something – anything – to help him forget the quagmire that his life had become. It would bring relief, if only for a while.

\* \* \*

On his march over to Ethel's, he forced himself to think about his diminishing relationship with Vin. He knew he was thinking of Vin in order to postpone the inevitable analysis of his relationship with Diane. He reflected on how he'd messed up with Vin and possibly hurt her too, and he wondered if he had the mentality, personality – call it whatever – to form an honest relationship. And that hurt even more. Although they'd decided on a pause while this investigation was ongoing, he still felt guilty about lying to her. He'd thought, with Dr Clare's help, that he was moving forward, but Josephine's words continued to ring in his brain. He needed to keep busy, to solve these murders. He would have to face his demons sometime – but not yet.

Ben was surprised that Dr Hendrick greeted him less coldly than on previous occasions, but he noticed a brittleness about the bonhomie. 'Come in, Mr Burton. We need to thank you. A very good send-off you organised. You did him proud. Now, what can I do for you?'

Ben went straight to the point. 'A delicate matter but one that will go no further. I know that Dobson was blackmailing you. I know that you were caught exposing yourself twice in your youth and Professor Dobson came to know about it. And now he's dead. You realise that this means you have a prime motive for murder.' Ben was pretty sure he knew that the answer would be negative but he asked the question anyway. 'Did you kill him?'

While he'd been speaking, Ben had watched Hendrick's face turn red, then an alarming shade of purple and finally a deathly white. He waited while Hendrick staggered back to his chair and sat down heavily. Hendrick put his head in his hands and Ben had to stoop to hear his muffled voice. 'I thought at last I was free.

Murdock then Dobson, both dead. A stupid prank in my youth and it's haunted me all these years. Now you. What do *you* want of me?' He laughed bitterly. 'Another thirty pieces of silver?'

'I want nothing from you except the truth. Did you kill him?'

Hendrick looked up. His face took on an ugly expression as he hissed. 'I want nothing from you except the truth! What makes you so different? You a saint or something?'

Ben's mind was immediately taken back to Fisher's description of the altercation he'd heard in Front Court the day before Dobson's murder. The hissing man. Here was the hissing man. It must have been Hendrick. Ben took a step back and readied himself for an attack. Maybe Hendrick was the killer after all. 'You argued with Dobson the day before he was killed. Things were coming to a head. What did he threaten you with?'

Suddenly, all the stuffing went out of Hendrick and he slumped in his chair. 'He wanted me to take some evidence to the police. I could tell he was scared – terrified. He said it was about another member of College and it was important – someone whose crime was far worse than mine. He threatened to tell the police and the College authorities about me if I refused.' He picked up a framed photo from his desk and showed it to Ben. It was a happy family snap showing Hendrick with his two children, a boy and a girl. 'He said they'd take them away. I couldn't let that happen.'

Ben's mind was whirring fast. They'll fake them anyway. Not fake but take. They'll take them anyway. Dobson had threatened him with the loss of his children. 'So you killed him.'

'No! There and then, I could have. I would cheerfully have strangled him but instead I agreed to take his evidence to the police. And then he was murdered.'

Ben asked quickly, 'Do you have the evidence?'

'He gave me a sealed package. I didn't know what to do with it when he was killed. I've kept it hidden. I've been frightened ever since, terrified. If he was murdered for this, what chance do I have?'

Ben put a hand gently on the other man's shoulder. Hendrick jumped at the touch. 'Have you told anyone else about the package?'

Hendrick shook his head.

'Are you sure? Think, man!'

'No. No-one, not even my wife.'

'Give me the package. Say nothing to anyone. Do you hear me. Tell no-one.'

Hendrick nodded and pulled some books out of his bookcase. Hidden behind them was a slim envelope securely sealed with tape. He picked it up as though it would bite him and handed it, at arm's length, to Ben. 'Take it! Please take it. I didn't open it. I didn't want to know.'

As he took the package, Ben felt the stirrings of pity for Hendrick's dilemma. He knew how he would feel if someone had threatened to take his children from him. Maybe Hendrick had been recruited, but this man was not an accomplished spy. If he had been, he'd have found a better hiding place and he'd have known who to turn to.

\* \* \*

Ben knew he was deliberately withholding evidence again and he should, by rights, take the package straight to Vin, unopened. Instead, he took it home. He put on latex gloves and spread a sterile plastic sheet over the worktop. He carefully removed the slim package from his pocket. He turned it over three times. Brown paper envelope, nothing on the outside save the initials P. T. There would be fingerprints, probably just his, Hendrick's and Dobson's – maybe Murdock's too. With a sharp knife he slit the tape at both sides and carefully prised the envelope open. He emptied the contents on to the sterile sheet. Some photos tumbled out, face up. He picked them up by the very edge, being careful not to smudge any fingermarks they might carry. The first looked like an innocuous holiday snap. Pedersen's face smiled up at him surrounded by three boys aged, he thought, about seven or eight. The children all had their arms round Pedersen's neck and were also smiling up at the camera. The background and the faces of the children suggested the photos were taken somewhere in the Far East. That would fit with Pedersen's area of study. Ben wondered who had taken the photo. It didn't seem to be a selfie. The second showed the same scene but with another man, unknown to Ben, in the same pose with the same children. Presumably, this man had taken the first photo and Pedersen had taken this one.

As Ben put these two aside, the third and fourth photos were uncovered. Ben dropped the pile of photos on to the sheet. Even holding them made him feel dirty, defiled, disgusted. He stared at them in disbelief. Each photo showed one of the same two men subjecting one of the boys to anal sex. The boy looked terrified. A tide of bile rose in Ben's throat. He just managed to get to the sink in time to empty the contents of his stomach. He spent five minutes dry retching and, when his stomach had stopped heaving, he stood up straight and rinsed his mouth. He splashed his face with cold water, then took a long drink of water and several deep breaths. He knew there were more photos that he had not seen. He thought back to the session where they'd been trying to solve the clues and was reminded of the reaction of the liaison officer who still had flashbacks from her time at Obscene Publications. Tie and dye. Suspecting that the further photos contained no happy ending, Ben decided that the rest of them would go unseen to Vin. He carefully scooped them into a pile, still only touching the edges and returned them in the same order to the envelope. He knew that he would feel better if he resealed them tightly but that might further destroy evidence. He was well aware that he would get a bollocking from Vin. He found her in his contacts and waited for her to answer.

# Chapter 35

He sat bolt upright, all senses on full alert. No sound – only the sounds that had been in his brain – pounding his head and freezing his body into total torpor. He could still smell the cordite and feel the heat of the bomb blast. He could see his dead wife, even though he knew he was now awake. The sights and sounds and smells of his dream slowly receded and his breathing gradually returned to normal. His heart slowed to a regular beat as he consciously breathed as his yoga teacher had taught him. Two dreams now in quick succession. Was he heading for another crisis? He shook his head as he brushed that thought into the deep recesses of his mind.

He was at a loose end. With nothing to occupy him, he wandered the house like a caged bear. He'd been told, in no uncertain terms, not to tamper with any more evidence. He was waiting for an emergency appointment with Dr Clare, scheduled for tomorrow. He'd been loath to say how desperately he needed to see her, and the wait seemed interminable. He tried to concentrate on the two murders, Dobson's and Sister Theresa's. It was becoming increasingly evident to Ben that the murders were connected and had paedophilia at their heart. That was now all in Vin's hands. All he knew was that the police were having some difficulty in finding Pedersen. And they still hadn't unearthed the heavies that had attacked him. There was no more he could do, so with great reluctance, he had had to turn his mind back to his own problems.

No. First he'd find the copy of that newspaper that Sister Theresa had left in her cell. He knew that this was a displacement activity – putting off the evil hour – but he did it anyway. He found the paper and began to search through it. He looked carefully, as Dr Fursley had done, at every picture. And there it was! A picture of the self-same man whose photos had so disgusted him – Pedersen's partner in crime. In the paper, the man looked normal, ordinary, professional. He was wearing a sober suit, sitting in the foreground of a large sober-suited group. Ben leaned over to read the caption. *'Twenty GPs from Cambridge and surrounding villages visit the new paediatric unit on the Addenbrookes campus.'* He read on. *'These local GPs have volunteered to be at the forefront of new technologies in paediatric care. It will involve close monitoring of children in certain vulnerable groups.'* Christ! No wonder the nun had been alarmed. She had almost certainly been killed because she had shared her disquiet with her Mother Superior. He would do his damnedest to ensure that that woman didn't get away scot-free. He phoned Vin – voicemail. The message he left told her to look urgently at her emails. Then he wrote an email giving her the newspaper details, the background and pointing to the Reverend Mother as a 'person of interest' in their investigation of Dr Neville-Taylor. He knew that Vin would be beyond furious when she realised he'd sat on this evidence and was only now sharing it. There would be repercussions, but, at this time, that was the least of his problems.

Throughout this exercise, his mind's eye repeatedly wandered to the trap door of his attic, the attic that he hadn't entered for sixteen years. That long time ago, when his wife had lain dead in the morgue and he had lain almost dead in the hospital, Mo had organised the retrieval of their belongings and their repatriation from Belfast to Cambridge. Mo and Gwen had sorted the personal from the mundane and had organised their storage in the attic above. Soon he would have to enter that lost world and see if any clue had been left which would, he hoped, soothe his fears. He realised how much he missed Mo. Agnes had described him as 'one of nature's gentlemen'. So right. Face your demons, Josephine had said. He stared at the email to Vin in his sent box and made up his mind. This evening, when Katy was home, he would go into the attic and search through those memories. Now he had a newspaper to deliver to Vin and two burials to prepare for.

# Chapter 36

Christmas had come and Christmas had gone. He'd used it as an excuse. He decided it might spoil Christmas so he would have to leave the attic till New Year. That excuse had now become invalid. Their quiet family Christmas celebration was now history and a New Year's resolution had to be put into operation. It was now 2013 and he would have to begin his search of Diane's things. It was time.

He'd asked Sarah to come over and she'd brought Pam with her. He could hear Sarah, Pam and Katy in the kitchen and it seemed their entire conversation was centred on Michael. To put off his distasteful task, he listened at the kitchen door.

'Has he proposed yet?'

'No, but we have talked about having children, so it's getting serious.'

'Bloody brilliant! Can I be bridesmaid?' This was Katy. 'But not if I have to wear a yukky floaty dress. And you must know that pink doesn't suit me.'

'Hold on! He hasn't mentioned marriage.'

Katy was still full of enthusiasm. 'But he will. He loves you and you're just right for him. Go girl. Push him a little.'

Sarah added, 'Yeah. He needs someone to protect him. He's so naive, bless him. Remember when I told him that rappers are people employed to wrap presents and he believed me? And he'll be mega-rich, don't forget. He could fall for some scam. He needs you.'

Ben reluctantly turned away. Life was so uncomplicated for those three and he envied them. They'd offered to help, but he'd said he'd rather do it alone. He'd told them what Josephine had said, that it was time for him to 'face his demons'. And facing demons is a lonely business.

Josephine was right, of course. She was facing her demons and overpowering them. She would soon be coming back to Cambridge and Dr Clare would see her as an out-patient. She and Agnes had formed the bond that had been absent throughout her childhood and she was moving forward from a very dark place. If she could do it, then so could he. Maybe.

He took three deep breaths and pulled down the loft ladder. He ascended slowly. He had a torch but found that there was perfectly adequate electric lighting and a boarded floor. A neat pile of suitcases stood in the far corner. The rest of the attic was empty. He approached the dusty pile. There were three suitcases and that was all. Not much for the contents of a life. He lifted the upper two on to the floor and decided to take them in order, smallest first. The catches were old and reluctant to open but, with perseverance, he opened the lid.

Clothes. Clothes that suddenly brought Diane to life – in his memory, at least. That green silky dress that had so perfectly fitted her figure. He sat back as he remembered the last time she'd worn it. They had been attending a regimental do and she had turned heads, her long copper curls swinging behind her. She had accentuated her usual sensual walk by wearing very high heels. He laughed as he remembered that she'd had to take them off in the car on the way home, and had sworn never to wear them again.

He put the dress to one side. Underneath were usual, everyday clothes. They brought back the other side of Diane. Diane, the mother. What would she think of her two girls, now grown? He was sure that she would have been ultra-proud. Would they have turned out differently if she'd been around? Of course they would. He felt a tear trickle down his cheek as he was brought again to the realisation that that other world would have been different. Would it have been better? Who could know for certain but he was pretty sure that it would have been – for his girls, anyway. Guilt spread through him again, rising in a tide that threatened to sweep him away. Why had she come to the barracks on that day of all days? She'd never come during his time on duty. But she'd come that day. If only she'd stayed away, she'd be with him now. His suspicion had always been that she'd come to tell him that she was expecting their longed-for third child – but he'd never had the courage to ask – a positive response would have been too much. Two lives lost would have been far too much to bear.

Wrapped in her favourite jumper was a small, locked wooden box. He could picture it as it had always been, sitting on her bedside cabinet amongst the detritus of everyday life, pens, make-up, vitamins, nail scissors. She'd always kept it locked and the key on her key ring. He'd never enquired what was in there, had never thought to. He remembered when they'd bought it. They'd been on a trip to London, she'd seen it on a stall in Camden Market and she'd persuaded him to buy it for her. He turned the box over and discovered a second key attached to the bottom with flaking sellotape. A shiver ran up and down his spine. For no logical reason, he now attached significance to the box. Perhaps it contained evidence of her affair with Dobson, the affair that plagued him even though he was certain it had happened before he had known her. He found himself ambivalent, not wanting confirmation of his fears. As he sat irresolute, he could hear again Josephine's voice, articulating her new-found strength and sanity. He knew that his sanity would not be fully restored until he'd uncovered the whole truth about his wife's life; until he'd fully faced up to the past. He pulled the key from the remains of its binding and opened the box.

Downstairs, the three young women had left the topic of Michael and marriage and were discussing their career prospects. Sarah and Pam affirmed that they both wanted to be a Chief Constable somewhere and would ensure that they didn't apply for the same job, even though such a job lay at least thirty years in the future. They had moved on to advising Katy, in big sister fashion, what she should do with her life. The howl that came from the attic made them all jump. It was primeval, a sound full of negative emotions: anger, fear, hate, despair. The sound continued as they raced up the stairs and, in single file, climbed the loft ladder. Later, Katy would describe it as an animal cry of pain.

* * *

The call to Dr Clare had brought an immediate response. In the twenty minutes it took for her to arrive, Katy, Sarah and Pam had each tried to coax Ben down from the attic. He hadn't responded. He seemed not to hear anything. Katy had called on Mary, the neighbour who had provided food and company while Ben had been recovering from his mugging. She had managed, by gentle but firm persuasion, to get him to his bedroom. There he now sat, hunched on his bed wrapped in a blanket and staring into space. His daughters sat either side of him while Pam tried to ply him with hot sweet tea. He pushed it aside.

When Dr Clare arrived, she took charge of Ben. Sarah, as next of kin, gave permission for his immediate admission to The Friary. Katy had phoned Mo who was now on his way back to Cambridge. Pam had phoned Michael and he was now in attendance. By unspoken consent, they had closed the trap-door to the attic without investigating the cause of Ben's 'episode'.

Mary kept them all occupied while they waited for the ambulance to take Ben to The Friary. They packed a bag for him, they drank copious quantities of tea, they talked in a hushed fashion about what they might do to help. Mary took total control. She partially calmed their fears by telling them that Ben was strong, his resilience would see him through and, whatever had caused this set-back, he would recover.

# Chapter 37

*He's down. Be strong – now is the time to strike. He has the evidence. We find it or we take the girl.*

# Chapter 38

Early the next morning, as Ben lay sedated in The Friary, Mo, Sarah, Pam and Michael sat with Katy at the kitchen table. Mary had already provided so much help that they'd asked her to join them. She was making tea and toast for them all.

Sarah was adamant. 'No arguments, Kate. We're all going to move in while Dad's in hospital. Pam and me, Vin's given us two day's compassionate leave so we can get things organised but we'll sleep here every night till he gets back, and after, if needed. Then we'll think again. We need to be together.'

For once, Katy didn't argue with her big sister. 'Thanks Sarah. I didn't realise how much…' and she crumpled into tears again.

Mo enveloped her in a bear-hug. 'Come on lass. We've got to keep strong. For your dad. Let's decide what's urgent to do.'

Pam said brightly, 'I'm going to help Michael to run the business. I've got a week's leave owing so I can take that. I'm sure Vin will agree. And Mary says she'll join us if we need her.' Pam smiled across at Mary. 'I've been told librarians can turn their hand to anything.'

Katy sniffed and noisily blew her nose. 'Yes, thanks Mary. You've been great. I wish...' She stopped suddenly, blushed and changed tack. 'Dr Clare said we've got to find out what caused Dad to seize up like that. The sooner we can do that, the better, she says. So we've got to go into the attic. Who's coming with me?'

Sarah said, 'I think it should be me.' She turned to Katy. 'The two of us together – it's our dad, after all.'

Ten minutes later they came down to a silent kitchen. All eyes turned towards them as they crept back into the room. Both were red eyed. Sarah carried a single sheet of paper.

Mary pointed towards the front door. 'I'll go, shall I? Perhaps you need to be alone. This is family stuff.'

Sarah looked round at all their faces. 'No, Mary. Stay please. We need some wisdom. Someone who can see this from the outside. We've got a letter written by our mother to our father for him to read after her death. She didn't know it would be sixteen years before he read it.'

She took a deep breath and began to read aloud:

*'My dearest love*

*If you are reading this it means that I am dead and being dead releases me from promises I have made and oaths I have taken. Now I am free to tell you the truth and I hope you can forgive me for the lies I have told – the deceit I have lived.*

*Never doubt that I loved you from the moment I first saw you and that you and our two beautiful girls are the centre of my world. But I also inhabit another world, and this other world has surely caused my death.*

*I know you refused Dobson when he approached you, but I was not so circumspect. He recruited me and I worked in a small way in that shady world until our daughters were born.*

*That should have been the end of it. But when you were posted to Belfast, they had one last job for me. I was persuaded. I insisted on coming with you. You resisted, I insisted. If I'd listened to you, I'd probably be with you now and you would not have had to read this.'*

Sarah swallowed and shook her head. She looked over at Katy. The only sound in the room was the miniscule rustling of the paper being passed from one sister to the other. After a brief pause, Katy continued where Sarah had left off.

*'I did what was required of me. Through my source, I found evidence for them about a truly evil man and the truths that he held which could rock the nation. To protect my contact, I won't tell you his name – or the name of the villain I've uncovered. You might be tempted to go after him. Please don't try to find him. He's got me. I don't want our girls to lose both their parents.*

*I am so very sorry for the lies and the hurt and for leaving you and Sarah and Katy.*

*Love always*
*Diane'*

Katy finished reading and the stunned silence was only broken by the sound of quiet sobbing. Mo gulped and wiped away his tears. 'The poor lad, the poor, poor lad. No wonder he freaked. He's been blaming himself all these years.'

Katy added, 'He idolised her. He put her on a pedestal. I can't…'

Sarah finished her sentence for her, 'We can't even begin to understand how he feels.'

Katy wailed in response, 'But we idolised her too!'

Mo hugged his great-niece. 'I know dear, I know. But she loved you all. She says so. She was conflicted. Love of family – love of country. She thought this was the last time and then she would be free. But it all went wrong and she died.'

Silence again descended. Then tears were wiped, noses were blown. And hugs were given and received.

After a while, Mary asked, 'Can I say something?'

They nodded, so she continued, 'You said about having an outside view.' She shrugged. 'I'll do my best. I can see the pain you're all suffering, and Ben is in even worse pain. The person you thought you all knew, isn't who you thought she was. She doesn't say so in so many words, but what she's saying is that she was spying on someone in Northern Ireland. And she was killed for it. Added to that, if things had been different, she might have been with you now. It's hard to bear.' She paused for a moment. 'But we can't undo the past. We can only let it give some meaning to the future.' She paused again. They nodded silently as she continued, 'I've been talking a lot to Ben over the past few weeks, when he was laid up after the mugging. He values truth and it really distresses him when he can't be honest. I think the knowledge that he will find hardest to bear is that Diane was not honest with him. They were living a lie. And all this, in addition to having lost the love of his life. With Ben's permission, this letter needs to go to Dr Clare so she can begin to put his world together again. To start a new truth.' She smiled. 'And she'll be able to do that, I'm sure of it.'

# Chapter 39

'I'm so pleased you're all staying over. I couldn't have borne being on my own.' Katy gave a feeble smile to the assembled company. 'I don't think we should use Dad's bedroom. Doesn't seem right somehow. How about Sarah comes in with me, Mo has Sarah's old room and Pam and Michael can have the big spare? Then we'll all be on the same floor and I'll feel happier. Mary says she'll pop in after she's delivered the letter to Dr Clare.'

They busied themselves making beds and preparing a dinner that all except Michael would have trouble eating. They discussed what would need to be done to keep the business working as Ben would have wanted. Then they each went into their own little worlds to try to sort in their minds what this new information about Diane would mean to them.

They were sitting drinking yet another cup of tea when Mary arrived. As soon as she was through the front door, Katy and Sarah began bombarding her with questions. Mary held up her hands for silence and immediately the two of them subsided. 'Dr Clare could give me an update, thanks to Sarah giving permission. The good news is that he seems to be stable. He's been sedated and is slowly being brought back from that. I was able to give her the gist of the letter contents. I said that it was from Diane and contained news that Ben would find difficult to take. I gave her the letter and she will ask Ben, as soon as he is ready, if he will permit her to read it. She says he trusts her implicitly so she's pretty sure he'll say yes. I'll come back in the morning to see what's needed. And try not to worry. He's a brave man – he'll get through this.'

Soon after Mary had left, they all took themselves off to their bedrooms, though they knew they would have difficulty getting any sleep.

*  *  *

It was pitch black in the bedroom. Sarah shook her sister gently and immediately put her fingers to her lips to ensure silence. 'Shh!

Don't say anything. I heard a noise downstairs. I've checked all the rooms and everyone's asleep. I think we've got burglars.'

They went quietly into Mo's room. He was snoring with gusto. They shook him and Katy put a hand over his mouth to ensure he made no noise. Sarah explained that she suspected a break-in. While Sarah roused Michael and Pam, Mo dialled 999.

The entire posse gathered on the landing. Michael carried a cricket bat. Pam handed Sarah a pair of handcuffs and a baton. At Sarah's querying look, she whispered, 'Tell you later.' Mo carried a large torch. Katy was empty-handed and they ushered her to the back. They crept downstairs in single file and followed the sounds of surreptitious scrabbling coming from Ben's downstairs office. Someone was searching for something.

Pam motioned Katy to stay back. Then with loud yells of 'Get down, Police', Sarah, Pam and Michael rushed the room. There followed a short period of shouts, swearing, crashes and grunts. Katy moved towards the door but Mo barred her path. 'You wait here, lassie. Pam'n Sarah – they've been trained, and Michael's a big fella who works out. They got brawn. You got brains. Use 'em now.'

Katy retreated behind Mo as he moved into the room. He swung his torch, missing Michael by inches and landing a heavy blow to the side of the head of the largest of the three intruders. The man staggered sideways and slumped to the floor. Sarah and Pam lunged at the second and between them wrestled him to the ground. Michael caught the third behind the knees, waited for his legs to buckle before sitting on his chest and menacing him with the cricket bat.

After cuffing the two biggest intruders, Pam called out, 'Stay out there, Katy,' but Katy took no notice.

She entered a room that was in chaos, the floor covered with papers, books, overturned furniture. Two men were lying prone in the middle of the room with their hands cuffed behind their backs. The larger of the two was swearing loudly and offering a variety of reprisals against anyone and everyone. The smaller one was silent. A third man was cowering in the corner with Michael standing over him, threatening him with the cricket bat. Katy was the first to notice the tattoo on the neck of the bigger burglar. 'Hey, look. He's got a tatt, same as Dad described. I think we've caught Dad's muggers.'

'Shut up, Kate.' This shout came from Sarah.

Pam added, in a quieter voice, 'Katy, you mustn't say anything. We're going to arrest them so we need to keep quiet.'

Katy pointed to the third man. 'Who's he, then?'

Michael frisked the cowering man. 'His driving licence says his name is Pedersen.'

'Good. There's a warrant out for Pedersen,' said Pam. 'We've only got two pairs of cuffs so can someone find some rope for this one.' She pointed towards Pedersen with a look of disgust. Mo hurried out to find something to bind him.

Pam and Sarah moved back towards the door waving their batons all the while. Sarah shook her head and whispered to her friend, 'OK, Pam, the cuffs. You know we're not allowed to use them on our own account, so what gives?'

Pam looked shamefaced and whispered back. 'Vin told me not to tell anyone, including you. After the beating your dad took and the threat to him and your family, she thought it would be sensible if you were all together with protection. The protection was me, and you, of course. And Michael, with the bat.'

Mo came back carrying a stout roll of electrical tape and scissors and handed them over to Pam. He'd obviously been listening to the whispered conversation. 'And me! Don't forget me.' He pointed to the big burglar. 'I got that one.'

Pam was obviously in charge. 'Now we need to separate them.' She pointed to the cowering Pedersen. 'Sarah, take that one to the kitchen. Michael, you can have the big one in here and Mo and I will take the other one into the hall.'

With the larger burglar still effing and blinding, the smaller one yelling at him to 'Shut up' and Pedersen still trying to cower even as he walked to the kitchen, they saw blue flashes reflected on the ceiling indicating that their reinforcements had arrived.

# Chapter 40

'You're sure no-one was hurt? Eight days ago? Why didn't you tell me?'

'Because we had to sort out your issues first. And, as I said, no-one was hurt. It seems that DCI Wainwright took the threats to you more seriously than you did and made sure your girls were safe.' Dr Clare smiled. 'You see, you're not the only one whose job it is to protect the world.'

'But I've been here wallowing in self-pity while they've…'

Dr Clare cut him short. 'While they've taken on and overpowered the thugs that beat you up. They're fine, and feeling very pleased with themselves. They told me to tell you that your attackers plus Professor Pedersen are now residing in cells. And you haven't wallowed. You've done brilliantly, in a very short time. You've made a start on coming to terms with some unpalatable truths and you're beginning to look forward not back. Still a long way to go but I think your feet are pointing in the right direction and you know what to do to keep them facing that way. And your girls, well, it seems they can look after themselves, so you're not so indispensable after all.'

Ben paused while he took all this in. 'Yeah, could be.' He smiled. 'They are magnificent, aren't they. And they got Pedersen. Clever and brave. I'll thank Vin just as soon as you let me out of here. I'm a very lucky man.'

'Funny you should say that – about your DCI. She's been in touch and she wants a favour.'

'I certainly owe her. So, what can I do?'

'I was thinking it would be good for you to take your mind off yourself for a while, and get your teeth into something outside your family. She's come up with something to start with, if you want to do it.'

'Intriguing. But the big question is, will it get me out of here? I've been here eight whole days and I'm stir-crazy.'

'That's good! And yes it will. I'll have to give you a shadow, just to make sure I've assessed your condition correctly. Here's a question for you. I wondered if you would accept your neighbour, Mary, as a companion for the next few days? I was impressed with her when she came with your letter. Say no if you don't think it's appropriate.'

'No problem for me. But what about her work?'

'When she brought me the letter, she said she'd taken some leave to help your family run the business so she's already available. Your DCI wants you to talk to Pedersen. He won't talk. Says he'll only speak to you. She mentioned something about you both being from 'a Godforsaken hole of a college'. Says you'll know where that comes from.'

Ben smiled grimly. Yes, it would be good to be able to do something useful.

Alison Clare's parting shot brought him back to the realisation that others too had their problems. 'And I've now got to get down to finding out how Doctor Neville-Taylor got in here and to make sure that our security measures can't be breached by a homicidal doctor for a second time.'

\* \* \*

Vin ushered Ben and Mary into her office. After the introductions Vin looked him up and down. 'I must say, you're looking remarkably fit for someone who was supposed to be in full meltdown.'

Mary responded and the temperature in the room took a nosedive. 'Oh, isn't he. We've been looking after him. You can be certain of that. But, as you know, he's remarkably resilient.'

'Of course. Yes, he also recovered quickly from that beating, probably helped by our quick response in getting him to hospital.'

Ben was bemused by the frisson between these two women who had only just met. He thought he'd better remind them that he was present and could speak for himself. 'I need to thank you both for all the help you have given me in mind and body, and for looking after my family when I wasn't able to do so.'

Vin interrupted, 'As long as Taylor is out there, those precautions will remain in place. You don't need to worry.'

Ben continued, 'Thank you for that, but we do need to move on. Pedersen has said he'll see me, and only me?'

'Yes. But first, we need to agree that all communications related to this case will be kept completely confidential.' Vin turned to look directly at Mary.

Mary straightened herself so she was sitting at full height and nodded twice. Her voice was firm and clear as she carefully enunciated each word. 'Of course. Goes without saying.'

Vin turned back to face Ben and continued, 'We need to get something concrete on the murders. He wanted to be interviewed by my Apostles. I vetoed that. They're already suspended and under investigation for intimidating you and we're looking at any conspiracy between them and others. Then he suggested you. I've no idea why. Have you any thoughts on that, apart from your shared history of being at the same college?'

'Oh yes. He thinks I'm a Mason. I would imagine he thinks he might get some leverage through that. You should look at your Apostles as well. That might be the link in your establishment.'

Before Vin could respond, Mary intervened. 'Are you?' And to Ben's ears, she did not sound pleased.

He smiled. This was becoming a very interesting meeting, and not for the reasons he'd anticipated. 'No. But my father was one and he wanted me to join, so I know a lot about Masons. It was one of the many differences between us.' He could see Mary relax and wondered if there was history there.

Vin said, 'Can you keep up the pretence? We need him to cough. We have those disgusting photos of him and Taylor, Dr Andrew Neville-Taylor, that is, but we have nothing to connect either of them to the murders. Taylor had motive, means and opportunity for both but we have no proof. We reckon, for Dobson's murder, he was the killer and Pedersen, the watcher. We think Taylor killed the nun on his own. We've got search warrants for all their premises and officers looking for Taylor. For the past week, he's not turned up for work.' She smiled a sardonic smile. 'Now, I wonder why that is?'

'I think I should see Pedersen one-to-one.' Then Ben made a decision. For reasons that he could not identify, it seemed portentous. 'I'd like Mary to watch the interview. Not in the room but through your one-way glass. She has history with Ethel's so she might be able to glean something I miss. Is that OK?'

Vin looked frosty but replied in the affirmative. 'Of course. But no notes are to be taken.'

Ben could feel that a victory had been won, but he had no idea by whom.

*　*　*

Pedersen looked smaller than Ben remembered, and older. They shook hands in the customary manner, and Pedersen's first utterance was to confirm the assurance he'd been given that the conversation was not being recorded.

Ben nodded. 'No record, but I'm not at all sure why you asked to see me. Tell me what you want of me.'

'You're one of us. And I need someone to plead my case.' His next words to Ben came as a complete surprise. 'And I needed to warn you. You'll be next.'

Ben was not surprised by the content, but only that Pedersen had said it. Then he realised. 'You're scared, aren't you? After me, you think it could be you. And then anyone else who can finger him. Do you know if he's killed before?'

'I'm sure he has. I think he did a lot when he was working in Belfast. Over there, people disappeared regularly and no-one would testify if you had protection. And he had protection. He boasted about it once when he was drunk. Said he was invulnerable. I didn't pursue it. Didn't want to know.'

Ben could hear Vin's voice in his earpiece. 'Move on. This is wasting time.' But Ben did not want to move on.

'Did he tell you about any people he knew there, in Belfast? Mention any names?'

'No, I don't remember any. He knew Murdock. They were both in with one of those Protestant groups. He did say something about a woman called Moira. I picked that one up because women aren't his thing. It seemed odd but I don't know where she fits in.'

'No other names?'

'No.'

'Did he tell you who was protecting him?'

'No.'

'Any guesses – any clues so we can pinpoint his protector?'

Again the voice came in his ear, 'Move on. This is old news.'

Pedersen replied, 'I got the impression that Murdock was the go-between. That's all I know. They were a cabal together, Murdock, Dobson, Taylor. I think he killed Murdock too. No-one's been caught for it.'

'Was Taylor blackmailing you?'

Pedersen nodded his head sadly. 'Yes. One mistake. I was foolish enough to go on holiday with him once. There were some pictures. We had a set each. Insurance for both of us. Then mine disappeared so he had proof but I didn't. Dobson acquired mine – I don't know how – but that's why he was killed. He's certain you have those photos now. He wants them very badly.'

'Did Dobson tell you what he'd done with the photos?'

'No. He didn't tell us anything. Then Taylor got furious and just killed him.'

'Want to tell me what's in the pictures?'

'No, I can't. They disgust me. Taylor led me on and to my shame, I followed. So you don't have them?'

'No.' Ben could honestly answer in the negative as the photos were now in the hands of the Obscene Publications Squad.

'If you don't have them, then where are they?'

Ben didn't answer but had a question of his own. 'Dobson. Was he blackmailing you?'

'No. We always kept our distance. I didn't like him and he didn't like me. I didn't know he had my pictures till Taylor told me.'

'And who decided to get them back from Dobson?'

'Taylor engineered it all. Then he killed Dobson.' Pedersen formed his fists into a ball and pressed them onto his eyes. 'I can still see it. All that blood. It was ghastly.'

He looked up at the ceiling. 'I couldn't watch. Then, I opened my eyes and I could see, from his face, that he enjoyed doing it. That's when I knew for certain he'd done it before.'

'So what part did you play in Dobson's murder?'

Pedersen looked straight at Ben. 'No part. I didn't even know he had a knife. I went to persuade Dobson to give back the photos. I thought maybe Taylor would hit him but not that!'

Ben decided to change tack. 'What about DS Bennett and DS Burnham? What is your relationship with them?'

'Same as you. We meet at the Lodge, share information. That's all.'

'Do they know Taylor?'

'Yes. He's in the Lodge too.'

'Did they know what had happened? That Taylor had murdered Dobson?'

'I don't know.'

'Sure?'

'But I think they know he killed the nun. Or suspect, anyway. That's when I got really scared. When the nun died. Then I knew he wouldn't stop. Look, he's dangerous and devious. If he wangled his way into that secure unit, he can get in anywhere – even a prison.' His eyes were pleading. 'That's all I know. That's all I'm saying. I've been helpful, but I want something in return.'

'So what do you want?'

'I want you to find him. No. You won't even have to find him. He'll find you. When he's killed you, wherever I am, he'll come after me. I'll give a statement about Dobson's murder but only if I can have a guarantee that I'll never be anywhere where he'll be able to get to me.'

'And will your statement include evidence about the photos?'

Pedersen looked pityingly at Ben. 'What sort of an idiot do you take me for?'

Once outside, Mary and Vin joined him in the corridor. Ben shook his head. 'What a pathetic excuse for a man. I almost feel sorry for him.'

Vin's voice was full of contempt. 'Don't waste your pity on that one. Search of his house found a hidden dark web computer. Full of indecent images of children, some recent. He spun a sob story but it won't wash. He may not be charged with accessory to murder but we've got enough evidence of his other proclivities to lock him up for years.'

# Chapter 41

Ben and Mary were sitting in comfort, she with a glass of single malt, he with a soft Beaujolais. 'I must educate your palate about whisky. We could start with something soft and rounded, like your wine. I promise you, you'll come to like it.'

There was a crash from the kitchen as one of the younger generation dropped something heavy and breakable. It was followed by a forcible 'Bugger!' in Katy's voice so they knew who the culprit was.

There were four cooks, five if you included Mo who said he was supervising. Ben suspected that Pam would be in charge, as she was the only one with cooking skills which could be deemed in any way adequate. He was sure that they'd organised it so that he and Mary could relax together. Mary laughed. It was a soft, smooth sound. Much like my wine, thought Ben.

'Sounds like they're spoiling the broth, or at least throwing it over the kitchen. D'you think I should go and help?'

Ben shook his head. 'No way. They've got to get the hang of it sometime. Mind you, my stomach lurched when Katy said, "Welcome home. I baked you a cake." And then she said they're making enough dinner so "those hot policemen at the doors" could have some too.'

'She'll learn, and I don't know about "hot". It's freezing out there so they'll probably be glad of it. But Katy, now she could do anything she set her mind to.'

'Well, she's certainly been putting her mind to something. She has a surprise for us all, but said we'll have to wait until after they'd put the casserole in the oven.'

There was a lot of noisy shuffling and laughter outside the door. Katy led the way, carrying her laptop. She placed it so that her father and Mary could both see it. 'Gather round all of you. I have something amazing to show you.' She turned to Mary. 'You know we've been solving riddles to find out what crimes all the murder suspects had committed? Well, we all got quite good at it.' She turned to the gaggle behind her. 'Take a bow, people.' They duly bowed, including Mo.

As he straightened up, he rubbed his back and groaned. 'Ye gods, girl. Don't make me do that again.'

Katy grinned and continued, 'Way back in the summer, my Dad solved Stanley Murdock's murder but he was left with a key in an envelope. We couldn't make out what it was for or where it fitted. Well…' She made a drum roll on the coffee table. 'I've solved it! Well, me and Mr Google actually.' She clicked the mouse. 'This is a picture of the envelope. See, a square shape with Tom written inside.'

'Hang on young lady! I had that hidden in my room.'

Katy looked contrite for a nanosecond. 'Yeah Dad, but it was such an easy hiding place to find. And I had to make sure you wouldn't impede Santa Claus so I've found a much better place for it. I'll show you later.'

Ben didn't know whether to be pleased or worried so decided to be neither.

Katy continued. 'It was so easy that we just didn't see it. We thought Tom must be a person. But if you type in Tom Square Cambridge, look what you get. St Thomas's Square. So I went to have a look and there are blocks and blocks of lock-up garages.' She showed them the picture of rows of garages. 'I bet anything you like that the key fits one of those lock-ups. Drum roll please everyone. This is Stanley Murdock's hidey-hole.'

The news had given Ben a dilemma. Dr Clare had insisted that he still needed Mary as a chaperone, but he knew that, if he took her to the garages and they indeed found Stanley Murdock's lock-up, Mary would become more deeply involved. He was enjoying her company. She was easy to be with, but if there was going to be danger, she didn't need to be involved. She solved the problem for him.

'I think you and your daughters should go. Maybe Michael too – for more bulk – in case Taylor sees you. I can divert your police guard while you make your getaway. That sound like a plan?'

'Tomorrow then. OK everyone?'

\* \* \*

The ruse had worked and they were driving across Cambridge to the eastern side. The morning rush was over and the roads were relatively clear. Sarah drove, Katy navigated and Ben kept a lookout behind. He couldn't see any pattern in the cars so was pretty sure they weren't being followed. Michael had his cricket bat. They'd added Pam to the mix so they also had two police officers with expandable batons and handcuffs.

Katy had been right. There were several rows of lock-ups. It was deserted and secluded, a perfect place for nefarious deeds. It had that unkempt air of a place that was not regularly visited, except, as Pam had suggested, for drug transactions and the like. They decided to split up and look for garages that had not been used for some time, then Ben would systematically try the locks. If questioned, Sarah and Pam would show their ID and say they were looking for counterfeit goods. As a cover, it wasn't sanctioned, it wasn't foolproof, and they hoped it would not have to be used.

They separated and came back to Ben when they had a suspect garage. A quarter of an hour in, Ben gave a long low whistle. That was the signal that they had found the lock that matched. He waited till all had gathered, then unlocked the garage door and pulled hard. It was reluctant to open but eventually it gave. He raised it till it was fully open. He scanned inside with his torch. Then he scanned again more slowly. Then a third time, even more slowly.

The garage was empty.

There was a collective gasp of disappointment. Ben scanned a fourth time. Still empty. He moved forward and the others followed. They looked closely in all the corners. Nothing but leaves. They dispersed the leaves – still nothing. They searched the walls to look for loose bricks – again they came up with nothing. They scanned the roof and all they could make out was empty space.

Then Michael dropped his torch and before it hit the ground, it spun, illuminating the side of a roof strut. Ben's eyes followed the beam of light, then he trained his torch upwards. Barely visible, strapped behind the strut, and camouflaged by colour, was a single, small, canvas bag. Michael was the tallest. He reached up but was about a foot short of his goal. Pam looked up at the strapping. 'We'll need a knife. Has anybody brought a knife?'

In the subsequent silence, Ben brought out his pen-knife, glad that he'd been a boy scout and was prepared. He also brought out several pairs of latex gloves which the company duly donned. The silence was now palpable as Michael lifted Pam and she carefully cut the straps that held the bag in place. She dropped the bag into Ben's arms and Michael returned her to solid ground. They all stood in silence and looked at the bag. It was an ordinary, khaki, army surplus bag, long and narrow, fitting snugly the width of the roof strut. Ben broke the silence. His voice was strained. 'We'd better get back.' He placed the canvas bag inside a thin plastic bag, ushered them out and closed and locked the garage, then marched off towards the car, head lowered.

He could hear Pam's voice behind. 'Is he OK?'

He could hear Michael respond, 'He'll be fine. He just needs to see this through.'

Ben just hoped Michael was right.

# Chapter 42

No-one had quibbled when he'd said he wanted to look through Stanley Murdock's bag on his own. His reasoning, that it would probably contain incriminating evidence, had convinced them that the fewer people who were involved, the better. His ulterior motive, that of removing anything that might involve Dr Clare or any other innocents, and anything that linked Murdock to Diane, he had kept to himself.

If there was anything pertaining to Diane, he really had to be alone.

He put on latex gloves and upended the bag on to a plastic sheet on the floor of his study. There were several small packets, tightly sealed in plastic covers. They fell out in a heap. They were in various shapes and sizes, some much fatter than others. Each, he saw, had writing printed on one side. He counted them, ignoring for the moment, the writing. Twenty-four. Twenty-four victims of Stanley Murdock. Twenty-four people with secrets that had led them into Murdock's clutches. Dr Clare had had an affair with a married man. He knew about the misdemeanours of the Ethel people. He wondered what the others had done.

He started with the nearest – a name he recognised as a Cabinet Minister, so a call to Chris would be necessary. He knew that, as soon as he involved Chris, 'National Security' would be invoked and all the packages would be removed. All that were left, anyway. He continued his search. Next came a businessman that Ben had heard of; a fat-cat who was trying to become a press baron. Again of interest to Chris. The third name jumped out at him. A single word, 'Jacko'. That one he definitely needed to look through before passing it on to Chris. He put it to one side. He'd said he would protect Dr Hendrick, so his package also went to the side as did that of Dr Fursley. Next, there was a series of names that Ben recognised from Murdock's funeral – famous names – people who had seemed so happy to wave Murdock into the ground. Now he knew why. He had no interest in them so they would be passed on. Next came one marked Taylor/Pedersen. That one he would have to look at. Then, remembering the photos of those young Asian boys, he recoiled at the thought. He decided that he knew enough about those two already so could leave that package entirely to the professionals.

He felt enormous gratitude that he was not one of those people who had to look at that stuff every day and he wondered how they stayed sane. He sighed and continued his search. Dobson's was there – and after an initial thought that he might look inside, he decided that Dobson's secret should go with him to his grave. He put that one with the others he was keeping. Soon he found the one with Dr Clare's lover's name on it, Professor Hallfield. He put that one with his stash and went idly through the rest. He recognised none of the names. They were probably the good, the bad and the ugly from the funeral and beyond. There was no package with Walpole's or O'Connor's names on, and none with Dr Clare's. Of more pertinence to him, there was nothing with Diane's name. If this was indeed the totality of the blackmail evidence that Stanley Murdock had held then, at least, his wife had not been among them. The only link he had was Dobson's unsent letter. This haul had brought him no nearer to finding the identity of Diane's killer, so his immense relief that she had not been one of Murdock's blackmail victims was tinged at the edges with disappointment.

\* \* \*

By the time Chris arrived, there were just nineteen packages in their original state and one which had been opened and expertly resealed. Ben had opened the one entitled Jacko, copied the contents, then replaced all the evidence and resealed it so it looked the same as the others. The four he had removed were as yet unopened and occupying his safe place in the chimney. Nestling beside them was the evidence that Jacko, now deceased, had been a paedophile. Ben knew he would have to find a new safe place. Katy had already discovered it and, if 'the Services' decided to search his house, he was certain they would immediately find his cache. A lock-up would seem to be a good solution.

'You are one clever bugger. How'd you find these, then?' Chris had not been as careful as Ben, having just ripped open the packages and left his finger marks all over them. He didn't wait for an answer. 'Well, well, well. Lookee here. Our esteemed Justice Secretary, always banging on about integrity. What a naughty boy he is. Oh dear, he might be resigning any day now. And this one? Do we want him to be in charge of one of our influential newspaper groups? Could do. Might be useful.' He pulled out the evidence against Jacko. 'Now this was one evil bastard. Wish we'd had this when he was alive. Could've put the squeeze on him.' He flicked the papers in his hand. 'Died peacefully in his bed, just last year. Half the villains in Belfast realised they'd lost their protection and the other half heaved a huge sigh of relief. And the third half started out on their long-held retaliation strategy.'

Ben decided to ignore the faulty maths. 'Taylor and Murdock both knew Jacko and Taylor is in the same Lodge as Burnham and Bennett.'

'I know about your Apostles. Putting the screws on them as we speak. Your lovely DCI has been a mine of information. She's a real find. Wants to climb the greasy pole and I'm sure we can give her a leg-up.'

This only confirmed Ben's suspicion that their affair was coming to an end. It had been good for him and he hoped it had been good for Vin. He'd needed a relationship that was carefree and without strings, just as she had. But he knew that their paths were now pointing in opposite directions.

Chris riffled through the other packages sorting them into two piles. He pointed to the smaller pile. 'Serious shit, this lot. Intel that we've missed, but that fucker Murdock had it all. And bang up to date. Well, up until his overdue demise. We'll use this.' He pointed to the other pile. 'Small fry. But we'll keep it anyway. Never know, but any one of them might rise to the heights and need reining in.'

If Ben had had any compunction about retrieving the evidence against people he knew at Ethel's – people he knew to be 'small fry' who had made mistakes – Chris had removed it. They didn't deserve to be 'reined in' by Chris and his mates, now or at any time in the future. But Chris was still talking. 'Funny that there's nothing against your Ethel people.' He looked sideways at Ben. 'Stanley must have passed it on to Dobson. What d'ya think?'

Ben kept his voice level. 'Yeah. Probably.'

Chris laughed and mimicked Ben. 'Yeah. Probably.' He waved an admonitory finger at Ben. 'You've got form, my friend, for withholding evidence. It worked for us both last time so I'll say no more for the moment. But I'm not stupid. Now, to the business in hand. Your DCI agrees with me that we need to catch that bastard, Taylor.'

Ben interjected. 'I have a plan. He wants his photos. He thinks I have them. We should set a trap for him with me as bait.'

## Chapter 43

Chris had protested half-heartedly – saying he was supposed to protect his people, not put them into danger. But, with Ben's insistence that it was the best way, and that he was sure that Chris would protect him anyway, it was agreed. Ben knew that putting himself into short-term danger was the quickest way of catching Taylor. He also knew that, as long as Taylor was at large, he would continue to be in jeopardy. Better to get it over with, for good or ill. He had to put his trust in Chris – something he was not at all sure about.

Chris had arranged for all Ben's family to move out. Ben had insisted that they go to a safe house. Mo had refused point blank. He was going to Cherry Hinton to look after Josephine and Agnes and he could not be persuaded otherwise. Michael had insisted that he accompany Mo. Pam had insisted that she went with them as, after all, Josephine might also be a target. Ben had given up and had bowed to the inevitable, wondering how they would all fit into that small house. He was relieved when Katy and Sarah had put up no resistance and had gone to the safe house. They had left, in batches, under cover of darkness.

The police guard had ostentatiously been removed from the front and back of the house and Chris and four black-clad associates had inconspicuously moved in. When Ben had asked whether they were police or army, Chris had only shrugged and said, 'You really don't want to know that, do you?'

The black-clads were scattered, one in the back garden, one in the front and one somewhere in the house, Ben knew not where. Ben was now installed in his study at the front of the house, with Chris and a black-clad hiding in the same room. He'd been fitted with a stab vest. It was a long time since he'd had to wear one and he'd forgotten just how uncomfortable they were. The debate about stab or bullet had gone on around him with the decision being made that, if Taylor were to be 'tooled up', he'd be stopped before he got to Ben. And anyway, Taylor would want to get up close to 'encourage' Ben to tell him where his photos were. Ben was not convinced, but nobody seemed to be listening to him. The deciding factor seemed to have been that Taylor wanted the same package that he had tried to get from Dobson so would use the same modus operandi. Ben still wasn't convinced but he, the target, had been overruled.

Chris had arranged Ben's study to his liking. The room was in half gloom. Ben's desk lamp cast a pool of light encasing Ben and his immediate surroundings. A standard lamp had been brought in and positioned so that the door and pathway to the desk were illuminated. Ben had been placed in full view from the street but back from the window, which now had a bullet-proof screen in front of it. When he had queried that, he'd been told, 'We don't want him to kill you and get away, do we? Sort of defeats the object of the exercise.'

When Ben had remonstrated that that was unlikely, as Taylor was looking for evidence that he thought Ben possessed, Chris had replied, 'Look – he's a psychopath. He's unstable. He could do anything.'

If Chris thought that would reassure Ben, he was mistaken. Now they waited.

* * *

They sat in silence for five hours and, when it came, it was over quickly. Somehow, Taylor had managed to evade the black-clads outside and inside the house. Just after midnight, the brass knob on the study door turned with an almost imperceptible squeak – inaudible if any other noise had been present. Ben held his breath, and felt sure his two protectors were doing the same. Taylor slowly opened the door and sidled into Ben's study. He quietly closed the door behind him and stood with his back to it. His face was in shadow but Ben could see that he was brandishing a hypodermic syringe. His voice was silky smooth. 'Where are they? Give me the photos and I'll make it quick. Otherwise, a slow and painful demise – your choi...'

He never finished the sentence. Immediately a burst of gunfire left Ben, Taylor, Chris and a black-clad lying prone on the floor. The sound of the guns resounded in Ben's ears. He thought he must still be alive because he could smell the cordite. Either that or he was dead and was about to relive his nightmare dream for eternity. He could move his limbs, but that didn't prove anything.

Chris turned to the black-clad. 'Good work.' Then he grabbed Ben's hand and pulled him to his feet. 'Great outcome. Only the one down, I think.'

So, he was alive. Ben looked over to where a body lay. His first reaction on seeing the mess that had been Dr Andrew Neville-Taylor was that he'd have to get a new carpet. Odd, that. A dead man with his brains sprayed across the wall and his body bleeding all over his floor, and his reaction was mundane. But then he had nothing but disgust for the dead man. He turned to Chris. 'Your people all OK?'

Taylor's body was blocking the doorway. Chris grabbed his legs and pulled him further into the room. A smear of blood and brain followed the corpse. Ben remonstrated. 'Shouldn't we preserve the scene?'

'What scene?' was the terse reply.

Chris stepped over the body and left the room. Ben could hear the back door bang shut. A few seconds later Chris returned. 'The one in the back was out cold. He's coming round and making sense. As much sense as he usually makes, anyway. He'd tripped over a step and knocked himself out. Bit of a dickhead. He'll be leaving us.' This was the first intimation that the black-clads were Chris's operatives. 'You phone your family. Tell 'em you're OK. But nothing else. Understood? And I'll organise to get this lot cleared up.' He pointed to the spreading crimson stain. 'Bit messy, that. Want the same colour carpet?'

* * *

It took just five hours for Ben's study to look better than it ever had. The pock marks from the stray bullets had been filled, the walls cleaned of the pink and grey gunge that had once been Taylor's brain, Then they'd been repainted and the carpet replaced. Ben had insisted that he wanted the walls painted a bright sunshine yellow. The supervisor of the painting team had looked dubious. He'd shaken his head and had made that sucking noise that all artisans and engineers make when the client is so obviously wrong. Ben was eventually convinced by the argument that the stains might eventually show through a light colour. He'd been persuaded that a rich deep burgundy would suit the proportions of the room. And a sumptuous cream carpet would counterbalance the deep shades of the walls. Ben had given in gracefully and had been dazzled by the result. When he'd congratulated the team, the young supervisor had said, 'No probs. You do your job and we'll do ours.'

Then he was brought back down to basics. Amazingly, the underlay had not allowed blood to soak through to the floor-boards, so it could almost have been that nothing untoward had happened there. Except in Ben's memory. When he'd asked Chris what would happen to the body, the reply had been, 'What body?'

He knew then that Taylor and his nefarious deeds would be expunged from all records. Ben suspected that it was not Taylor's paedophile activities or the fact that he was a double murderer that concerned Chris. It was that he had known Murdock and Jacko in the past. That brought a niggle of worry about Pedersen. He asked Chris if Pedersen would suffer a similar fate? Chris's reply confirmed his suspicions and brought some relief, but not much. 'Nah! See Taylor knew Murdock in Belfast. They had history so we had loose ends to tie up there. Pedersen is just a paedo who got mixed up with a villain way above his pay grade. We'll see what he knows then get him extradited to Thailand. Course, he could get killed while he's waiting. They don't take kindly to nonces in gaol.'

# Chapter 44

'I'm spitting tacks. How could they do this? And you – you're part of it! Fucking, bloody spooks. Think you can run roughshod over the law. Well, I won't let you. D'you hear me? I won't let you.'

Ben thought he'd been prodded in the chest enough times, so decided he should intervene. 'Vin, they'll hear you all over the station. Do you want that? Let's go for a coffee. I have the key to a flat near here. We could talk there and you can shout at me all you like.'

She was getting into a tangle putting on her coat. He tried to help her but she shrugged him off. They set off at a pace to Josephine Finlay's flat over the fire station. Ben had been looking after it since Josephine had entered The Friary. He'd kept it ready for her return. It felt strange now bringing his latest partner – ex-partner – into the domain of a previous one. Especially as the previous one had hardly let anyone over her threshold.

As Ben made coffee, Vin wandered round looking at the pristine surfaces. Ben remembered the time he'd taken a book from the shelf and had put it back in a different place. Josephine had had to remove it from the place where he'd put it and put it back in the place it had come from. She had been a mess. She was making such progress and he was happy for her. He knew that his need to 'face his demons' was coming fast. He both feared and welcomed it.

Vin had calmed down somewhat. 'Bloody Chris. They've taken Pedersen. God knows where or what they're doing to him. Don't get me wrong. I've no truck with paedophiles, but he's my paedophile, not theirs. Now they say he'll be extradited to Thailand. It's out of my hands.' She stood up and paced the room. She had her shoes on. The old Josephine would have been apoplectic. Ben wondered what the new Josephine would make of it.

'Then there's bloody Taylor. We had to drop everything. No explanation. I gave them intel. I helped them and what do I get in return? My team worked bloody hard looking for him. We find out where he's hiding and we're just on the point of arresting him. A bloody paedo – and a murderer. And then we're told by bloody Chris to stand down. Stand down. I ask you. We had him! What am I to tell my people? Can't tell them the bloody spooks have got him.'

This was news to Ben. He knew Chris had engineered Taylor's death, but now he knew that Chris had also prevented his arrest and subsequent trial. And all because Taylor had links to Stanley Murdock, the UVF and the mysterious Jacko. He wondered how high up the chain of command Chris's orders had come from. The highest, was his estimation. This must be a cover-up from the top.

Vin was still talking. 'We had evidence. That's the thing. Two murders solved, a paedophile ring uncovered and firm evidence against bent coppers, and I can do nothing!'

Ben wanted to know the fate of DS Burnham and DS Bennett. He was sure they'd been party to his beating and the attack on his family. 'What's happening with your Apostles?'

'They've been interviewed by men in grey suits. God knows where they were from. They weren't the usual lot, not IOPC nor IPPC. They marched in, took over, cleaned out all the files then left. And the upshot? God this sticks in my throat. The upshot is that those two take early retirement with full pension. For God's sake, they colluded with bloody paedos. That's the last fucking straw!' And with that, she burst into tears.

Ben was unsure what to do for the best. He went over to her and put his arms round her. She didn't push him away. 'You could tell your people that Taylor's dead.' Here, Ben prevaricated a little. 'Caught in an ambush. I saw his body. You won't find it. Taylor's body's been spirited away. I'm not surprised those men in grey suits collected all the evidence. I suspect this is part of something much, much bigger – something way above our pay-grade – something that can't come out in court. So there will be no trials, no public restitution. They will erase all traces. And you're right, it's not justice, and there's nothing we can do.' But, as he said it, he was already thinking that Diane must have been mixed up in this somewhere, and he knew he wouldn't be able to leave it alone until he'd found out how and where.

Vin looked up at him. She looked so tired, so defeated, and he knew what she was about to say. 'I'm sorry. I was going to tell

you this over a nice dinner, but I've decided to go back to London. I can't stay here after this. I've been offered promotion in the Met. I need a complete new start so I think we should say goodbye now. I hope you find someone who can take care of you. You need it.'
And with that she kissed him on the cheek and walked to the door. She turned and smiled. 'We had fun, didn't we?' And then she walked out of the flat and out of his life.

Ben sat down on Josephine's pristine sofa and let out a long sigh. He was feeling relieved. Relieved because Vin's actions in taking the initiative had meant that there was no possibility that she would feel the humiliation of being cast aside. He had been cast aside. In Katy's terminology, he'd been dumped. Did he feel humiliated? No. Did he feel relieved? Yes. In Agnes Barrett's words, 'It was time.'

And Ben wondered, as he looked round Josephine's perfect sitting room and gazed through Josephine's picture window, who was it that had engineered that promotion in the Met? And how long would it be before Vin welcomed Chris and his 'fucking spooks' back into her life? Not long, he reckoned. He silently wished her well.

# Chapter 45

The sun was, at last, beginning to bring just a little heat. As he walked into town, Ben stopped to listen to a robin performing its requisite territorial function and he wondered how a sound so beautiful to our ears could be so threatening to other robins. He hoped that spring was in the air, and certainly a spring was in his step. He was feeling a profound sense of relief. He was in that space where one burden had been lifted and another had not yet fallen. He was relishing his postman duties; he would bring relief to sufferers and for that he was glad. He'd pushed his own problems to the back of his mind again, so that he could enjoy the pleasure and serenity that his deliveries would bring. For these people, their tribulations would soon be over. He envied them.

As he arrived at Ethel's he glanced up at the rooms that Dobson had occupied, now given over to Dr O'Connor. His thoughts turned to Dobson and his redemption, the restitution that he had performed in his final days. No-one would be allowed to know that Dobson had endeavoured to pass evidence of his killers' crimes to the police. Hendrick was to have been the go-between but Hendrick had been too terrified to do anything other than hide the evidence. And, no-one could be told that, in a final act of bravery, even with a knife at his throat, Dobson had not divulged the location of that evidence. Had he done so, it was inevitable that Dr Hendrick would have been Taylor's next victim. It saddened Ben that no-one would ever know of Dobson's last heroic act. At that moment, Ben decided that an endowment should be made to the College from Dobson's estate and in Dobson's name. He deserved that much.

Dobson's pack of evidence had been destroyed unread. Ben had three still-sealed packs of evidence from the lock-up, one destined for Dr Clare and Professor Hallfield, one for Dr Fursley and one for Dr Hendrick. Ben had made up a further sealed pack – containing Dr, soon to be Professor, O'Connor's bogus degree certificate and the real one. Following the demise of Dobson, O'Connor had been voted Bursar of Ethel's and, in this guise, Ben was sure he would be able to view and, if necessary, expunge any evidence of his subterfuge all those years ago. He was returning these packages to their rightful owners, and he had an inkling that, although it was contrary to official rules, Chris was on-side. This brought the thought that maybe his and Chris's values were congruent, partially anyway. In his present mood, Ben found this amusing. He had found no package of evidence against Professor Walpole but he wanted to see him on another matter.

He'd made arrangements to go to see Peter Hallfield first and then on to Ethel's to see the others. Hallfield had been effusive in his thanks, especially as he had not had to confess to his wife in what were probably her final weeks. She would be allowed to die with dignity, without the trauma of having to acknowledge and deal with his infidelity. For that, he said he and Alison would be forever in Ben's debt. As Ben had left him, he had said, 'If there's ever anything I can do...'

As he entered Ethel's, Ben announced his arrival to Mr Fisher in the Porters' Lodge. Fisher was in an expansive mood. 'A very good morning to you, Mr Burton. Things are beginning to look normal again, thank goodness. Police have gone; they kept walking on the grass in Front court and they left muddy footprints all over the place. I kept telling them. But did they listen? No class, no respect for tradition. Glad to see the back of them. Can get back to normal now. But then, terrible that it was one of ours as did it. But, at least, it's all cleared up.'

'One of ours?'

'Oh, I thought you'd know. The Master sent word today. She's been told that Professor Pedersen has admitted killing Professor Dobson but will be extradited to Thailand to face charges there first. We haven't been told what the charges are but no matter. We've been told that he'll be there for long enough for us to move on from this whole dreadful business. Of course, the Master's only told those who need to know and we've got to keep it to ourselves. Got to protect the reputation of the College. The word outside is still that it was a robbery gone wrong and the trail's gone cold, so we're telling everyone to make sure to lock their doors. But it just goes to show, you never know people, do you?'

So Chris had been covering his tracks at Ethel's as well. Ben was beginning to think that Pedersen would never arrive in Thailand. Did that worry him? Yes, it did, despite seeing those disgusting photos of Pedersen and Taylor. It was becoming apparent that anyone who knew about this cover-up – or was even sitting on the periphery – was vulnerable. So, it followed that he was vulnerable. He would need to keep Chris onside. That might mean doing his bidding again. Not a thought he relished.

'Anyway, Mr Burton. Drs Fursley, Hendrick and O'Connor are all gathered in Professor Walpole's rooms. Shouldn't tell you this but they've ordered champagne – so they're pleased it's all over too.'

But not for the reason you think, thought Ben.

\* \* \*

They were indeed, gathered. And a small cheer arose when he entered the room. Professor Walpole hobbled forward and slapped him on the back. 'Well done, dear boy.' He turned away from the others and winked at Ben. Then he said aloud, 'Shocking about Pedersen, but I never did trust him. All that hand-shake nonsense.' He turned back to the assembled company. 'Anyway, we all owe you a debt of gratitude. Didn't prepare a speech. Can't abide those stuffed-shirt eulogies. Suffice it to say, we've been talking and we know that Dobson had personal information about all of us that we didn't want others to know. And now, mercifully, that has fallen into the hands of an honest man. So, young man, what do you have for us?'

Ben handed his sealed packets to Drs Fursley, Hendrick and O'Connor. 'I haven't opened them but I'm pretty sure that they contain the information you need. Professor Walpole, there is nothing for you. I think, perhaps, it was destroyed when the perpetrators knew it had no value.' Ben turned to the others. 'I'm delighted that you can all relax now and get on with your lives.'

Champagne was handed round to all but Dr Fursley. Ben went over to her and pointed towards her glass of orange juice. 'Does that mean what I think it means?'

She grinned at him. 'Early days and we're not telling anyone yet. But yes.' To Ben's eyes, at that moment, she looked beautiful. He could only describe her look as a glow emanating from within; she shone with inner peace and strength. She took hold of his hand and squeezed it. He was completely overcome when she added, 'We are so grateful to you. If it's a girl, we're going to call her Clare. If it's a boy, he'll be Ben.' Ben had to use one of his own white handkerchiefs.

They all, in turn, thanked him for giving them back agency over their own lives and then they drifted back to work. Ben was left holding an empty glass and deciding how to ask for help from Professor Walpole. He was pre-empted by Walpole himself. 'You'll be wanting my assistance, of course. Tell me all you know about Murdock, Dobson and your wife. Then I'll see what else I can find out. You'll need Mary. Absolutely indispensable. You realise that, don't you?'

'Why will I need Mary?'

'Oh, you'll find out, dear boy. Soon enough.'

# Chapter 46

Breakfast time. They'd assembled again round the kitchen table, the family plus Pam and Michael. Ben was enjoying having a full house and would miss them all when they returned to their respective abodes. Mo was harrumphing. 'Bent as bloody nine bob notes. Call 'emselves coppers? Criminals, that's what they was. Tried to fit you up and I think they was involved in getting you beaten up. And now they're getting away scot-free. Bloody disgrace to the force. See, in my day…'

Sarah butted in. 'Uncle Mo, they do things differently these days. Some things are better, some are worse.'

Mo nodded sagely, while Ben was thinking that, from time immemorial, all sorts of bent people had been shuffled up, down, sideways or out in order to keep up appearances. But he let it go.

He'd described, in a very truncated fashion, the events of the previous day. He'd told them how hacked off Vin had been that there were to be no charges and that Sarah and Pam were not to give her a hard time and to try to persuade others to be kind to her. To explain the lack of any arrests or charges, he'd told them that decisions had been taken way above Vin's pay grade and there was nothing she could do.

Michael said quietly, 'Something to do with my Uncle Stanley, no doubt.'

Ben was not sure who else had heard this aside, and he decided to ignore it.

Mo was yet to be mollified. 'Well. Taylor's dead and good riddance. Killing Dobson was one thing. But killing a nun. Why, that's...' He ran out of words for a moment then found the one he was looking for. 'That's sacrilege. Agnes is praying for the poor old girl. Don't hold with all that stuff meself but it makes her feel better. Pedersen's off to face the music in Thailand. Don't fancy his chances. But what makes me mad is them scrotes getting away with trying to fit you up. It gives the Force a bad name.' He paused for breath. 'Feel better now I've got that off me chest. Anyone want another cup?'

Ben decided that Mo would probably have been incandescent had he known that those 'scrotes', whether knowingly or not, had assisted two paedophiles because they were fellow Lodge members. Yes, the scrotes had tried to fit him up and had been instrumental in organising his beating. That had been bad enough, but consorting with paedophiles, that he found unforgivable. So far, they'd got away with it. He shared Vin's view that justice had not been served. He would have to see if Chris could intervene.

He smiled at his uncle and replied, 'Yes please. Now that Agnes has taught you the gentle art of making tea that's drinkable.' Before Mo could respond, they heard the plop as the post arrived on the doormat. Katy jumped up and ran to collect it. She brought it back and riffled through it, picking out one long envelope and dropping the rest on to the table. She disappeared with her letter into the hallway. After a wait, they heard a whoop and she came rushing back, all smiles. 'I've got it! I've got in.' Katy waved her letter above her head. She turned to her father. 'I've got in. Whoohee! Maths with physics at Ethel's and then I want to move into computer science.' She looked at her father and her smile disappeared. 'I thought you'd be pleased.'

He managed a smile. 'I'm sorry, Katy. It's the shock of all that's happened recently. I am pleased. Of course I am. I'm absolutely delighted for you.' And he realised that he was. 'You know I'll miss you.' He looked around the room. 'But none of you is far away. Maybe I'll take in lodgers to fill this place! Anyway, congratulations. You'll have to have a party to celebrate.' He held up his hands. 'No oldies. I'll go out. But Mo's in his second childhood so he might like to party with you.'

And he was thinking, Mary might like to go out to eat somewhere. He ought to thank her properly for all the times she'd supplied him and his family with food and support. And he needed to find out why Henry Walpole rated her so highly, why he thought her indispensable. He gave Katy a big hug and all the family gathered round to join in with their noisy good wishes. He looked at his younger daughter – all grown up and ready to fly the nest. He would miss her. How he would miss her. He knew that Ethel's was changing and he knew that the Ethel's of today would look after her. Maybe she'd join Professor O'Connor in his important work with the medics. It meant that the last family tie had been loosened and he was free to pursue the truth about Diane. It was coming closer – becoming inevitable. And that scared him.

## Book 3 – Bury the Pain

Only by returning to Northern Ireland and finding the truth about his wife's death can he gain peace of mind. But, in finding his own peace, he uncovers a plot which could destroy the fragile peace in Northern Ireland.
February 2013
Ben Burton is recovering from a complete breakdown caused by finding evidence of his wife's double life. He discovers an old photo from their time in Northern Ireland but can't remember who took it. He finds a coded message. 'Find Moira then find Kevin's cousin. You'll know him when you see him.' He sets out to crack the code.
With Mary's help, he uncovers evidence that Stanley Murdock and Jeremiah Knatchbull, a mid-ranking MI5 officer, led a plot to commit genocide in Northern Ireland and that plot is still ongoing. Knatchbull has now risen to second tier MI5.
Ben must seek him out and outwit this powerful adversary …

## Book 4 – Bury the Past

is still turning somersaults in my head!

Printed in Great Britain
by Amazon